SAVING THE GHOST

M E Fuller

Cover designed by M E Fuller
Additional photo credit for forest pathway image, Judith Connor

This book was made possible in part by financial support from
Five Wings Arts Council with funds from the McKnight Foundation.

M E Fuller
www.mefuller.com

Printed in the United States of America

First Printing: February 2019

M E Fuller LLC

ISBN: 9781793818362

ACKNOWLEDGEMENTS

To the many people who encouraged and supported me in the struggle it's been to write to this story, I say, "thank you." It hardly seems enough.

Saving the Ghost is an important story, I believe, and I wanted to do it justice. So, thanks and a high-five to my readers, Judith Connor, Katherine Christianson, Sheila Ross, Melissa Birch, Roslyn Nelson, and Jean Bergstrom who gave me much needed feedback. And to my listener, Keith Vettel, thank you for your patience.

To these accomplished women who tried to help me get this right, I thank you—my editor Angela Weichmann, Laurie Parker, and Bonnie West.

Thank you to writing group members for their critiques, Audrae Paul, Charlie Johnson, Darrell Pederson, Donna Sali, Jan Kurtz, Janice Bradshaw, Kathleen Krueger, Lauren Nickisch, Susan Smith-Grier, Julie Jo Larson, Beverly Hamilton Abear, Robert Peterson, Diane Schlagel, and Diane Carlson. Thank you, Jodi Gray for your medical advice and to Art and Ray Owen for exposing me to the Dakota life.

Financial support was provided by Five Wings Arts Council with funds from the McKnight Foundation. They exist to help regional artists create words and pictures for everyone else.

To anyone I've missed, my apologies.

To Colleen "Blues Queen" Frey

CHAPTER 1

Before sunrise, I leave for Capitol, steeling myself for the two-and-a-half-hour drive ahead. Puffed up red-tailed hawks perch on tree limbs and power lines, waiting to snatch unlucky field mice and voles from their foraging. The images of meaty deer cadavers, bloated and ravaged by crows and eagles, linger, accompanied by the rhythmic road noise of tire on tar, a steady beat that measures my time. Off the main highway, rough and broken pavement takes me into Capitol. The pines, deep in snow, are near enough to brush the car as I pass. Their fragrance is intoxicating. I should have brought some gin.

Why am I doing this? I'd like to believe it's about me being nice to an old lady, giving her a chance to see her oldest brother blessed and buried. I know this is a lie. I will never believe he's dead if I don't see his carcass. And I need an excuse to show up. A four-hundred-mile out-of-the-way excuse.

When my mother, Virginia, called my office to tell me Billy had died, the sound of her voice went off in my head like an air-raid siren. She insisted I inform his sister Mercy of his demise. Even after forty years of silence between us she expects that I will do as she asks. I can't believe she gave a thought to Mercy—probably saw this as her last opportunity to frighten me witless. A shudder runs through my scalp and my face flushes hot.

Mercy at eighty-six still lives way the hell up north in the old logging and railroad town where she was born. I like her. She's always been good to me. I'm happy to help her out from time to time, no matter how far away she lives. It's Virginia's touch on my life that has me twitching. I feel like an uncertain hare smelling an unseen fox nearby that's closing in.

Mercy is waiting at the window when I arrive at her small backwoods home and bustles out of the house with her best friend, Nellie Jane. No need for me to get out of the car, but I do, to collect their overnight bags, but first, to hug them both. They kiss me and call me honey and try to fight me for the luggage. I smile at the look of them. Mercy is round and soft. She reminds me of a Parker House roll, risen dough on the counter, oven ready. Nellie Jane is more muscular and straight of stature, the daughter of a Scottish trapper and logger, her mother, Lakota. She favors her father's side and once had quite the mane of auburn hair. In the summers she sports a bounty of freckles, adding color to her fair skin on face and arms.

I pack the ladies into the car and ready myself for the long trip ahead. The soft chatter of the two friends rises and fades off in rhythm with the thumping of the tires on the old highway. The whir of the engine's fan, set on high to keep heat circulating, distracts. I want to sleep. I want to be going the other way. I wish the sun would shine. But the sky is one color of gray, all the way into Minneapolis.

Today, at the First Presbyterian Church of Saints and Sinners or Whatever, we will send my father, Billy McInnis, off to the netherworlds. He can eat my dust tomorrow. I've given up two days of my life on his death. A couple more days and I'll be done with him for good.

The parking lot at the church is packed. I can't believe what I'm seeing. *Who would give a fuck that Billy died? Maybe I have the wrong day, the wrong funeral.* I pull the car up to the church entrance, get the ladies out and through the wide, double doors. The room is as packed as the parking lot. The noise from mourners is deafening. A young man approaches to hand us programs for the event.

I ignore the bulletin and ask, "Would you take these ladies to the family pew? I need to go park the car." It's obvious that he is unsure about the care of old people. He stands, mute.

"Aunt Mercy, take this young man's arm and he will escort you and Nellie Jane to the front pew." Mercy ignores his reach and begins, with Nellie Jane in tow, to get herself down the church aisle.

I am relieved to be alone again, if even for a few minutes. There is no open parking space for a full square block. I circle until I spy a car leaving the church lot, pull in, and park. I need to call Ned before I get caught up in the funeral madness, but first, I close my eyes. I hear myself sigh. I feel the air in the car cool quickly. I don't want to leave this solitary space, but I can't leave my aunt and her friend on their own.

"Hello my sweet husband. How are things with your sisters?"

Ned's oldest sister died the same day that Billy evacuated the planet. She was beloved by her siblings, the first one to go. Ned is in Texas, holding down the fort with his sisters while they try to regroup into a smaller family unit.

"We're all right. It's hot as Hades in Texas. I'm glad to hear from you. How crazy is it there?" Ned's voice soothes me.

"Give them my love and tell them how sad I am for you all." I can hear a duet of sister voices saying *we love you* from the background.

"I just have a minute to check in. The old girls are already in the church, waiting for me. I'll take them to our house tonight and home tomorrow."

"Okay." Ned's warmth fills me, but I still want a drink. "Talk later. I love you."

"You, too." We disconnect, and I re-enter the world alone, into the bowels of a church where heaven and hell coexist, to see my father, that abusive son of a bastard, in his coffin.

I make my way up front, where the ladies are waiting for me. It does not surprise me that Virginia is absent. It was bad enough I had to hear her voice. I haven't seen the woman in forty years either and I do not need to break my winning streak. Aunt Mercy stands before I can sit, gesturing that she and Nellie Jane want to view her brother's remains at the altar. They go on ahead as I settle myself in the pew not intending to go near the coffin.

There's something beautiful about Nellie Jane and Mercy holding one another close, tight. They move as one body toward the coffin to witness the death of the asshole I called Daddy. I watch as they make their way down the aisle of the modern, sparkling-clean chapel. The floors are so highly polished I wonder for a moment if the women will slip and fall.

How would anyone ever find the comfort or solace the Bible promises—so I've heard—in a place like this? It has an unnatural smell of waxed floors topped off with an odorous bouquet of smoldering candles. There are horrendous other scents of perfumes, aftershave colognes, and I swear a whiff or two of whiskey. I turn my head to look behind me, and indeed there sits an old man with a flask poking out of his sports coat pocket. I'm tempted to ask for a swig.

My gaze shifts to inspect the church interior and halts at an architectural Jesus captured in iron, installed on the wall straight ahead. There's a condemning look in his eye. I thought Jesus was supposed to love the little children, yet here, in His house of worship, I feel judged for Billy's monstrous acts on my child's body. *Someone should have done something. I should have done something.* Shame stirs terror that creeps up my spine. My heart flutters. *Please, no panic—not today.* I distract myself in a stare-down with the iron Jesus.

And Jesus cried with a loud voice and gave up the ghost.

I wonder where Billy's ghost has settled. It's probably unsettled whirls of dust devils in hell. *Ashes to ashes, dust to dust.* I'd have cremated him, just to be absolutely sure he could never rise from the dead, but Virginia wanted to keep his corpse intact, to be buried in the military cemetery with a twenty-one-gun salute she wouldn't show up to hear. I intend to miss that part of the festivities. I don't trust myself around Billy and guns at the same time, even if he is already dead. He *is* dead, and I thank the resurrected, chapel-ensconced Jesus for that. Billy is silent as he lies in his casket. He's gone.

Who are the others in the congregation of mourners? Could they be friends of my parents? I can't conjure an image of Billy and Virginia out on an evening with good friends, laughing, joking, playing bridge, or dining. Yet the place is filled. Maybe they're Lodge cronies, who've come out of respect for the financial windfall Billy left them. Virginia was clear that she would see nothing from his fortune and that I should expect the same.

A collective gasp escapes from the mourners seated at my back. I focus on the altar where Mercy now holds Nellie Jane, who has collapsed. On my feet in a flash, I sprint down the aisle. Mercy is on the floor with Nellie Jane, stroking her forehead. I kneel, extending my arms around them both, like a mother shielding her babes from harm. Mercy looks up at me with eyes that spook me to my core. She looks terrified.

The other mourners are crowding us. I stand and hold my hands up to push them back, to give the old women some air. They retreat to their spaces in pews, too noisy in their mumblings as they go. I glance down at Aunt Mercy. She and the minister are helping Nellie Jane to her feet. I step back to allow them to move away from the casket and back to their seats when I notice an old man stopped in a wheelchair in the west aisle. By the look of him—the wavy white hair, the scowl on his face—I know he's my uncle Terry, come to his brother's funeral. He is aged and frail. His face is ghastly pale with unkempt facial stubble. His hair is in such disarray, I wonder if he owns a comb.

However he's learned of his brother's death, what would compel him here, to see the body? There was no love between the brothers. Does Terry have a eulogy in his pocket? Perhaps we should compare notes. He seems mesmerized by the scene at the altar where his sister Mercy tends to her friend. Mercy, in turn, is unwavering in her attention to Nellie Jane.

I watch him try to rise up out of his wheelchair, but he can't lift his old body. He's slow to settle himself back down in the seat. He struggles to turn the chair around. I think to help him, but I don't move. Now he turns the wheelchair to face the doors. He grinds along, using all his energy, it seems to me, to move back down the aisle from which he'd rolled into view. I can't tear my gaze away, but still my body does not move to help him. I fixate on a bright orange student notebook sticking out of the backpack harnessed to his chair. It makes me think of a highway flagman, signaling caution to oncoming traffic.

A person who looks to be a care attendant stands in the doorway. Terry must have arrived by Med-Van. I can't think. I let him go. He's gone from my thoughts as an aging couple support Nellie Jane and escort the two ladies to their seats. I sit next to them in the oaken pew, my arm about Mercy's shoulders as she comforts her friend.

Mercy and Nellie Jane, color returning to both their faces, sit shoulder to shoulder. Mercy's fingers stroke the red hymnal secured in her lap, opened to the appropriate page for the next song of "To God Be the Glory" or some other dirge. Nellie Jane hums a near-inaudible song of thanksgiving. I recognize the words, *pilamaya, wopila.*

The reverend is wrapping things up. The grieving and the grateful—me—stand as one to close the ceremony. In the death of my father, all are united. To God be the glory, indeed. Billy will be put into the ground later in the afternoon. There is nothing more to worry about from him.

As I prepare to leave the reception—a lavish expanse of buffet and booze laid out by the Masons and their auxiliary—I feel an unstoppable rise of panic settle into the core of my body, radiating through my arms and into my head, bringing with it a cold as complete and severe as death itself.

CHAPTER 2

It's late afternoon, and I need to get out of here, to get home. Mercy and Nellie Jane are buckled into their seats in the back of the car. I wrap two blankets—scored from my Minnesota-winter-weather emergency kit—around their legs and feet. The women are tired and colorless. I notice they're holding hands. I hope they'll fall asleep on the two-and-a-half-hour drive north to my home in Breeson.

We stop for bathroom breaks a couple of times. After each stop, I hurry to settle the women back inside the cooling car. I'm on edge. My nerves are raw. Even my skin feels raw and tender. I cannot wait to get home to shower and climb into my bed, to sleep a soothing sleep. I'm tired, worn down from nearly sixty years anchored to my father, the child-molesting monster. He's dead, but I still wear him like a worn and filthy jacket rescued from the dump. He is in my mind like a fist in full delivery of a crushing blow. *Ellen*, I speak to myself in a silent tongue, *don't*.

At last we're home. The women are sleeping. I'll have to wake them. My phone vibrates. Ned is calling. I don't answer. He needs to hear from me, but I have nothing to give him now. The ladies, awake, are getting out of the car as I unlock the front door. I retrieve our overnight bags along with a basket of sympathy cards shoved into my unwilling hands on the way from the funeral reception.

“Give these to your mother, will you?” spoke a nameless, unknown mourner.

I dump the cards along with the sympathy cash and checks in the trash can. I’ll keep the basket. It’s nice and will be useful.

Reheated turkey vegetable soup and a side of warm cornbread covered in cream will help the ladies to sleep through the night. Mercy manages a prayer to Jesus before dipping into her soup. Nellie Jane, in her way, sets aside a little food. “For the spirits,” she’d say if I asked. I didn’t ask. I don’t bother with a plate for myself, but the ladies eat with gusto. Both women are excellent cooks themselves and love good food. Ned’s cooking never disappoints them. His meals are not fancy, but they are hearty, wholesome, and flavored with his special touch of love and care. There is renewed color in their faces. I leave them to finish their meal and visit while I head for the shower.

The bathroom fills with steam as the water pelts my skin and scalp. I slather my skin with moisturizer, slowly towel my mid-length graying hair, then take my time at the mirror, inspecting my face with a questioning eye. Have I aged since yesterday?

I catch a glimpse of my little girl self, always present in the bathroom, mirrored in my memories. I sigh and shake my head, run my fingers from my forehead through the slick scalp, and send the memory packing. *Not today. Not now.*

Satisfied that the reflection is my own again and no worse for the trouble of the day, I reach for a robe stored in the linen closet—not my favorite one with the bunny-ear hood. I surround my body with the plush terrycloth, tying the belt tight around my age-expanded waistline. I’m ready to face the others but not ready for food. I have enough to chew on with thoughts churning. Sleep will help. We all need a good night’s sleep.

The old girls start to clear the table. I wave them off to the guest room.

"Go to bed. I'll do this."

There was a time when Ned's sister and daughter visited, and we set up the guest room for them. Though the room is dusted and vacuumed weekly and included in the seasonal ceiling-to-floor cleanings throughout the house, no one has used the room or slept in the beds in many years.

After clearing the table, I dry my hands, hang up the towel, and go check on the women. They're already in bed, eyes shut. Before I close the bedroom door, leaving Mercy's and Nellie Jane's resting bodies behind me, I take one last look at them, snuggled into quilts Nellie Jane made for Ned and me when we married. They look, for a moment, like two little girls on an overnight, smiling happily, lost in their dreams of fun and childhood secrets only friends as close as sisters might know.

Memories rush in a flood of my summer nights with my cousin Missy, up in the loft, up in the north, safe under soft, summer-fresh quilts. Safe. The earlier cold in my bones awakens. I shiver, but I will not give in. Not today.

I sleep hard and late. It's nine o'clock when I open my eyes. I'd hoped to be on the road back to Capitol by now. I dress in jeans and a sweatshirt, tousle my hair, and head for the bathroom to apply a touch of makeup and some lipstick. I feel refreshed but in a mood. I'll have to let it go. A long and tiring day lies ahead. My aunt and her friend deserve better from me than what I have to offer right now.

Coffee. Coffee might help brighten my mood—or at least give me the strength to keep it quiet.

The two women look up when I walk into the kitchen. Mercy is the first to speak.

"Good morning, dear. Did you sleep well?"

"I did. Thank you." I want to quip, *like the dead,* but I hold my tongue. I kiss her on the head as I pass by on my way to the coffee. "And well into the morning, it looks like."

From the window, the day appears sunny, mild, and dry. I kiss Nellie Jane, too, and then sit down with my coffee.

"When would you like to leave for home?"

"Anytime you're ready, dear. Anytime you're ready."

"Let me fill my travel mug."

I retrieve our coats and Mercy's hat, which she takes in her hand. Church is over until Sunday. No need to wear a hat today. Out in the car with the women buckled in, Nellie Jane talks about plans for her spring garden.

"I may have to have a sturdier fence this year. The bears took more than their share of berries last summer."

I listen with half an ear. I don't like how I'm feeling—nervous and jumpy. I wish Ned was back. I smile, imagining his lovable face, feeling his emotional generosity. He's the absolute extreme opposite of me and my closed-off, tightfisted, ready-to-brawl, snide way of being. He is respectful of my emotional wounds, well-preserved and shoved to the back on a shelf in cold storage. He sees humanity in me that I can't find in myself. He's the beauty to my beast. He doesn't pry and listens well when I go off on a rant, upset by some injustice or slight. And he doesn't mind. It's not in his nature to mind. He's like Mercy in that way.

The long drive to Capitol is quiet and uneventful. A pileated woodpecker flies across the road. I hear Nellie Jane whisper a chant and begin to hum. She is acknowledging that bird. It calls back in a piercing announcement, unlike the more determined voice it uses when claiming territory.

We've crossed over into the magic of the north woods. I'm told that the shift in reality I feel whenever I come this way might be a magnetic effect from the iron range. I would believe that, and probably should, but I've felt this same shift in other places, places without iron, places Nellie Jane says are sacred or ceremonial. She taught me to put a name to things like this, *wakan*. I've always had these feelings, a sense of some sort of something else, but I never talk about them. I'm sure they're symptoms of deep neurosis. I don't want confirmation.

I round the bend of the old logging road that feeds into Capitol. Houses are stick-built or mobile, scattered here and there. Few homes are in sight of one another. Most locals live outside of town, in the woods, off hand-hewn pathways worn through by rusted, well-used pickup trucks.

Out of a population of fewer than sixty, most are old men, many in their late eighties to mid-nineties. Men live long lives here. I suspect they wear their women out with hard work and isolation, so women die earlier, leaving a slew of untidy, undisciplined bachelors to litter the landscape. Alcohol is the drink of choice after a mug of morning's strong coffee. The area has only recently shown signs of an urbanized population, seasonal folks bringing their 4K fun races and chic athletic garb. But the winters are rugged and not for the latte crowd.

I reach Nellie Jane's home first and walk her into the house. It's parka-worthy cold in here. I run the water in the sink to be sure the pipes haven't frozen. I turn the thermostat up to sixty-eight. On my way back to the car, I hear a window open—so much for warming up the place. The drive to Mercy's is less than two blocks and down a slight hill. I help get her settled too.

"Thank you for everything, Ellen. I'm so glad to be back in my house. I love you, dear." Mercy delivers these words with warmth and a soft caress to my cheek. "Would you like to stay for some fresh coffee?"

"I would, Mercy, but you're tired. I'm tired. Would it be all right if I call you tomorrow to check in?"

"That's fine, dear."

She tries to mask her relief. I picture her falling asleep in her reading chair as soon as I'm out of sight.

Back in the car, I let the silence of this wild place overtake me, just as it did when I was seven years old. I know my mother did me a favor by leaving me here that first summer. Maybe she saved my life. Memories of that summer are alive in me as I travel the empty highway, away from Capitol, heading toward home.

CHAPTER 3

In the morning, after three cups of coffee at the kitchen table, with a throbbing headache, and in a foul mood, I open my emails to calculate how far behind I am in my work. The spring season has just begun, and next year's summer launches are not yet on the boards, so I have some breathing room. Good. Once sales reports for May are in, I can think about next year's forecasts.

I'm grateful that I found my niche as a style consultant for top-shelf retailers. I didn't know that was a career until I met a number of stylists at a color conference. I'm good at what I do—a talent I discovered as a little girl, exploring deep in my mother's closet, fingering the brocades and chiffons of her ball gowns. She wanted me to be a secretary. I'm not good at taking dictation. I like to give it.

That marketing degree paid off, thanks to my best friend CiCi's dad. I wanted to go into sociology, but he steered me toward a self-sustaining future and away from a self-indulgent one—serving others and all that. He knew I would have to take care of myself and keep a smart distance from the other walking wounded.

LuLu and I step outside to stroll around the yard while she does her dog thing. Most of the snow is gone. The yard is drab in browns and grays. I look forward to the first spring blooms, but that will be a while yet. I shiver from the chill. Even though the sun is bright and warm, the air is damp, and a stiff breeze attacks my skin like a hatchet. This is March, I remind myself, a bitter month. I consider scattered branches shed from two river birch trees and a cottonwood. LuLu dances around my legs, begging me to throw sticks. She would chase after them all day, but my arm won't hold up to that. I leave them for Ned to clean up.

Back in the house, I grab one more unnecessary cup of coffee and walk back to my office. I sit down at the computer, stare at the screen. I open a fresh document, intending to build a work plan for the coming quarter. But I can't think about anything except Billy. *Why?*

I want to cry, to scream, but instead I write a letter to myself, the self that needs to stop obsessing about the past. This is a voice I haven't heard from in years, not since I chose to live and not die.

Death by car accident was on my mind at this particular time of year, every year. Depression came with the first sniff of autumn and was a full tenant in my brain by December. But by some heroic act of will, I dismantled the mechanisms of depression and emerged as a thriving survivor. For ten years I've been depression free—not sober—so I don't get a chip or a cake or an atta girl. But then, I don't have a group to acknowledge my anonymity. I'm in recovery in secret.

Dear Ellen,

You worthless piece of shit.

Start over.

Dear Ellen,

You are the child of two worthless shit piles.

That's better.

You have to get past this. He's dead. He has inflicted all the pain and damage he can. Yes, that was a lot, but it's over. There will be no more surprises. It's time to live your life, live your life. Just do it.

Yours in hell,

Ellen.

I read my letter over and over, silently and out loud. Then I write a response, the quick and the dirty of truth.

Dear Ellen,

Shut the fuck up.

Yours forever,

Ellen.

I print the letter and stick it up on the bulletin board to the right of my chair. I swivel to the side to stare at the words. Shame and panic surge.

"*What do you want, Ellen?*" The words screech in my ears.

I don't know. I feel lightheaded, like I might pass out.

"Think!"

I cry out, tears streaming, body shaking. The dike to my walled-off childhood fears springs a massive leak. The barricade that protects me from emotional catastrophe is weak and worn and can no longer bear the pressure.

I want a jury to convict. I want a public trial and condemnation. "I want prosecution!" I'm screaming now. "I want him to stand trial. I want him dead!" I cannot catch my breath the pain is so deep and the panic so great. "God damn him!" I scream and disintegrate into a sniveling mess. *Why now? Why now?*

I feel his crimes against me even as I feel something new and unfamiliar rising up to fight him. He cannot defeat me if he's dead. I can expose him now, without fear of retribution. Pulling myself together, I begin to breathe, and wipe my face and nose. There is one person who can still stand trial. Virginia. I need to have it out with her. I want to make her cower and cringe. Adrenaline soars through me. I will pulverize her.

"Sorry girl." I scratch LuLu's ears, the ears that have been perked and attentive. She shoved her nose into my side at my first outburst. "It's back to the sitter for you."

I grab my coat, jump in the car, drop LuLu off at Annie's, and speed toward Minneapolis. When I arrive at Virginia's, I'm poised for the kill. She has not yet been evicted by the Masons from the house that Billy gifted out from under her. They will wait a respectable time for the widow to grieve and gather her things. Maybe thirty days. I smirk.

In my car, in front of her house, I remember the day I left home. It was two days before high school graduation. I was seventeen. CiCi had rented a two-bedroom apartment near campus in St. Paul. She scored a part-time job with a local rock and blues radio station as an assistant producer, which actually meant go-fer. She majored in music, but not to teach. She was equipping herself for stardom, to hit the big time, to run with the big dogs.

The pay at the radio station was lousy, but her dad said she could keep it for spending money if she got a roommate. He'd pay for everything, as long as she got a roommate.

When CiCi asked me to share the apartment, I couldn't help but ask, "Your dad is okay with this?"

She laughed, shrugged, and smiled. "He will be."

CiCi's parents were quiet in their support of their daughter's best friend's dreams. They cared about my future and wanted good things for me. Billy and Virginia hadn't made plans to send me to college. I'd have to work for another year and save every dime before I could enroll. I'd have to do it on my own. With CiCi's help, I could.

Finally, the day came that I could move in with CiCi and out of the nightmare with my parents. I squirmed in my seat on the school bus, anxious that CiCi might already be waiting for me at the house. The last day of school meant a half-load of bodies on the bus. Most of the other seniors and their junior girlfriends had taken off early from school for graduation booze parties. The laughter and shouting bounced off the vehicle's tinny insides. My ears rang from the noise.

I nibbled at my fingertips, careful to hide my full-on nail-biting obsession. I couldn't keep my fingers out of my mouth. My nails, ragged to the quick, looked red and sore. *Why didn't I take the rest of my stuff with me this morning?*

As the bus ground on, I lowered the window by my seat to feel the warmth of the sunny afternoon on my arm. Outside, kids of every size were set loose upon residential neighborhoods, free from the restraints of school for the summer. Panic rose up to take me down. *Please don't let them screw with me today.*

I jumped off the bus at the street corner and listened to it roar off as I ran the half-block to my parents' house, recently sporting a For Sale sign on the manicured front lawn. A cardinal was singing nearby, and I could hear a mom in a kitchen, clanging pots and pans, probably cooking the family meal.

There were no cars in our driveway. I'd be safe from my parents for now. My key turned in the lock at the front door, the door I was never to use, not under any circumstances. I rushed into the spotless, showroom-quality living room that had never been lived in and only visited by a few.

My dusty school shoes shuffled across the stiff blue floral carpet. I wanted to leave a lasting mark somewhere. *Kilroy was here*. I chuckled to myself and then I didn't care. CiCi would be here any minute.

I raced upstairs to grab the few personal items that remained in my sad little bedroom. I was sorry for the pain and loneliness and fear I'd brought to this place. No one, not even a little bedroom, deserved what we got together. I was happy for the room that new people, maybe nice people like CiCi and her parents, would live here.

"Out with the old," I said aloud as I grabbed my toothbrush, hairbrush, and alarm clock. My mother had already stripped the bed.

I'd not been allowed to hang pictures or tape anything to the Federal blue and cream satin-sheen wallpaper that spoke of Virginia's taste, not the style of a teenage girl. I'd thought about asking to take my wrought iron bed since I had no money to buy another, but I didn't want to carry more memories with me.

There remained a few small, barely perceptible spots of brown here and there on the carpet. These spots of my blood had refused Virginia's efforts to fully expel them. Once Billy stopped having at me, she could have replaced the carpet. What would have driven her to vacuum over those blood stains day after day for ten more years? I shuddered.

CiCi honked the horn of her 1968 Toyota Corolla 2-door princess carriage. She had it painted pink and added chrome wheels. It was all flash and girl. I opened my canvas purse and threw in my stuff. I wanted out of there before Virginia or Billy made it home.

Skipping down the stairs, I was intent on knocking artwork askew with my elbow. That hurt me a little, but it would hurt Virginia more. I took a leap off the final step and nearly took a tumble. Righting myself, I hopped to the front door, still wide open to the elements, and ran through, stopping cold on the first step, nearly crashing into Virginia. I glared at her and pushed past. I was free. Screw her. *I'm gone, baby, gone.*

The door handle to CiCi's car, slipped out of my grasp and I hit my knuckle against the door panel. I cringed. Fitting, I thought, that the world would fight me on my way out. My back was to Virginia. I absorbed the wince from pain. She would never see me vulnerable again. Not ever.

I wrestled that door open, threw my stuff in the back seat, climbed in next to CiCi, and stopped myself from slamming the door. It wasn't necessary to beat up on the princess carriage.

I looked at CiCi and grinned. "We're outta here!"

A barking dog down the street snaps me out of my memories and back to my present plan to destroy Virginia. Two cars are parked in her driveway. One is a Lexus and the other a Mercedes. I haven't seen either parent for a good long while, so I can't guess who owns which. I pull in behind the Lexus and park. That turned out to be a good choice.

CHAPTER 4

I pound the door with its bronze knocker. I beat that door over and over, hoping to take off the head of its smiling angel. Angel. Really.

Virginia answers clad in an ecru lace and copper-colored silk nightgown covered with a matching silk robe. I burst in before she can get in a word.

"Hello, Mother. It's time we talked."

Startled, she gathers herself to present an unruffled composure. "You'll have to leave, Ellen. I have guests."

"You have guests?" I stare at her robe, then reach a finger out to lift its tie to reveal more of her nightgown. "Guests? How many men are you screwing this afternoon?"

"Ellen!" she screeches.

Her boxer-clad lover—a quite trim, silver-haired Viagra user—is halfway down the stairs. "What is going on here?" he shouts. He sees me and sprints back the way he came.

"Cover up that erection, old man. Virginia has a guest," I shout after him.

Virginia pushes me toward the door. "Get out of here!"

"Sorry, Mommy, I'm here for a chat. It's been a while. You may as well sit yourself down. I'm going to be here for some time, I imagine."

Virginia tightens the sash on her robe. "I will call the police to have you removed."

"Go ahead. I can talk to you, or I can talk to your social media pals or a publisher or a lifestyle columnist. There are many outlets for personal stories rich in family drama, like our story."

I've got her attention. Exposure to her peer group is the ultimate humiliation for a social climber like my mother. How could she spin this story to make herself look good? She knows there's no way out but to listen to me.

She takes a seat in an exquisitely upholstered, stiff-as-a-board cream linen high-back drawing room armchair, generally reserved for visitors. The chair is designed to discourage anyone from staying for long. I don't give her a chance to pick a more comfortable spot. She looks out of place.

I realize my mind is out of place. I look at her—her, not my memory of her. She's old. She's *old.* She doesn't know me. I don't know her. I'm caught off guard, surprised by my own history rising up like a specter with the death of my father, as surprised by it as Virginia is surprised to see me. *Why am I here?* And then I remember. I contain a blackout rage.

Lover-man makes his escape. Without a nod or a word to Virginia, he gives the door a healthy slam on his way out. Will this story make the rounds at the club? I hope so. I hear the Mercedes engine fire up and the tires squeal in their escape from the driveway. I imagine the marks his tires left on the concrete, leaving one more man-made mess for my mother to clean.

The court of two, with no evidence to admit and no jury to convene, begins with a diatribe from me, the sole witness and law.

"Why did you let him do it, Virginia? Why?"

She is stoic, upright and still.

"You had your own money, and lots of it. Why didn't you leave him, take me out of here? Didn't the bloody sheets and underwear—oh, and the bruises and blood on me, your little girl—didn't that spark some care, some guilt, some emotion of some kind?"

Virginia holds herself stiff and wordless. There isn't a hint of a nervous twitch or a reddening in her face.

"You've got nothing? Would you like me to demonstrate what he did to me?" I begin to pull my pants down.

"Stop it!"

"Why?"

"There is nothing to be done now." Her face passive, her tone icy cold, she dismisses his crimes against me along with her unforgiveable negligence.

"Okay. What about then? You suggest something could have been done earlier?"

"Just stop it, Ellen."

"Remember that night when you came home from playing cards with the neighbors, the night you called from the bottom of the stairs for the babysitter? There was no babysitter, remember? There was only a bloodied child, cowering in her room. Do you remember how you gave me hell for being a mess? Do you remember? I remember. I remember every single breathless moment of terror and pain. Remember? You left me alone to go to the neighbor's house for a game of Bridge. You left me alone with him!"

I pace in front of her, jeans undone and lying loose against my hips.

"You used to have your Bridge club to our house, remember? I liked watching you make the fancy sandwiches, and I liked helping you clean the house. I loved the smell of the furniture oil on the rag you gave me to use when I polished the side tables."

I felt myself drifting out of passion and into softer memories. My voice lowered.

"And you let me dust your figurines. There was a pair of alabaster doves on that three-tiered knickknack shelf. And a crystal ashtray you used on special occasions. And a smiling alabaster Buddha. I touched everything as if each was an exotic, priceless treasure."

Sitting down on the sofa, I pause to remember. I stare at her, board-stiff and silent.

"I knew you loved those things. You had other pieces, beautiful and delicate, that Billy destroyed in his rages against you. Did you think I didn't know that he beat you? Did he rape you, too?"

Her expression did not change, but my feelings did. I felt sad now, not rage, deep sadness.

"Each time I dusted, there were fewer objects. I kept rearranging them to fill the empty spaces." I rose to my feet and move closer to Virginia, vengeance usurping more tender feelings.

"But on that Saturday, there was no dusting or polishing or baking in the kitchen. I had a cold knot in my belly when you told me you were going out for Bridge. I tried not to cry. You ignored me when I begged you to take me with you. You ignored me and went off to dress. *You'll have a babysitter tonight*, you said without a glance my way. *She'll be here soon. Your father is going out as well.* But he didn't go out, did he?

"I thought the sitter would play with me, so I went into my room to look for the Parcheesi game. *I'm going now*, I heard you call out from downstairs. I heard the back door close. I knew the sitter would be here soon enough. I began to walk down the stairs with the game box in my hands when I heard Billy at the front door. He was telling the babysitter she wasn't needed. I crept back up the stairs, making not one bit of noise. He couldn't know I was home. I heard his footsteps on the stairs, coming closer to the top. He passed by my bedroom door. I squeezed my eyes tight and tried to crawl inside my own body. I didn't dare breathe. I set the game box down next to me, terrified the marbles might rattle, and sat cross-legged on the carpet."

"Ellen—"

"Shut up! I don't know that I can stop myself from hurting you if you don't shut up."

She keeps still, and I continue.

"I knew what would happen if he found me home on my own. Every opportunity you allowed him to get at me, he took full advantage. I will forever hear my pleas for him to stop. Every time, it was the same. He was unrelenting in his mad assaults on me.

He'd rip off my panties or pajama bottoms and toss them on the floor. He rubbed his penis on me until he was hard. Then he stuck it everywhere, in my mouth, in my butt, pushing it between my legs until it was inside of me. *Do you like this, little girl? Do you love your daddy?* I'd beg him to stop, but he'd tell me to stop whining. *You need this* he'd say and go at me again. *All girls need a good fuck."*

I'm engulfed in memories. I can't slow down to think about what I'm saying.

"But that Saturday night was different. I sat still as a stone until my legs ached, and my ankle fell asleep. When I thought I couldn't take it anymore, believing I might be safe from him for once, I heard him open the door to your bedroom. There was a soft tapping at my bedroom door. *Are you in there, little girl?* I held my breath. I saw the knob turn. I almost passed out from fear. He opened the door, staring at me sitting on the floor, and then he grabbed me by the arm, yanked me to my feet. I stumbled, unable to put weight on my tingling ankle.

He dragged me, mumbling, to the bathroom. He ran water in the tub, testing the temperature with his free hand. He kept my arm in his grip. He let the water fill the tub as he let loose of me and dropped his shorts."

I fight to keep my wits. I will never get another chance like this for a face-down with Virginia. I close my eyes, suck in as much air as I can, and charge at her again.

"I had to pee. I spoke in the smallest voice I could muster: *I have to go to the bathroom.* He said nothing as I got up from the floor and sat on the toilet. I let the hot pee flow out of me. I wished I could go with it. As I reached for the toilet tissue, he raised his flat penis to my mouth and pried open my teeth. *Suck it.* He stunk of cigarettes and whiskey and other awful smells. *Suck it!* He stood tall above me. He clenched his hand nearest to my face into a tight, fighter's fist. I couldn't breathe. I tried to do what he asked, but I wanted to throw up. And then he raised that fist and plunged it into my compliant belly, pushing my face off his penis with his other hand. I banged the back of my head onto the toilet tank. I must have blacked out. The next thing I remember, we were in the tub of water."

I glare at Virginia, expecting her to crack, but she holds her own. She's a tough cookie, my mother. I take a deep breath and hammered out the rest of the horrible memorial to my father.

"He held my body onto his fattened penis, moving me across it, back and forth, a finger stuck up in me. I was naked. He was naked. The water was cold. I shivered. My teeth shivered. I stopped breathing. He pushed me out of the tub and ordered me to get him a towel. I slipped on the wet tile floor. I grabbed hold of the vanity while I reached for one from the towel rack. *Nice ass, little girl,* he said to me—words I will never, ever stop hearing. I handed him the towel, then ran back to my bedroom, slammed the door, and put on my robe. But it didn't warm me. Everything in me and about me was cold and wet."

I'm almost out of force. Recalling it, hearing out loud everything that lived in the darkest parts of me, I'm resurrected. But not as a cowering child. This is risen evil, and it threatens to choke the life out of me. I fight off an urge to stammer. My mouth dry, my throat hoarse, I make myself slow down. My words now must be controlled. I let myself wonder if she knew—she couldn't possibly know—how bad it got that night.

"Did you ever once ask yourself why I was such a bloody mess when you got home? Remember, you weren't home, right? You were having fun and snacks with the girls. Were you laughing? Did you give me a thought? Of course not, because you hired a sitter who hadn't arrived by the time you left. You couldn't be bothered to wait one more minute to be out of that house."

The barest of flinch passes across Virginia's face. I push on, harder.

"He followed me into my room and threw me on the bed, punched me one more time in my tummy. He pushed and pushed his penis between my legs and into me—his huge body inside my small one hurt, worse than ever before. Did you get that bit, Virginia? *Than ever before*. And let's not forget I was a mere seven years old."

And still nothing from my mother. Nothing. I feel I must be living in some other world where things—bad things—don't matter, don't have meaning. Have I exaggerated? Does she not respond because…because…why wouldn't she have some reaction? The unreality in this moment of absolute exposure catches me up in a great and hungry fear. Have I been wrong? Am I crazy?

But then my head is filled with the sounds of the springs on my mattress squeaking with his pushing and grunting and profanities. I can feel him pulling my hair until I think it might rip off my head.

"I knew he was going to kill me, for real this time. I could feel my insides shifting. It's an indescribable sensation of knowing—not actually feeling—that you're being ripped apart from the inside out."

I know I'm near blackout with rage. I tell myself to take my time, but I can't listen. My heart is beating out of my chest. My limbs are weak. Yet I can't show weakness.

"The sound of your voice calling for the babysitter from the living room stopped him. And honestly, I don't know why. Another thrust or two, and he would have had it all—brutal sex with his child and an ultimate final flourish of her death as she bled out. You likely saved my life, so maybe I should be grateful. What do you think?" I can't wait for an answer.

"I'm home, you called upstairs to the babysitter who'd never set foot in the house. *I can take you home now.*

"*Fuck,* is all he said as he pushed off me and left my room, but not until he heard you set foot on the bottom stair, calling out, *Hello?* He never touched me after that. But how he touched me then."

And then I take my pants all the way down to languish about my ankles. I spread my legs in front of her face and describe every intrusion I can recall. I turn my back to her and bend over, continuing with the list and styles of assaults committed by Billy on his young daughter.

Virginia manages to wriggle her way out of the chair and away from my exposed behind. She stands and brushes herself off while smoothing her silk nightgown, barely ruffled by my explicit display.

"Leave now."

I pull up my pants, zip my zipper, spit at her well-manicured feet, and lurch out the door, leaving it wide open to the bitter weather—certainly no colder or harsher than my mother.

In the safety of my car, I back out of the driveway, running high on adrenaline. *What was I thinking?* I quickly turn into the curb and stop.

I can't feel my arms or legs. My face feels huge and hot. I am suffering, unsure, frozen. I gasp for air and spirit. The need to flee frees my paralyzed limbs so I can drive. *Get out of here. Go!*

I head for Northway Liquors. I'm not sure how much whiskey I have with me, but I know I can't be caught short. Not tonight. Twenty minutes later, with a bottle of scotch secure in my overnight bag, I head for Bristol Suites, my hotel of choice whenever I need to stay in the city for business. The parking lot is full. I find an open spot at the end farthest away from the front door. With bag in hand, I feel the cold evening air bite through my jacket.

"Jesus!" I shiver while my teeth chatter.

I enter the lobby and see signs at the conference room entry announcing a fundraiser for a high school hockey team. The hallway is flooded with high school boys, their families, and exuberant cheerleaders.

"Welcome, Ms. McInnis. It's good to see you again." My favorite concierge, Alfred, is on duty. "We do have a room, but it's a single. Will that be all right?"

I nod, hand him my credit card, and sigh. I can't wait another minute to crawl into pjs, bed, and a whiskey. The adrenaline rush is wearing off. Now shame and utter despair sweep over me like a tornado tearing up a Midwestern prairie. I am smashed to emotional smithereens.

Once in my room, I open the whiskey and pour myself a drink. I settle into a white hotel robe—stiff, not soft, like my robe from home, in its surround to my body—and sit on the bed, drink in hand. With the first sip of whiskey, the panic subsides. My mood changes from whipped dog to a more settled state of satisfaction. I humiliated Virginia.

I flip on the hotel television to catch the early evening news. I'm hypnotized by the flickering light cast from the screen. I hear sounds of two children in a race down the hallway just outside my door. There's laughing, an "Ouch!" crying from a little girl, muffled voices, and then the slamming of a door.

The screen from my phone lights up. I don't want to talk to anyone tonight. I intend to drink myself numb and stay that way for a day or two. But exhaustion overtakes me, and I fall asleep. I am wakened much later by a constantly vibrating phone. I fumble for it, tangled up in a blanket and sheet. The phone falls to the floor. I roll out of bed, step on the damned thing, and bend over to retrieve it, jabbing my toe into the base of the nightstand as I try to crawl back into bed.

"Fuck!"

I see my neighbor Patsy's face grinning at me from the phone.

"Crap. What's wrong now?" I mumble.

I answer, but then drop the phone again. "Hold on, Patsy." I reach for the phone on the floor. "I dropped the phone! Okay. Got it."

"I'm so sorry, Ellen, but I thought you should know. I got a call from Crystal Swenson. You know her. She's an ER doctor at St. Clara's." She's crying and breathless with hurry to speak the words. "She said your mother's body was found a few hours ago by a close friend. It looks like suicide. She asked me to tell you, so you'd know before the authorities reach you. With your father just gone and all, well, we thought you should know. Please don't tell anyone that I told you. Crystal would be in so much trouble. I'm so sorry."

I am speechless. I sit straight and tall on the edge of the bed, looking at the phone, staring at the screen. I cannot respond.

"Please don't let anyone know that she told me. Ellen? Ellen, are you there?"

I click off the phone, then stand. I walk to the hotel window looking out over the twinkling lights of the city. *She's dead. She's dead. What have I done?*

I sleep without booze, without conscience and wake after ten a.m. to streaks of bright morning light leaking through the heavy window coverings. Before dressing, I take a long look at my body in the full-length dressing mirror. Aging skin doesn't look good, but that does not distract me today. I think about how I used my body to shame my mother into suicide.

I always felt alone in the world, but that was never true. I just didn't know how to connect, except with CiCi. Yet no matter how open she was to me, I used her like a life raft, my grip on her never relaxed. Now, feeling disconnected again, adrift, floating, free, I'm loose in a world for the first time without a shadowland of monsters and ghouls in pursuit.

CHAPTER 5

I ignore the phone calls from the police until the end of the day. Would I come to the morgue to identify the body? There is no one else to do it. The next morning, I stand in the Medical Examiner's office, being prepped for the viewing of my mother's corpse.

"Please, come with me, Mrs. McInnis." A young assistant speaks to me at my back in an efficient tone, not making a request.

We're joined by a distracted detective who is late and in a rush. They escort me to an elevator that takes us down one level to a concrete block tunnel. The floor is also concrete, painted gray. The walls are painted white. The sounds of our footsteps slap in my ears as they ricochet off the hard surfaces. There is nothing to soften the noise. The fluorescent lighting burns my eyes. My head begins to hurt.

I am terrified to see my mother's body in the company of the detective, who must know her death was my fault and will accuse me. The gates of hell will open to swallow me whole. My mind clouds, stifling any thoughts that could help thwart the rising panic in my chest. My heart pounds in my ears. I might pass out.

We enter the room where her body waits for me to give the final nod of acknowledgment, that yes, these are my mother's remains. I look at her, vacant of life. There is nothing here to suggest our mutual disregard of one another.

The streaming tears are, I suppose, an involuntary reaction to relief, but the cries come in heaving waves that leave me gasping for air with tears pouring and snot bubbling from my nose. I am a baby again, just popped from the womb into the world as I came, cut away from a cold, loveless mother.

The young assistant catches me as I begin to teeter. He walks me out of the room and to a chair in the empty, institutional hallway. He pages a nurse, who arrives quickly with a sedative.

"No." I shake my head and wave her away, grabbing at the tissues poking from the small box she places on my lap. The waterworks flow freely. Tissue after tissue is spent and tossed to the floor. I can't stop heaving from shock. A breath. A second breath. Good. It's coming. Calming.

The nurse whispers too loudly to the assistant, "I've got to get back. Can you take it from here?"

As he nods, I burst out laughing. "I've been reduced to an 'it.'"

The nurse is horrified. I brush off her apology. She scurries away down the hall. I stand, set the box of tissues on the adjoining chair, and straighten my shirt. I dry the last of my tears and reach back for one more tissue to go, just in case.

"I'm ready," I say to the assistant and the detective, who has been standing back from the eruption of emotion. He doesn't look the type to engage well with others outside of the interrogation room.

We walk back through the tunnel of death. The assistant leaves me with the young detective to return to his office, he says. The detective stays with me through the elevator ride, even to the lobby doors of the hospital. I think I may have misjudged him. Perhaps he is more a kindly sort. I thank him and offer my hand with a weak smile.

At the exit door he stops me. "Mrs. McInnis."

I turn to face him.

"I understand you argued with your mother on the day she died."

His manner is accusatory. It hits me like a Golden Gloves champion's sucker-punch right under my chin. I take the assault like a pro, still standing, yet I drop my shoulders in a show of defeat, then bristle.

"We always argued," I respond with my back to him and my face to the wind.

The next day I receive a call from Virginia's attorney. Would I come to sign some papers… as Virginia's only heir, blah… blah… blah. She couldn't give me love or protection, but she could make me wealthy from her parents' estate. I can't fathom what may have been in her mind to leave me anything. My father left her nothing in his will. I'd have thought she'd follow his lead. Two days later Virginia's reported suicide made the front page of the *Trib*. It is suspected that she was overcome by grief at the recent death of her husband. *Yeah, that's what happened.*

I will not attend her funeral. I need to go to Capitol to talk with Mercy. I want to tell her the truth. All of it. I can't stand myself right now. And why? What did I do? The accusations scream in my head, she killed herself because of me. *But it wasn't because of you, Ellen. It was her fear of exposure. You got to her. Take the fucking win!*

Mercy will give me sympathy. She will be appropriately outraged. She will open her arms to me and love me like the baby I am. She will hear me. She will understand and forgive me. I surrender to the idea and make a plan to go back to Capitol, stay a couple of days, and have the last word in the closing chapter of my family book of horrors.

Maybe I'll pick up LuLu to bring along this time. She could have a good run, smell up some wild things, and hang her head out the car window for hours, sniffing up the wonders of the world. I call Annie, who has LuLu with her on a spring vacation with friends in Sioux Falls. I miss the cuddles LuLu offers. She is a rescue who rescued me. I miss her almost as much as I miss Ned.

CHAPTER 6

I open the door to Patsy's pounding. She is inside and talking before I can say her name or hello.

"I heard you were interviewed about your mother's death. How are you?" Patsy has recently changed the color streak in her salt and pepper hair from aqua to yellow. She's a few years older than I am but as light of heart as a bear cub.

"In honor of spring?"

"What? Oh, yeah. And I've got a new girl, so we have matching dos." She beams at that, then switches to a more serious face. "So, what happened? You didn't tell them about Crystal, did you? Oh Lord—I'm sorry to make this about her."

I point her toward the living room, where she sits on the sofa. "You talk." She waves her hand at me, dismissing herself from the conversation.

"The police interviewed me because her nosy neighbor, Helen, saw me come and go. But she also saw Virginia's lover flee the residence shortly after I arrived. So, I met with a detective at the precinct station, after I had to identify her body at the morgue. But really, the interview amounted to nothing. He didn't ask. I didn't tell."

"Didn't tell what?" Patsy leans in for more story.

I tell Patsy every ugly detail of my brief but savage exchange with Virginia, so alive in the telling that I forget she knows nothing of the abuses in my young life. I fight to maintain composure even now. I feel dark and dangerously close to screaming, yet I speak in a small, tired voice that sounds hollow against the raging waves of condemnation at work in my head, in my chest.

"I gave her a choice between social humiliation and scandal that she'd never live down, or she could listen to me. She chose death over both. Couldn't she have left a note, saying *Gee, kid, sorry for everything*, before she ate every pill in the house? I could still expose her, I suppose. But that wouldn't help anything. I'd probably come out the horrible daughter who pushed her own poor grieving, freshly widowed mother, to kill herself." I end with sarcasm: "You know how bitter and unforgiving children can be."

Patsy has lost all color and sits rigid, hands clenched into fists. "Jesus, Ellen! Holy crap! I never knew… you never said a word. Jesus!"

Up until this moment, only CiCi and Ned knew about my childhood. I feel deep shame, even though I know, I *know*, there is nothing to be ashamed of. I stand, put my head down, begin to pace. I feel the panic start, crawling up my back and pounding in my chest.

"Yes, my father, Billy, raped me repeatedly from age five until I was about seven. Virginia not only didn't stop it, she punished me for it. I think he stopped coming at me once I had a good friend, CiCi, who might expose his acts to her parents. My father was an opportunist, not a fool."

Patsy remains immobilized by shock. I don't care that I'm dumping this all on her. I don't care. And then I look down at her, because I do care. A sense of a reality of now makes a cautious approach into this bizarre time trap I've dragged us into. I want to stop, to spare her. But she can see I have more to tell. She waves a hand to gesture that I should continue.

"I couldn't stop myself from having at Virginia. I didn't shove the pills down her throat, but I certainly forced her hand. Billy's death threw me. I thought I'd be happy with him gone forever, and I suppose I am. But the permanence of his absence equals pardon for his crimes. I can't handle it. And I took my crazy over this out on her."

I have to sit down. I need a drink.

"The worst of it is when I saw her, she was *old*. I hadn't seen her in decades. I can't rid myself of her face, her form—someone I don't even know anymore. Yet she was the same. Just old."

For now, I have no more tears but still want a drink.

"Gin?"

"Please." Patsy, usually exuberant, wears a look of shock, likely mirroring my own. "Yes, please."

Back with two gin and tonics, I hand a tumbler to Patsy, and sit again.

"Virginia didn't care about Billy any more than I did. I thought that since he'd left her nothing, she might be pissed off enough to crack a little bit with me. But no. She was so cold, impervious to anything I did or said. She responded to my actions with one word: *leave*. That was it. Until I heard she overdosed, I had no idea I'd affected her at all." I sigh, feeling horribly discouraged and exposed.

I send Patsy on her way home, still early in the day, thoroughly shaken and fluid in gin. She can drink more, longer, than anyone I know. I call Mercy to arrange a time to visit. I tell her I will arrive on Sunday, after church, in time for Sunday dinner. She sounds tired but welcoming.

The gin I had with Patsy is not doing the trick. Menial tasks are mind-numbing, so I have an ambitious plan to distract myself by giving the house a thorough cleaning. This too is Ned's territory. He prefers that I leave domestic chores for him, because each time I'm asked to do anything around the house, I whine my way out of them as quickly as I can. But for him, to honor his homecoming, I will do this thing.

I grab a bucket from the cleaning closet in the hallway and start in on the kitchen floor. On my knees, like a nun at the convent, I begin to scrub with a brush, harder and harder. I attack the floor, not moving an inch from the spot where I first knelt in this cleansing, self-flagellating enterprise. It's not helping. The memories, the questions, tumble over and over, like balls in a bingo basket.

"You've been over this and over this," I mutter to myself in anger as I scrub. I begin to cry, again. "God, make this stop!" I know I'm screaming and slap the floor in defeat until my hands burn. The word *stop* sends me into deeper grief and sobs. I crumple on the floor and cry myself into exhaustion.

There's pounding at the back door. "Are you okay?" Patsy shouts as she pounds harder.

I raise myself from the floor, soaked in dirty water and suds, slipping in the mess. I manage to get to my feet and to the door. It's barely open when Patsy storms through.

"What in the hell is going on? I could hear you in my basement!"

"Come into the living room," I say as we track through the wet, soapy mess on the kitchen floor. "I'm sorry. I didn't realize I was so loud. It just came out."

Patsy holds me and asks if I want a sedative. "You know I've got a stash."

Her offer makes me laugh. "No, thanks. I just have to catch my breath."

"How about I order some food, and we watch a movie tonight? I don't think you should be alone. Girl, you are struggling." Patsy has her phone in hand, ready to dial.

"Pad Thai."

"Done."

She makes the call while I stretch out on the sofa. I try to breathe. It's difficult at first, the panic keeping pace with every breath. The food arrives, and with it, Patsy hands me another gin. We settle in to watch mind-numbing television until I fall asleep.

It's ten hours later when I wake to the smell of frying bacon. Patsy says she stayed the night in the guest room. She hands me coffee. I can smell the sizzling bacon fat hanging heavy in the air. I open the kitchen blinds. The sun is shining. Things almost always seem better in the morning, when the sun is glowing, warming a room.

Thank you, Patsy, I think. *Thank you for not leaving me alone.* I consider her friendship in this moment and feel I've not done enough to show how lucky I am to have her as a friend. I will have to do better in the future.

"I'm going to visit my aunt in Capitol, my father's sister," I tell her. "I'm going tomorrow, in fact. She's in her eighties. I'm afraid to tell her all this, but I'm driven to do it. I want some level of familial acknowledgement. And she always, always loved me. I'm afraid, though, that I will hurt her by telling her about the monster that was her brother. What if she dies from the shock? I'll never recover from the guilt!"

Patsy jumps in. "You can't know what you can't know. Go gently. Test her with a little bit of the story. See how you both handle it."

“Part of me holds her responsible—some. She could have helped me out when I was a kid. I spent summers with her and her husband. They must have known something was wrong. I feel she deserves to know. But I get confused between wanting what I want and doing the right thing. If I’m honest, I’m still looking for someone to pay for my pain. She’s a nice old lady—but there it is.”

“You’d better get clear on what you want, then, if possible. That’s a tough one. Do you want me to drive up there with you?”

Tears well up, on automatic now. Everything gets an instant emotional rise out of me. “You are beautiful, do you know that? You know, it means everything to me that you are so supportive. I don’t know how I’ll ever thank you.”

Patsy smiles a sunshine-warm smile. “No need. I want to help if I can. And I’m right here.” She puts her arms around my neck and kisses the top of my head. Patsy is short, no more than five-foot-two to my five-foot-eight. Still, she gives me a motherly finish with a flourish to our sad and awful conversation.

I cry a little more, then wipe my tears. “Enough!” I say. “Let’s eat!”

I pick at my food while Patsy starts collecting dishes. “I don’t want to leave you with one more mess. You’ll have to redo that floor, you know.”

One more mess.

Patsy leaves around 1:30, but not without an admonishment. “If your aunt is the important family anchor you say she is, I’d be careful about approaching her with this. Really. It’s all so fresh. You’ve said yourself that you’ve been blindsided by what you’re feeling and the memories. With your mom’s death too, it’s too much for you. It’s almost too much for me. If you have any thought of dropping this on her, expecting that she can fix it somehow or take responsibility… could you take some time, think, feel it through?"

I know she's right, but I don't know how she's right. My thoughts are run over by my hurt.

"I'll think about that. And Patsy"—I reach for her and hug her hard—"Thank you. Thank you."

I have to call Ned. I have to.

"Hi, sweetie. How are you?" The sound of his voice sends a wave of longing through me. I miss him so much. "I'm getting my stuff together to head home tomorrow. I miss you."

"I miss you too." I try to hide my emotion. I don't want to overwhelm him with my needs and tears.

"Are you holding up? I got twenty or more emails about your mother, but not one from you. You must be a mess. Is anybody with you?"

I take a moment to respond. "I know. I'm sorry. I had a meltdown, and then I had another meltdown. Patsy came over a couple of times and propped me up. I thought that when my father died, it wouldn't be anything to me. But both of them—it's uncomfortable to be me right now."

"What about tonight? Will someone be with you tonight?"

"Patsy's next door if I need her. She's been amazing. And tomorrow I'm going to the cabin. Patsy helped me see that if I pounce on Mercy right now, out of knee-jerk need, I could harm her and our relationship. I've got to get myself grounded, centered, something other than swirling in madness." I pause to take a breath. "You know how visits to the cabin can settle me down."

Ned is silent, generous in allowing me to ramble. I take note and appreciate but can't stop talking long enough to tell him.

"There's so much you don't know. Honey, I can't go through it all on the phone. Will it be okay if I'm gone for a few days after you get back? Will you be all right?"

"I'll be all right, but now I'm doubly not sure about you. It's still wicked cold up north, you know."

"Yes. Yes. I know. I'll get the winter gear out of storage. And I'll call Freddie to have him go over and turn the heat up and make sure the cabin is plowed out. I think he sent me an email last week after that big snow, saying that he'd plowed."

I wish I could be home for Ned, but I just can't. "I'm sorry about this, Ned. I really am. I'm overthinking, and I'm obsessing. I have to get a break. The isolation and cold might force the break I need."

"I think I understand, but I also think we should do it together. And I need you right now, too." He sounds both certain and pleading.

"Ned, I'm stuck in a place I haven't been in for decades. I can't relate to us, only to me. I'm collapsing. I'm fighting for my sanity. It's running away, almost too fast for me to catch up. You can't help me. I don't see a way you can help. And I'd be useless to you."

"I'm going to have to work harder at teaching you what love and marriage is all about." He sounds sad, even lonely.

I hate myself for pushing him away, but he isn't hearing me. "You saying that makes everything much more painful," I blurt without thinking. "I can't meet your expectations or needs right now." My voice fills with desperation. "I'm in trouble. I don't know how else to tell you. I can't have your needs pulling on me now." I know I'm being ugly and hateful.

"I hear your desperation. Obviously, we have more to talk about." His tone softens. "Will you call me tomorrow before you leave?"

I force myself to find some kindness in me to give to him. I don't want him to worry, even though I know there is plenty to worry about.

"I'll do what I can. You know where I'll be. If anything changes, I'll let you know. I'm really sorry, Ned. It's not that I don't know you need me. I just can't do more than what I'm doing. I'm truly, truly sorry." I feel sick.

"You're not alone. Ellen, I love you. Do what you need to do, but remember to check in. We'll regroup when we can. Meanwhile, I will be home. That's where I'll be."

I say goodbye, hang up, then fall to the floor in sobs.

CHAPTER 7

The first time Virginia drove me up north to Capitol for the summer, I was scared to go away and scared to stay at home. As she drove on and on, I made a game of watching for wildlife dead or alive. I spied woodpeckers and a fox and a coyote. I saw a bloated carcass of a porcupine, and two raccoons, one half-eaten by crows that flew off the meat when we drove by.

"Stop fidgeting!" my mother said. "You'd better behave, or your aunt Mercy will put you out with the dogs. A coyote will get you for sure!"

My mother was glad to get rid of me but hated the bother of the trip. I overheard her say that to my dad last night before I went to bed. He mumbled something I couldn't hear.

I tried to think about something good, but my mind gave me something bad, the last day of first grade and our class party. We made a line at the teacher's desk to pick a chocolate cupcake with a fat strawberry on top. As I walked back to my desk, my tongue lapped at the soft, buttery frosting, knocking the strawberry loose. It rolled down the front of my green striped cotton blouse, the one with the smocking on the front. I wet my pants as I watched its steady stain mark a path through the embroidery threads and along the dainty mother of pearl buttons. I knew my mother would kill me.

The other kids pointed and laughed, catching the attention of our teacher who grabbed my hand and marched me to the bathroom, huffing and murmuring about a different job. My other hand let loose of the cupcake, which dropped to the checkered linoleum floor in our wake. Smashed and splattered, the cupcake made one more mess for someone else to clean up. I could hear my mother's scolding voice in my head: *One more mess for me to clean up.*

I wasn't dry when the bus came to take us home. I sat by myself, smelly, my shirt stained. I wanted to die. A cold crawled up from inside my belly and made my teeth chatter.

At the bus stop, I jumped off and ran the two blocks to my house. There were no cars in the driveway. Relief. I raced to the back of the house, ripped open the screen door, and turned my key in the lock, letting myself into the kitchen. I scrambled upstairs, tripping twice, to clean myself and change clothes before anybody got home. I hid the stained shirt under my mattress. I'd figure out how to get rid of it tomorrow.

I heard car tires grazing the asphalt driveway. I looked out my bedroom window to see my father getting out of the car. I wet myself all over again.

But I can't wet myself in the car with my mother. That would be the death of me for sure, so instead of thinking backward, I watched ahead as the trees flew by the window. I counted two more dead raccoons on the road and then I saw a deer with two spotted fawns making their way into the tree line.

"Look!"

My mother ignored me. She cranked up the Big Band radio station and smoked until the air in the car was blue. Some days she'd open the quarter window, set her wrist on the door panel, and let the smoke stream outside. But not today.

I squirmed in my seat, sneezed, even coughed, before I begged her to open the back window for fresh air, but she wouldn't do it. She didn't like the road noise. I hoped we'd get to my aunt's house before I choked to death.

We zigzagged through a tiny village, passing different kinds of houses and barns. This wasn't at all like my neighborhood.

"We're here," my mother spoke for the first time in forever. "This is Capitol." She pulled into a yard. "This is your aunt Mercy's house."

She didn't turn off the engine or bother to get out of the car. She waited in silence as I stepped out with my suitcase. I stared at the small log two-story house. I heard Virginia—I used my mother's real name when I was really mad at her—pull away at my back.

I stood alone in the turnaround with my small black suitcase, smelling like a house afire. I didn't know what to do. I was afraid to stay outside by myself in case there was a hungry coyote nearby, but I was afraid to go up to the house too. I tried not to cry. I imagined myself small as a mouse. I didn't want a wild creature to notice me. I was hungry and stinky and scared. There wasn't a noise, not even from a bird. There wasn't a puff of wind to cool my skin, growing hotter and redder with fear. And I had to use the bathroom.

I heard a car coming and turned myself around. It was Aunt Mercy and Uncle Jasper.

"Well, honey," Mercy exclaimed as she climbed out of the old blue pickup, "we thought you were coming tomorrow!" She reached out to hug me, stinky as I was. "Whoo! Let's get you cleaned up and get some lunch in you."

Jasper's giant hand was on my head. I flinched, only for a second. He was gentle as he stroked my hair. He flashed me a sunny grin. "Good to see ya, child!"

Jasper led the way into the house, snatching my small suitcase in his great, large hand. Aunt Mercy led me into the bathroom for a shower. She dried me off with an oversized towel and walked me upstairs to find my suitcase resting on one of two pine log beds. I could smell bacon cooking downstairs.

"BLTs, smells like," Aunt Mercy said with a smile. She left me to get dressed. "We'll be ready for lunch when you are."

My cousin Missy ran home from her friend's house when she heard the lunch bell ring outside. Uncle Jasper had rigged up a rusty cowbell that clanged three times for meals or any other reason a child might need to be summoned home.

Missy and I sat at the sprawling log table, eyeing each other, smiling, and devouring our sandwiches. I'd never had a BLT before. It was delicious. I finished my milk when Missy, getting up from her chair, asked if we could be excused to go outside.

Aunt Mercy nodded. "But only after you clear your place from the table."

Missy showed me the huge vegetable garden, pointing out cabbages, lettuce, beets, and tomatoes. Most plants were newly sprouted, some showing only a few leaves.

"Just wait," she told me, "to see how big the cabbages grow!"

She walked me through the small town, pointing out who lived where, which dogs were friendly, and where the best raspberries grew for picking in July. We stopped to rest in the sun on the wide porch of the co-op store, swinging our legs, greeting people as they came and went. It was a busy little town. Everybody was nice. I decided right then that I would live in Capitol forever, somehow. I'd find a way.

That night, I made a nest from hand-sewn quilts, my eyes and cheeks peeking out above the colorful cotton edging. I held the smell of pine logs in my nose, imagining the world of forests and wild things on the other side of the window, past Aunt Mercy's vegetable garden. I wanted to stay awake to listen for coyotes, but my body wouldn't wait one minute to go to sleep.

The next morning, Missy and I fished off the shore of Lake Makwa. We carried our poles, a jar of worms we dug from the yard, and a metal pail for the fish. We filled the bucket with water and set it under the trees past the shore, out of the bright sun.

We caught seven sunfish—bluegills and pumpkin seeds. We crouched to peer at them swimming in the bucket. We tossed them bits of worm. They tried to jump for the bait, but it was too crowded in the bucket. Water splashed all over us. We couldn't see who got the worms.

It was time to go home anyway. The pail, full of water and fish, was too heavy for us to carry. We tipped it a little to let some of the water out, but we dropped it. It fell over on its side, sloshing water out the top, letting its cargo loose in a flood. We'd kept the fish in the shade of the young pines off the shoreline so they wouldn't get too hot in the sun. Now the lake, their lifeline, was too far away. They gasped and flopped in the duff beneath the trees. We grabbed at them to save them, to pick them up and toss them back into the lake, but their fins cut our hands. There was a lot of blood and a lot of dying.

We ran home and told Nellie Jane, Aunt Mercy's best friend—a real Indian—all about what happened. She offered us stringers and showed us how to use them.

The next day, we took Missy's weather-worn wagon along with us to carry our stringers of fish, but we forgot to bring a bucket of water. We hauled the strung-up, gasping, flapping sunnies home in the wagon, a good twenty-minute walk. We felt awful about the dying fish in our wagon. We tried to drown out the sounds of death with loud singing, but our hearts felt guilty. We committed a terrible sin, and we knew it.

Nellie Jane came along the following day to show us how to clean the fish on the shore. "They won't suffer too much, and we'll have a good supper." She glanced up at us—"Nature's gift to the two-leggeds"—then went back to cleaning our catch.

We watched as she scaled and gutted a bluegill. Its golden saucer-size eye stared at me as she cut through its belly. It heaved, gasping for life, while she worked.

We didn't go fishing after that. Instead, we took up rock hunting and looked for abandoned bird nests. Once we hid from a family of black bears lumbering along the tree line at the edge of a meadow hidden within the pine forest. We didn't move a muscle and held our breath until the bears moved on, though we wanted to jump up and run to play with the cubs.

Nellie Jane didn't have any kids of her own. I dreamed she was my real mom. When I was born, somebody gave me to the wrong people, the mistake was discovered, and a kind doctor called Nellie Jane to come and get me. We lived together in her cabin among the drying herbs and hides. We sang songs together, her songs. She tapped her sacred drum while I shook her woman's rattle, letting the small seeds inside rustle against the skin of the dried gourd that made its shape. We ate turtle soup on Wednesdays, and I saved every shell.

The memories of that first summer are alive in me as I travel the empty highway north to the cabin in Ely. I feel as safe there as I did as a little girl with Nellie Jane in her cabin in Capitol.

It's right to delay my trip to see Mercy. I'll tell her everything later. Now I need to go to the cabin, the icy, silent cabin, and scream until spring thaw.

CHAPTER 8

It's 4:00 when I arrive in Ely. Another twenty minutes, and I'll be at the cabin. It's not yet dark, but twighlight is on my heels. I arrive at the cabin, a classic rustic log two-level structure. Grabbing my gear, I walk up the few entry steps to a small porch, swept clean, occupied by an empty weathered rocker covered in snow. I know I've made the right decision to come here. I feel better already.

There is a stack of wood outside the back door. I'll have to get a fire going. No point in being in the cabin if there isn't a crackling fire.

I drop my things in a heap inside the doorway and climb the stairs to the loft. I pull bedding from the loft bedroom, carry it downstairs, and drape it over the rustic pine sofa in the main room, in front of the wood burning stove. It's way too cold yet to sleep upstairs tonight.

I check the thermostat. It's set to sixty. I push it to seventy-five, run water in the kitchen faucet, and flush the toilet. Broken pipes would send me out of here. But I don't want to deal with frozen pipes or any mundane maintenance tasks. I'm the only maintenance job that needs attention right now.

I store food and water in the kitchen. A bottle of scotch is made handy on the sofa-side table before I snuggle into my sleeping bag, with my down jacket wrapped around a couch cushion for a pillow. I leave a stocking cap on my head to hold in heat. My feet are snug in wool socks I found in a drawer in the loft. I'll probably wake up in a sweat when the room comes to temperature, but I'll never get to sleep if I'm cold.

I feel calm creep through my body as if I'd downed a dram of whiskey. I let myself drift. I am alone, completely alone. I am free from tears and heartache and upset. I am exhausted, but I feel centered and stable for the first time in a week. I feel more myself—the self I built over the years, the self that matters. The self of control, that learned to keep the past in the past.

And then I see an apparition, a lady in white.

She is absolutely white, like porcelain clay. Her features are distinct. Her hair is long and flowing with no braid or curl. She is covered by a robe. She lies on her side and seems to be traveling through the ethers on an alabaster stream—though she is not in motion. Her stare is blank, but I can sense her will to move along in the alabaster waters. There are spurts here and there of blood, brilliant crimson in color, in sharp contrast to all the white on white. I am reminded of a white rose with a drop of blood from a finger stuck by its protective thorn. But it isn't that. I know it isn't that.

As I watch, the woman rises, supported by male figures, one on either side. There is no recognizable support beneath their feet, but they remain upright. Around them, surrounding them, are hideous faces of brown and gray, large noses and eyes, gargoyles.

I remember these creatures. As a child, I once saw them in the trees near our new house. I was six. It was a time when new neighborhoods rose out of former cornfields and spread like a plague across the Midwest. I was exploring on my own at the edge of a farmer's oak grove, not yet bulldozed, though I could hear the workmen and heavy equipment not far from where I wandered.

I looked up into the old trees, trunks deeply ridged and in many places scarred where branches had broken off in a time ago windstorm. The leaf canopy was lush with a bounty of young, green acorns that were meant not only to sprout new mighty oaks but to feed bears and squirrels and other wildlife come winter.

It was up in those trees—not on a branch, but within the leaves themselves—that I first saw troll-like creatures. Their faces were misshapen, their eyes rolling. They were watching me. I tried to ignore them. But once I'd seen them, I knew they were there. I was afraid to run and afraid to stay. I started to cry, kept my head down low, and hoped they would not bother me if I just kept walking on.

Once past the grove, I sped home, hoping they were not in pursuit. When I reached my back door, I risked a glance. I was alone. They had not followed me. I wondered, were there monsters hiding everywhere in the world?

The first time I was alone with Nellie Jane in her cabin among the hides and skins and dried herbs, I remembered those scary creatures and shared my frightening secret with her. She smiled at me as I told her everything, and she gave me an understanding nod. She told me then about the little people.

"I was about your age when I first saw them in the woods. My grandmother laughed at me when I ran home, afraid as you were afraid. She told me they are everywhere, but not everyone can see them. The little people, she said, trade for their favor. They can bring harm or health. What they bring depends on how well their request is heard and if there is an understanding of how to accommodate their wishes. If they get what they want, they will make peace."

She told me that the little people are often found in the less inhabited spaces in the world. "That's why children think there are monsters under the bed." She chuckled. "It's the little people. No one ever goes under the bed, unless there is a dog in the house. When there is a dog in the house that sleeps under the bed, children never fear from monsters in their rooms."

"What do these little people want?" I can see my child's face, expressive in wonder and concrete belief.

"They want their space. They will share if you acknowledge their right to it and if you feed them well. Everyone in life wants a good meal and an undisturbed corner to call their own. The little people are no exception. They like food and coffee and tobacco. They like things that come from the earth."

I get up from my cozy nest in the sleeping bag and pull on my heavy boots—the ice-cold floor bites through my wool sock-clad feet. Maybe the little people want something from me now, to trade for peace of mind and soul. I look for coffee and food. In my search, I find an old pack of Marlboros. I didn't expect to provide tobacco.

I forgot to bring a new coffeemaker. A mouse chewed through the cord on the last one. Instead, I find a saucepan and fill it with water from the stash I brought along. I dump some coffee into the water once it's boiling, remove the pot from the stove, and let the brew steep. While the coffee is steaming, I retrieve a small plate from one of the knotty pine cupboards to use as a dish for the spirit food.

I am glad no one can see me. I know I'm not crazy to act this way, but I wouldn't want to explain myself to anyone, except maybe Nellie Jane. For one wistful moment, I wish she were with me in this, in this ceremony.

Digging through my stash of food, I find a hardboiled egg, some grapes, and a granola bar. I put a little of each on the plate, add one of the cigarettes with the filter torn off, as Nellie Jane demonstrated so many times, and pour a little hot coffee over the lot. I set the plate outside on the porch.

"Mitákuye oyás'iŋ," I shout into the night as Nellie Jane taught me when I was so young.

The words call to all the relatives, the living things, even the grandfather spirits living in the souls of the rocks.

I then call out, *"pilamaya,"* thank you, to all the unseen world.

Peering into the black of the northern woods' night, I shiver and race back to my sleeping bag, ripping off my boots and tossing them across the floor. I crawl into my toasty sleeping bag. I hear myself humming.

When I wake, it's early dawn. I can see through the kitchen window a faint lightening of the skies. I remember everything that happened the night before with vibrant clarity. Coffee. I'd made coffee. I want coffee.

Stretching out of the sleeping bag slowly, like a cautious cat testing its next move, I determine just how cold it is in the cabin. It's at least twenty degrees warmer than the night before, but the floor is still icy. I pull on my boots, hopping around on one foot, then the other.

I stoke the stove and add two more logs to the few embers glowing underneath the wood ash. I look for the saucepan with the spirits' coffee to put on the stove to simmer. It's nowhere.

Where the hell did I put the damn pot?

I check the pegboard that holds the pots and skillets—it's sitting pretty, right there, next to the cast iron griddle.

What the hell? There must be two of them.

I take the pan off the pegboard, intending to fill it with water from the jug on the counter. The seal is intact on the jug, the one I used in the night.

What the hell?

The other two jugs are sitting on the floor, half frozen. There is no pack of old Marlboros on the table.

What in the hell? I must have dreamed the whole thing.

I throw open the front door and scan the porch. No plate.

"Crap," I whisper to myself. "Damn."

And then I start to laugh. Nellie Jane would have gotten the joke and laughed with me. "The spirits are sneaky," I could hear her say as if she stood beside me.

I remember a favorite line from the movie *Thunderheart*. The Graham Greene character was jealous of the young FBI Indian kid. "You had yourself a vision," he complained. And I laugh again. It's good to hear laughter, especially coming out of me.

Sitting on the sofa, warming my hands on my coffee mug, holding it close to my face, feeling the steam rise into my nose, I close my eyes and think about the woman in white and blood. I think she could be the first wound, the first hurt. At that first wound, that's when we give up the ghost of our innocence. I picture my little girl self at the first attack. Life comes through water and blood in many hungry, jeering, taunting forms.

"Feed the spirits," Nellie Jane would say. "They will bring you peace."

I pull a chair up by the woodstove to move closer to the radiating heat. Sipping my cowboy coffee brew, I sit for hours moving only to add wood to the stove or to refill my cup. My mind is blank. I've never been so calm in all my life.

CHAPTER 9

My morning walk through the woods follows distinct pathways made by snowmobiles and wildlife. The early-spring sun is warm on my face. Soon the ice will disappear, and the airiest of greens will unfold as a halo around the waking trees' branches.

There is an urgent energy about me that shovels the deep sickness from my soul and leaves it in heaps for the melting warmth to dissolve. I stand still and listen to the dripping of the melt from tree limbs. Damp, cool smells flush my nostrils. A rabbit or squirrel skitters not far away. There is a scream, that horrible scream produced by rabbits in the clutches of predators. *Hell in Eden.* There is evidence of moose and deer. Bear are rousing from hibernation. Young cubs are eager to explore the outer world and push their mamas to wake. But I see no bear scat, for now.

Thoughts of bears bring thoughts of berries, and I realize I'm famished. I head back toward the cabin. My thoughts are loose and unfocused. My boots slush along the path, when a prehistoric squawking scares the living daylights out of me. I've flushed up a wild turkey. The adrenaline rush from primal fear wakes me up and urges me on my way.

Near the cabin now, I see a man standing on the porch. I freeze in my tracks, hoping he will not turn to see me. I watch silently from behind a massive pine, wary, then realize it's Ned. He must have driven straight from the airport. I can see his car now, parked on the other side of mine.

"Ned!" I call out.

He turns and waves, throws open his arms. "Come to me baby." He grins.

I reach him. He buries me in his arms, among the folds and fluff of his old down parka.

"I wondered where you'd gotten to," he says. "I spotted your tracks and was about to follow them." He picks up a bag resting in the sunlight on the porch. "I brought dinner."

I am so happy to see him and tell him so with a deep, unflinching kiss. "What time is it?"

"It's only 8:30, but I didn't want you fretting about what we'd eat for dinner."

I laugh. "It was not on my worry list today. I have so much to tell you. Let's get you in and warmed up with some coffee."

He steps out of our hug and picks up his bag. "When was the last time you had a full meal?" he asks while walking ahead of me into the warmth of the cabin.

"I don't remember. I had a hardboiled egg in the middle of the night, I think. Oh, maybe not. I'm not sure."

Ned starts taking his things up to the sleeping loft—I stop him.

"Honey, I'd leave everything down here until this place is warm. I slept on the sofa last night."

I put more wood on the fire. The cabin is coming to life by the grace of the warmth churned out by the wood-burning stove. Back downstairs, Ned puts his arms around me. "I've missed you."

He kisses me. It is a long and lovely, soul-warming kiss. It feels wonderful to be in his arms, to smell his smell, to connect.

"Let me get breakfast started, and then we'll catch up with full stomachs."

I forgot how hungry I am. I poke through the bags of groceries he brought and find a raisin pie, my favorite. Bakeries and restaurants don't offer straight raisin pie anymore—only the sour cream variety.

"Where did you find this on the way from the airport in the middle of the night?"

"I did stop at home, and there was one left in the freezer. Happy?"

"Oh, so happy! Thank you, sweetie!" I blow him a kiss.

He cooks ham and eggs as I tear into the pie. He brought some apples and oranges too. I sit quietly watching him, sipping my coffee and feeling content. If he'd arrived yesterday, he would have walked into a raging storm. Today—though unnerved at the terrified turkey I scared up and confused about the night's dreams—I am okay. Settled. I'm glad he came. I close my eyes and drift.

He breaks the silence. "Tell me everything." He serves up the plates, then shuts off the burners on the stove, trailing a slight, stomach-churning odor of propane gas. He pours himself a cup of coffee and sits next to me on the sofa.

"Let me get one mouthful in first. But you first."

Ned flashes a half-hearted smile. "We need to talk about our losses, together. That's why I came. I can tell you the Texas family details—and I want to. Everyone sends love, by the way."

I nod, my mouth full of eggs.

"But first, I'm worried about you and how you disappeared from me. You can't just drop out of sight when you're in trouble. We're in this together, remember?"

My fork falls from my hand and clatters to the plate. "Wow!" I say with a bitter tone.

Ned never talks to me like this. I don't like it. But truth is, I did ignore him, and I am glad to see him now. I set my plate on the floor and face him.

"So start talking." I try to sound interested, but I'm angry.

Ned takes the cue and eases me into the conversation he wants to have by filling me in on his sister's funeral details. The other siblings are sad. He feels sorry for leaving them. He promised to return in a few months, if possible, and invited them to come north, if they'd like.

I think the latter is the better idea. I'm not a fan of Texas, any part of it. I certainly don't want to go visiting Texas in June or July. I've been in the northern climate too long to handle a southern summer.

"You know that Jessie and Laura don't get along," he continues. "They never have. Both depended on Sallie. Now she's gone, and they each want to turn to me. I hate to see them this way, but they're going to have to work it out. I can't, I won't, move back to Texas."

"That's good to hear—not that they're having trouble, but the not moving to Texas part. You'd be going alone, you know."

I'd go mad in Texas, cooped up inside in the summer to beat the heat. Like most Northerners, I live for the summer months, when I can be outside without bundling up in layers of outerwear. Only on the most humid days would I stay indoors with the air conditioning turned on. One of the minor reasons my mother used to leave me with Aunt Mercy in summer was because she liked the house closed up but didn't want to be closed up with me.

"It's tough to see everyone aging. I know we won't see much of one another in the next few years and we'll all start dying off. It's what we people do."

"Ned," I soothe him, "we'll try to get them up here. Maybe in August. It'll be too hot for us, but it'll feel like winter to them."

We finish our meal and small talk, clean up the kitchen, and nest together on the sofa in front of the wood-stove after I add another log to the fire. I relish the comfort that sweeps through me from Ned's arms.

"It's your turn," he says, sighing. "What's been happening to you that has you in such a state?"

I tell him about my many meltdowns and how I was rescued by Patsy. "I couldn't hold it in. There was this double grenade explosion in my gut, in my head. I could feel myself splattered in living pieces out of reach. I couldn't…" I'm out of words. "It all came out, and now she knows." I'm shaking. "I hope she can be trusted with this."

"What difference would it make if she told the town?"

I shudder. "I don't want to be the poster child for adult children of familial abuse."

"I can understand that. But you do know you share this space with thousands of others, don't you? Maybe, probably, millions."

It's dangerous to try to reason with me. Ned trips a live wire, and I explode.

"This is my story. Mine. It doesn't translate to any other story. It's not a story. It's my fucking life. It has affected every part of my fucking, awful life!"

"Slow down, Ellen. Slow down." Ned draws back from me.

"Don't you dare minimize my life and then tell me at what speed I can speak of it. God damn it, Ned! This is exactly why I didn't want you here!"

I get up and pace away from him. I feel destroyed all over again. Ned is supposed to be my ally, my safe place. But he is just like everyone else. He doesn't have a clue.

I glare at him. "I know you're grieving, and I'm sorry. I'm sorry I can't help you. I can't. I cannot make what's happening to me normalize into the casual swapping of details—'Oh, and this is what happened to me last week.' Fuck. I'm blown up. I am shrapnel. And if you can't hear what I'm telling you, then you need to be someplace else until I get some balance back."

Ned keeps pushing. "You're in trouble. I can see that. I may not understand everything that's going on in you right this minute, but I see you're in trouble. I lost someone I love, and you lost someone you hate. There's a universe of difference that I may never understand. You don't want to be minimized? Then don't minimize me!"

Ned's anger shocks me, and then I blow. My rage is complete. I am betrayed by everyone. It's always about their needs, what they want, how they want it. There is no fucking comparison to be made.

"You fucking don't get it. Your grief over the loss of your dear and lovely sister is normal. Everyone can relate. What is happening to me now is not relatable. This is not loss. This is…Jesus Christ! I can't tell you what this is! This is why I didn't want you here."

"Do you want me to leave?"

"I don't care what you do. But if you stay you have to let me have my nightmare no matter what it looks like or sounds like. I'm not looking for advice. I'm not even open to comfort." I can't look at him. "You can't correct me or steer me away from what I'm facing. I don't fully understand myself what's happening. And I feel even worse now—who knew that was possible—because I want to comfort you. You want to be in this together. Well, that means being *in* it, not taking away the enormity of whatever this is that I'm facing. I'm fragile in every single cell."

Ned sighs. "Okay. Okay. I get it. Well, I get there's something to get. I'm lost. Maybe I don't get it."

I smile and lightly punch him in the chest. "That's the spirit, old boy! First steps." I sit down again next to him. I put my face into my hands, stroking my own skin. I look up at him. "It's like the house is on fire—who will we save first, the baby or the bigger baby?"

We are both exhausted by the fight. We sit together, quiet, for a long time, until I need to bring in more wood. As I stack a pile by the stove and load another log, I know I can speak now without flinging knives with my words.

"Honey, I really am sorry. I love you. You know I love you. I've been undone by the deaths of my parents. I wasn't prepared for this. I thought my wounds were healed. I guess they're not. I feel as crazy as I've ever felt, as though no time has passed, as though nothing has changed."

Tears make runways on my cheeks. Ned draws me closer and strokes my hair while my head rests safely on his chest.

"I'm sorry too. Perfect storm, I guess. We're just caught in a perfect storm."

That night, feeling safe and secure and understood, I fall asleep after considering how fortunate I am to have Ned in my life as my partner. If this had happened to me during my first marriage, I maybe would have let myself free fall into insanity. Maybe I wouldn't have fought it off. My thoughts shift to CiCi and how she put Ned and me together. She's so smart about my life.

I used to wonder what was wrong with Ned that he would want me, my gruff and edgy next to his soft and deep. But I came to see over time—through great effort on his part—that he finds me fascinating and loves everything about me. I know that my self-reflecting lens is chipped, but I've come to accept his love as fact. It is abundantly evident in his treatment of me and how thoughtful he is sometimes, like now, at the expense of his own needs.

He shouldn't have let me hog the grief spotlight, but he conceded. Unlike me, he isn't wounded by every slight, every loss. That super sensitivity sets me apart from him and other people. He can find his way through sadness without coming unglued.

We sleep in the loft. The walls are warmed and no longer cast a deep chill into the room. I fall asleep, snuggled into Ned, happy and safe.

I wake inside a dream to find myself at the base of a hill. Eagles are circling overhead, three of them. There is a fourth off in the distance. It is albino. I wake up in a panic just as the three hovering eagles descend upon me and begin to tear at my living flesh.

I am terrified and sweating. I feel for Ned to ground myself in the here and now. Then I get up with as little fuss as I can, wrap myself in a warm blanket from the foot of the bed, and pad my way downstairs.

Ned had turned down the damper on the stove before we went up to the loft. There isn't much fire left, mostly embers and a small piece of charred log. I add another chunk of wood and open the damper. Flames fly up from the coals in a crazy flurry. I am mesmerized for a moment, but the heat is too intense. I shut the stove door.

It's quiet in the room but for the snapping of a log and the sizzling of moisture under the flames. I hear a soft scratching in the kitchen. A mouse, I imagine. I check the counters to be certain the food is secure in containers, then I curl up on the sofa in front of the stove, wrapped tight in my Hudson Bay blanket, and close my eyes.

Instantly I'm back at the base of the hill. My bones are picked clean. The albino eagle sits on my wrist, lifts a small bone from my outstretched hand, and flies away. From the top of the hill, I hear drumming and the sound of an eagle bone whistle.

In the morning, Ned wakes me on the sofa with a kiss and a stroke to my hair. "You okay, honey? Couldn't sleep?"

I reach for his face, pull it too me, and give him a good-morning kiss. "I had a dream, then I was cold, so I came downstairs, added wood to the fire, and fell asleep."

I do not tell him about the dream, though it is alive in my mind's eye. It's too much to capture in the smallness of words. I don't want another fight about words. I'm sick of talk.

We agree to each head out this morning, so we eat a quick breakfast, clean up the cabin, and pack our separate cars. I want to go on to Capitol. He wants to go back home. We hold each other for a long time as we say our goodbyes. I'm ready to face Mercy.

CHAPTER 10

It's an easy, back roads drive to Mercy's house. When I arrive, I collect my overnight bag from the trunk and shut the lid. All is quiet except for the chatter of sparrows and a squawking blue jay not far off. Before entering the house, I stand for a moment to listen and smell and absorb my surroundings. I hear children laughing in the distance and think of my time with Missy here, when we were young.

Mercy doesn't respond to my rapping on her door, so I let myself in. She won't be far away. Probably at Nellie Jane's or at the church with the other ladies of the town, doing some manner of good for others.

As I put my things away in the guest room, I realize it's been hours since I've had any coffee. It must be tea-time somewhere, and up here in the sturdy north, it's coffee and pie time. Sure enough, there's half a pumpkin pie stashed in the fridge. Pie plate in one hand and a warm coffee pot in the other, all thoughts of searching for Mercy vanish.

Aunt Mercy stayed in the north woods settlement of Capitol, her birthplace, when Uncle Jasper died. When Nellie Jane lost her husband, she returned to Capitol, where she had spent summers with her aunt Millie. She didn't want to stay on the reservation. She wanted to be near her best friend, Mercy. The two old women are left to each other for companionship and support, as Nellie Jane has no children and Missy lives in France.

I've always loved Mercy's house. It rambles from the entryway mudroom through the kitchen—barely modernized—into a front room with a large picture window that overlooks an uninterrupted view of jack pine, white pine, and tamarack forest. At the east end of the front room there's a small niche area, a nine-by-nine-foot cubicle that once served as the only bedroom. It was placed with intention, so sunrise would fall in line with the workday. Get up. Go to sleep.

Off the front room, other areas sprung over the years: two additional small bedrooms and a large bathroom that includes an area for laundry, storage, and canned goods. Within its walls, on the west end and down a surprising stairway under a trap door, is a cold room, seldom heard of anymore, that keeps fresh foods fresh without refrigeration for months. It's an ingenious idea.

As a child, I was afraid I would be stuck in that room, chilling underground with the cabbages, carrots, and fresh cow's milk. I was used to being forgotten. I imagined myself curled up by the apple basket, waiting for Mercy to find me when retrieving apples for a pie. It was a silly fear, of course. Missy would never have forgotten about me. But still, I was afraid to go into that room alone. I would scamper out as quickly as I could, usually with an armful of lettuce or a pail of tomatoes.

I wander through the house with my mug of coffee to warm my hands in contrast with the cool temperature in the room. I notice the many quilts and rag rugs. The few photographs. There is one picture of Missy and me when I was seven years old, my first summer here. We're kneeling by Able the Golden Retriever.

We fought over him to be our bed buddy every night. We pushed our beds together so we could both cozy up to him while we slept. I remember how much I loved his stinky dog smell—except when he was fresh from a swim in the lake. He died in a hunting accident the next fall. We grieved. Able was my first love in a young life that had known no other love. His death was a devastating loss for both of us.

I hear Mercy at the door and return to the kitchen. She's in the mudroom, removing her jacket and scarf, hanging them up on a wooden hanger that rests on a large nail in the wall.

"Hello, dear," she says. "I'm so happy you could come back to spend some time with me. I've been to Nellie Jane's. We've been gluing up that old rocking chair. You know the winters are so dry—the wood shrinks something awful."

"I've had most of the coffee, but I could brew more." My arms wrap around her small frame, and I give her a peck on a cold cheek. "Oh, you need some warming up!"

"I'm fine. It's quite lovely outside today. When the winds are calm and the sun is bright, it's cold, yes, but pleasant for walking."

"I've also had some pie. Excellent as always. Have you thought about dinner? Can we invite Nellie Jane?

"I don't think so tonight. We're both still quite tired from all the activity of the last week. Maybe we can bring her some breakfast rolls in the morning."

"Rolls sound fantastic!" I say with enthusiasm, remembering how delicious her warm cinnamon rolls taste.

We sit at the kitchen table, once my favorite place in the entire world. Mercy does look weary and small. And old—older than I noticed before. Maybe I need to keep my confession to myself this trip. I pat the brown-spotted, paper-thin skin of her hand.

"I can see you're still tired. How are you otherwise now that the funeral is over and you're back at home?"

"I love to be home. Always." She gazes out of the kitchen window, away from me. "But if you mean how I'm feeling about the death of my brother, I honestly do not know." She sighs. "He was a complicated and difficult man. He was the same as a boy."

She turns her gaze back to me and is silent for a moment. I can hear an old wind-up clock ticking in the other room and feel a chill. I get up to locate the thermostat and turn up the heat a little.

"I heard about your mother, dear. We had a paper this morning. Are you all right? So much more loss for you." She looks stricken. "And Ned too. How is he and his family? Has he returned?"

"Ned is fine. His family is fine. He's home, taking it easy. I'm all right, for now. There's a lot to think about. Ned would say there's a lot to feel. I'm getting a bit confused between the two."

We go into the living room to continue our talk. A beautiful antique lampstand with a newer frosted shade is positioned near her chair, perfect for reading along with a worn ottoman at her feet. I tuck the throw around her and sit down in an overstuffed, oversized lounging chair covered in green floral chintz.

"My mother's suicide—so unexpected. Of course, I hadn't seen her in decades. My mother and I were not close. I think you know that. She and my father were an odd couple and not good parents. Their deaths have left me with a storehouse of unanswered questions. I didn't realize I had questions about them until they were gone. I hope you can help answer some, at least about my father's family. There really isn't anyone else I can turn to."

I am a coward. I hope that by deflecting the truth of my mission—to find out what went wrong with my father—into a seemingly harmless stroll through family memories, I'll be able to get the information I need without upsetting Mercy.

"I didn't know your mother well," she begins. "And your father and I had little to do with one another for many years, as you know."

I sit back in my chair, seeing that Mercy remains relaxed and has taken the bait. My breathing slows, though my heart is still revved to race.

"I'm sorry to hear that you and your mother were estranged. It must be hard for you, now, to think of her." Mercy's voice is tender and soothing.

I feel like such a liar. "Not really. I learned early on to fend for myself and not look back. I like to move forward with things, not get stuck in old ruts on the road. But this is all a bit much. I'll admit to that."

Mercy offers a slight smile. "Whatever I can do to help, I'm happy to do."

"I would like to know more about you and Terry and my father as children. I know nothing of your parents, my grandparents. I'd like to learn whatever I can about where you and I are from, who our people are. I was never curious but now I feel like I should know these things, like they might matter, somehow, make a difference in my life. By the way, I forgot to tell you that I saw Uncle Terry at the funeral. At least, I think it was him."

Mercy seems to ignore my words. "We should move back into the kitchen, where there is more light. I'd like to get a chicken in the oven and prepare the vegetables."

We rise together, nearly in unison. My tall, sturdy form dwarfs her petite, soft body. Even tired, she's still straight and steady.

The shadows of late afternoon dance on my spine as I sit with my back to the kitchen window. A fresh and lively spring is on its way. The last grasp of winter always seems to carry an evil intent. Bad things can happen at the change of seasons, especially when winter is forced to retreat from an encroaching sun that brings the thaw and stirrings of life.

Mercy adds herbs and pepper to the chicken. She sets it to warm briefly in a pan on the stovetop while the oven reaches temperature. She retrieves a rutabaga from the vegetable storage bin in the small pantry and peels and chops it without speaking a word or looking up at me.

I ask if I can help, but she says nothing. I'm not worried. I know her well enough to understand she's thinking deeply about my questions. I give her the time she needs.

The lowering sun shines on her face. The ding of the oven timer sounds. Mercy finishes preparing the rutabaga, slides the roasting pan into the oven, and fills a pot with water to set it to boil on the stove. She scrubs, then pierces two baking potatoes found in the pantry and nests them alongside the roasting pan.

She straightens up, dusts off her hands on an old flour sack towel, and smiles at me. "Let me refresh your coffee." She takes a container of shortbread from the cupboard next to the sink and places four cookies on a small, delicate china plate painted with wild violets. "Here dear, a little something to hold us until dinner."

She sits down with a glass of milk and picks up where we left off in conversation.

"I can tell you—my mother, she was beautiful. Like a queen she was. Her name was Flora. Flora McIntyre. My brother William, your father, was always in trouble. We didn't know what drove him, but he would quickly become angry over the smallest thing and lash out in violence. My own father was kind—unless he had a whiskey. And then he too became violent and unpredictable. We kids were always afraid of what might happen next when he'd start drinking." She looks tearful. Her face flushes red. "He was most hurtful to my mother, who was so soft and light and generous with her love."

"So he was always like that? Billy, I mean."

Mercy pats my hand to soothe me as though I am a small child again. "With William gone, it's time you know the story of your father. I couldn't tell you about him while he was alive. I didn't know how you would handle hearing bad things about him. But more, I didn't know what he would do if he knew the truth had been shared. I was quite afraid of him—all my life. Terry was too. We all were." In earnest, she takes both of my hands in hers. "Do you want me to continue?"

The water on the stove boils. Mercy lets loose of my hands to place the chunks of rutabaga in the water. She'll mash them when cooked through. I'm uncertain about what I see in her face. I can't read her. *Did he do the things to her that he did to me? Unthinkable.*

"What about him?" I ask. "Aunt Mercy, you're scaring me. I haven't told you how he was in our house. I'm scared he hurt you as he hurt me."

"What do you mean, Ellen?" Her look is sharp and fearful.

This is my opening, and I cannot hold back. I tell her everything. I tell her how he raped me, beat me, screamed at me, and how my mother did nothing. I tell her about the blood, the fear, the pain. I tell her how alone I felt. I begin to sob. I stand up to grab some tissues, wipe my tears, blow my nose, and calm myself. Then I tell her how grateful I am for those summers here to feel the love from her and Jasper and to play with Missy, like any other child would play with a friend.

"I've been angry and confused all of my life." I feel shattered, again. "I've felt absolutely on my own in every situation. They say that no man is an island, but I know better. I've lived alone, cut off, surrounded by furious seas raging against the tiny island of me adrift in unreality and turbulence. If it wasn't for CiCi and Ned, I doubt I'd ever have become any kind of decent human."

I stop, take a breath, and confess the worst of it. "Mercy I have such hate in me, words fail."

Mercy's eyes are closed.

"I'm sorry to put so much on you all at once. But this is what I wanted to do—to tell you, tell someone who might care, before there's no one left to tell. I think I'm getting better at handling this every day. You need to know that. And with Billy dead in the ground, I don't think I'll be afraid anymore. But I'm so angry."

Mercy stands as tall as I've ever seen her, her body like a lumberyard board—straight, not warped. I see strength in her. And determination. I've said something that reveals a side to this old woman that I've never seen before. I should have told her years ago—even when I was a child. Maybe she could have done something to help me then. She extends her arms to me and I slip into them, as any sad child might, to be surrounded by love and understanding.

"With both of them gone," I say, "I've been overwhelmed by a need to confess, I suppose. And to be heard by someone who might have a heart about it. He broke me, Aunt Mercy. They both broke me. Now that they're dead—well, I can't pull myself together. I feel like the time I've spent trying to overcome and be strong and move forward was all a waste."

My back quivers from a flood of adrenaline. I am exposed again and terrified, but I can't stop talking. I stand back from her eyes and look down at her soft face.

"And then for my mother to kill herself—Mercy, it was my fault. I threatened her with exposure if she didn't at least acknowledge the abuse she allowed. But she wouldn't do it. *She wouldn't do it.* She killed herself rather than acknowledge the pain she allowed in her only child. She chose to kill herself. I can't . . . I don't . . ."

Mercy reaches up to me and hugs my neck and kisses me. "Oh, dear child. I knew your mother was cold, and I knew your father the way I knew him. But I never ever dreamed that he'd . . ." She trails off into silence.

I touch her arm and sob. "Please sit." I choke out the words. "Please."

She returns to her chair, her gaze turned again to the kitchen window, into the stunning colors of an early sunset. Smells from the roasting chicken and steaming rutabaga fill the room.

I have confessed to her. I'm flooded with shame and fear.

She fills our plates and serves a meal that neither of us will eat. We sit in complete silence for close to an hour. I clear the dinner plates, put the food away, and empty into saucers what remains in a jar of homemade applesauce. The sweet, acidy tang of the Haralsons with a touch—not too much—of cinnamon is something we both can eat. *Pablum.*

We wash, dry, and put away the dishes, our movements a clean and careful dance for space. Our silence is not awkward. Rather, we are at rest in the relief and shelter it provides.

I wait for Mercy to continue her story or say something more about mine. I know how selfish my confession is. It's what everyone warned me about. Panic and relief both come in waves, one pushing the other up or down. I hope Mercy will survive this, maybe help me. I'm certain my confession does matter. Maybe now, *maybe now*, I will know what it is to be part of, not separate from, family.

We retire to the front room. Mercy sits back in her rocker with the small footstool supporting her legs. I curl up with legs under me to nest in the cushy chintz-covered chair. The room is dusky and begins to cool as the sun sets. I turn on a few lamps and turn the heat up a little more.

"I don't know what to say, what I can do." She seems carried off by my confession, and diminished.

I must have a better self in me that cares about the effect I've had on her, but I only know relief. I feel connected with her now, like I've responded to an altar call and Jesus has touched me, cleansed me, and called me His child. This is what I came for. I knew she would save me.

"Dear," her voice is soft but determined as she turns to face me straight on. "I think it's time to tell you about your father. Maybe that is the thing I can do for you. I don't know."

Mercy begins her story of Capitol and how she lived here as a girl and a young woman. I am eager for her words.

CHAPTER 11

"Capitol and the surrounding areas remained rural," she begins. "Our small hamlet here in the woods wasn't ever going to be a sophisticated town or grow to city size. In the twenties and thirties, even the forties, we could read about advances in science and technology in the *Superior Journal*. But none of that had arrived in Capitol. There were few cars, mostly trucks, for the most successful townspeople. The railroad that inspired the birth of Capitol still carried iron ore and lumber to the shipyards in Twin Bays. Perishables and other equipment were delivered by rail to the co-op. Many trade goods were still brought by foot or by horse.

"The growing season was short, but every family and even the bachelors had a kitchen garden that produced plenty for canning and winter storage. There was no shortage of game. People ate what they killed. For those not craving high society and pampering, this place was an Eden. For those who needed a taste of society and pomp, there was the Women's League and the Moose Lodge. The town had a bar, access to hardware and home goods, a school, and two churches—pretty much all anybody really needed. It was a good enough life—except when my father erupted into one of his rages, which happened often enough to keep our household on edge."

Mercy falls into a reverie, softening her gaze toward the wall behind me. She rhythmically strokes the soft yarn of a crocheted blanket at her side.

"Mother was the most beautiful woman you could imagine. She was loving and nurturing. If her parents had lived closer, rather than in Michigan, I think she might have taken us all to them for safety. In those days, there was no way to leave."

I sit quietly, absorbing every word. The urge to shame myself subsides. As she talks, I feel some measure of relief, though I'm still exhausted from my own sharing and a little shaky. I'm on the verge of a panic that I struggle, as always, to hold at bay.

"Ours was a small farm that my father, Matty, cleared of timber. Each spring, frost would heave up a new crop of rocks. He used the work horses to haul them to the rock fence line, raising it ever higher each year with the smaller stones. Then he tilled the ground, planted, and tended the produce like it was beloved. All of us would help. William would throw small rocks at me or a handful of dirt in my eyes. I would cry. Matty would get angry and tell me to stop whining. William would laugh and pelt me with stones and dirt again. He could be so mean."

"Aunt Mercy," I interrupt," why do you always call my father William? Terry is always Terry, but Billy is William."

Mercy nods. "He was the elder son. In those days, still, he was considered the heir, so his Christian name was used, out of respect." She adds thoughtfully, "Habit, I suppose."

She continues her story.

"Once in a while, your grandfather would look up from his farming and gaze at us, his children." She smiles. "I would run to him in those moments, and he would swoop me up and spin me around. I laughed and laughed! He was a beautiful man until he started drinking." Her smile fades into a dark past, place, and time.

"We had ten acres, still referred to as the McInnis Farm. It's unlikely that anyone but hunters have visited there for five decades or longer. It was our home, our farm. One year, Dad won a blue ribbon at the county fair for his potatoes. He was so proud. He brought us home from the fair in the early evening. Then he went on to the bar in town to buy a round for everybody in celebration."

She clutches her hands together as her body stiffens. Her face loses its softness while her eyes well in unshed tears.

"That was the worst night of my life. Changed my life. Changed everything. He killed my mother that night."

Panic surges into my chest and throat. I can hardly breathe.

"*What*? What are you talking about? Jesus Christ, Mercy!" My curse is involuntary and the wrong thing to say.

Mercy winces. "Please, dear."

But even those words are a weak defense against the devil released into this room.

"That night in 1940, my father murdered my mother. And William, your father"—she pauses for only a beat until releasing a last chilling truth—"he killed our little sister, Eleanora. He beat her to death. I can still see them all. It will never leave me."

My father killed a child I never knew existed. He was a child killer—his own sister. This enormity is more, far more, than my mind can accept. I feel myself shuttering down. Panic explodes in my every cell, roiling through a flood of flashbacks of my father's attacks on me. My entire body is in the deep freeze of shock. My teeth chatter. I cannot hold my jaw still. The cold inside of me bites deeper into my ravaged soul.

That could have been me. I know now, for certain, that had my mother not come home when she did that night when I was only seven years old, my father would have killed me. He would have killed his child for want of sex and to beat someone else to death.

"Terry was the one who ran to get help," Mercy continues. "He got the Mikkelsons from across the road. It was Jake who shot my father dead. He hit William too, wounding him enough to make him stop his attack on me. It wasn't until later that we realized our two youngest brothers, only eight and nine years old, ran out of the house and into the night, into the wilderness, alone."

Two more boys. Oh, God. I know what the wilderness is like that swallows Capitol.

"Mercy! What happened to them?"

My voice sounds at a great distance from where I sit, as if speaking from another country through a crackling connection. My being is breaking up, like ice at spring thaw. To save myself, I am removed to that other country, safe from the disintegration of reason.

"Everyone searched for days, but they were not found. Even though Terry saved me by getting help, he's never forgiven himself for the violent death of Eleanora or the loss of our young brothers. You see, he and William both beat her at first. Even though Terry stopped and ran to get help, well, it was too late for all of us. I couldn't help. Mama was dead. Eleanora was in a heap, dying, on the floor across the room from me. William had just punched me in the face and the stomach. I couldn't get to Mama."

I can hear her pain. I want her to stop talking. There are blankets in the hallway closet. I leave Mercy to retrieve two, one for myself and another for her. I know this cold will not be warmed by wool or even the flames of hell, most likely. She thanks me, clutching the blanket around her throat. She looks as cold as I feel.

I can see the beatings. I can almost feel Terry's moment of clarity—his sister's blood on his hands. Her shrieks—I can hear them. But he stopped. My father could never stop. Maybe that means there's something decent in my uncle. Maybe it's his survival, like mine, that ties me to him, draws me to him—not just that he was abandoned by his family.

"The law took Terry in for his part in the assault. He did his time, but when he was released, the Mikkelsons would not allow him to come home. They adopted me, as you know, but didn't trust him. By the time he was released, he was like an animal—a different animal than William, but just as vicious."

Mercy looks up to make eye contact with another place, another time of sadness and regret, brought into this room with her story.

"After his release, Terry's disappointments compounded until he tried to hang himself. That's why he's crippled as he is. When I finished nursing school, I let him live with me until I married. I tried to help him. I told him over and over that a twelve-year-old boy in that situation—well, it wasn't his fault. Nothing is so simple in such violent chaos."

Mercy cries.

Grasping my trailing blanket, I kneel by her side. I hold her face and rock her and tell her I love her. Her tears make a steady stream down her gentle face. She is more caught in memory than in the moment, while I am caught in a stranglehold of very present horror.

There were six children, not three. Three are dead along with my grandmother. My father did this and his father. I float into the ethers—a place with no conditions—as I picture the bloodied floor of that cabin and the bodies of an innocent mother and child. I see myself at seven, standing in that rough-hewn kitchen among the bloodied, dead and dying.

These are my people.

Still on my knees, rocking back and forth under the blanket, stuck in the muckiness of truth, I rest my head on Mercy's leg. She automatically, I suppose, begins to stroke my hair. I clasp her hand and hang on with all my might.

How did I not know that Mercy was raised by another couple? Yes, I knew the Mikkelsons had been in the picture, but I didn't put any of this together. Why would I? I knew her only as my aunt, my father's sister.

And I really thought this all started and ended with me and Virginia with Billy. There's too much. Too much.

To rise out of this nightmare, I need a distraction. "Would you like a cup of tea?" The words sound weak and stupid in my ears, next to all the other words that populate this cozy space.

"Perhaps some sherry."

I almost smile when she says it. Leaving her to wipe away her tears, tears that have welled from a sorrow-fed river since she was fourteen years old, I am off to hunt down the aperitif glassware and the sherry for both of us. The sticky, sweet liquor feels good in my mouth and throat and warms me in an instant. Mercy sips her sherry in silence.

"Does Missy know?"

"We never talked about it," she answers, savoring heaven's nectar. "There was no reason to talk about it. Missy had a good life. I made sure that your father and Terry kept their distance. They didn't live nearby, and we did not share in family celebrations. We just didn't talk about it."

At that, Mercy rises from her chair, tells me she is too tired to continue, and goes to bed.

I stay up, struggling in the dark with visions of an enraged William McInnis murdering his sister while his own father murders his angelic wife, the mother of six. Six. I can see it too clearly. It could have been me. Hell, it was me. Wicked Willy and his lovely bride, Virginia, stole from me safety, security, nurturing, love, indulgence, cooing, support, encouragement, training. Everything good that a parent should give with loving abandon to their child was denied me. I got nothing from them but fear and hurt. And this too, it seemed, was Billy's legacy to Mercy and her siblings. Unspeakable. Unbelievable.

I think about the hard work it's taken to hide my truth while trying to heal from it as well. How in hell had Mercy done it? How had she survived these monsters and turned a soft, motherly cheek to the world?

I long for stable, tender Ned.

CHAPTER 12

I dream in the night of vague horrors that keep me restless and wear me out. In the morning, my face is puffy and reddened from tears. My nose is stuffed, and a slight headache nags at the base of my skull. Coffee will put this right. Coffee is and always will be my best friend.

Mercy is still sleeping, even at nine in the morning. Usually, she's up before the roosters, she's told me. It will be late morning before we make it over to Nellie Jane's.

I set about making some fresh pecan rolls with lots and lots of caramel. Yes. Sugar. Carbs. Better than valium are these.

I still can't shake the residue of shame and shock loaded up in my body. I know I need a walk. I need to shake off the impact of Mercy's story. I can't make myself do it.

Relax, I tell myself. *Give yourself a minute.*

My mind rumbles up in aftershock. We will walk up to Nellie Jane's in a little while. That will help.

I hear Mercy stirring in her room. The baking rolls fill the kitchen with their delicious aroma of burnt sugar. Is there anything better? I pull a cooling rack from its cupboard, set it on the countertop, find oven mitts—hand crocheted in autumn yellow and red with brown yarn loops on the side to accent the design—and wait out the last ten minutes before the timer goes off.

Mercy arrives in the kitchen, dressed in blue knit slacks with an embroidered maple leaf on her sweatshirt pulled on over a white cotton turtleneck. It is now ten after ten.

"Good morning, dear." Her voice is newly awake to sounds. "Did you sleep well?" She looks awful—her face is gray and puffy, masking the deeper lines around her mouth.

"Good morning," I reply with a kiss on her plump cheek. "I slept as well as could be expected after what you told me last night." I hug her close, letting compassion for her flow in a rush. I hand her a cup of coffee as she sits at the kitchen table.

"I hadn't realized how upset I was until I got to my room," she says. "I don't know what got into me. It's such an old story, you know. I've had a lifetime to live with it, as though it's an everyday sort of thing. It has been my life to keep it all under wraps." She pauses to consider her words. "All of it." She gazes at me, quizzical. "Are you all right?"

I nod and stare out the kitchen window, looking beyond into the outer world in its march to springtime.

"Mercy, there are precious few people I've told *my* story to. It has an unreal quality of fiction for me. The truth has held me hostage for as far back as I can remember. And now, knowing that you have kept this other secret for your lifetime—I can't seem to catch my breath."

The timer dings its cheerful alarm. I grab the oven mitts to pull the rolls out of the oven. I set the pan on the rack at rest and waiting on the counter. I wash and dry the baking dishes.

Once done, I leave Mercy to her coffee while I head for the shower. After I dry my hair and get dressed, I call Ned.

"Honey, Mercy told me the most gruesome story about my father last night. Can you come up here? I guess there's an old family farmstead from her youth. I want to find it, and I want to tell you everything."

"I'm not doing anything that can't wait. LuLu is still with Annie. Let me pack a bag, and I'll try to be there around 4:30. How's that?"

"Okay. Great. Thanks, sweetie. I'll see you in a while."

I'm grateful. I need him to ground me.

Mercy made her bed and put a load of sheets in the wash while I was on the phone. Back in the kitchen, she's fried some eggs for breakfast. Oranges, warm rolls, and eggs. I would have been in heaven except for the reality of being in purgatory, approaching hell at supersonic speed.

I take in a forkful of eggs and cut off a chunk from a cinnamon roll with enthusiasm. I feel better and hungry because I know Ned is coming.

"Ned is coming up this afternoon. He steadies me, you know."

She sips her coffee but picks at her food. "You know I love to see Ned whenever I can. He is a lovely husband for you."

"Aunt Mercy, you have to eat something." I sit with her as she labors over the orange and eggs. "How on earth have you managed to be so well adjusted?"

She smiles. "The Mikkelsons were wonderful to me. They couldn't have done a better job of stepping in where Mama left off." She closes her eyes to recall her mother. "I think she may have whispered to them a time or two: *Take care of my babies.* I'd like to believe she did. I believe it even now." She opens her eyes, moist and soft. "And with Nellie Jane becoming my cousin—well, it's always been a wonderful thing. You knew, didn't you, that her mother was Katey Small Horse Martin, Millie Mikkelson's sister?"

"All I knew about Nellie Jane was my mother's warnings about Indians. Odd, isn't it, that for all of Virginia's fear talk, she left me for months each year within easy snatching range of Millie's kin. She used to threaten me with the gypsies, too: *If you don't behave, I'll give you to the gypsies.*"

I begin to clear the dishes and clean the kitchen so we can leave to visit Nellie Jane—that heathen!

"Truly, if my mother cared for me at all, she would have dropped me off with you and never came back."

"Yes." Mercy sighs and shakes her head. "I wish that had happened. But there is now, and you are here now." Mercy abruptly changes the topic. "You know, Capitol is the place where we—Nellie Jane and I—shared our summers, even once we were grown and married. Millie would take me to the reservation whenever she went to visit her family, and Nellie Jane was often left with Millie and Jake. They all claimed each of us as one of their own. We shared so many memories and adventures, just as you and Missy did when you were young."

I'm happy to hear her talk about good times. "I know I've said it before, Aunt Mercy, but those summers in Capitol were the best of my life. I am so thankful for those days."

Mercy nods. "We loved having you here. I hope you know that." Her expression is wistful, but her tone is sad as she continues. "As for Terry, I don't think there's more I can say. He's injured and will not recover. No amount of prayer will soften a soul that has turned to stone. Only God can work that miracle. I pray He will. I know you have a soft spot for him, but I would caution you to keep distance."

No matter the story last night, today is a new day. Nellie Jane would say, "*Wašté*," or "It's all good," and wash the bad away with a swipe of her hands. But I'm not Nellie Jane, and I can't just shake this off. I can, however, slide the remaining cooled rolls onto a serving plate and cover them with waxed paper to bring to Nellie Jane. It's time to head up to her house for a visit.

"Shall we go? Are you ready?"

Mercy is eager to get outside for our short walk to Nellie Jane's house.

Though the days are edging toward spring, it is still quite cold, and the snows are not entirely melted away. The sun offers a sweet touch of warming rays on my face. As we walk the short distance up the hill to Nellie Jane's house, we see evidence that deer have wandered through. A light dusting of snow reveals their tracks. It looks to be a group of at least three, probably a doe with yearlings.

Had we left Mercy's house even an hour earlier, we would still have heard the morning chatter of songbirds and the pounding of woodpeckers and the cawing of ravens. With the sun heating up the mid-day, there is a comfortable quiet. I hear a faint scurrying of rabbit or squirrel, but that is all, except for the crunching and shuffling sounds made by our feet walking.

At Nellie Jane's, we open the weather-worn wooden gate to her yard. I hear the metallic click of its latch behind us. We cross the small front yard and enter the door without a knock.

"Nellie Jane!" Mercy calls for her friend.

I head inside the house, where I drop my boots in the entryway and carry the fresh rolls to the kitchen. Mercy stays outside, making her way to the rear of the house, where she can see Nellie Jane through an open gate on one of the wooden-slat fences surrounding her various gardens. There are fruit trees and places for flowers and vegetables. The fencing is useful in deterring the deer but not always successful.

Her berry patch is unprotected and is regularly raided by a black bear family when the berries are at their peak. Nellie Jane is vigilant. She knows when to pick the best fruit before the bears take their share.

Nellie Jane is stooped over a row of cloches—bell-shaped glass plant covers—in the garden. She holds a handful of freshly cut kale and a bunch of young spinach. Just before the first hard freeze, she sprinkles seeds mixed with a handful of soil over the ground and covers them with the glass bell jars. The seeds sprout under the cloches with help from the heat of the spring season's sun.

I pull on my boots and go outside to join them. I can hear them talking as I come around the house.

"Good morning!" Nellie Jane greets me as she straightens up. "You're just in time for lunch. I thought I'd make us some scrambled eggs. I have some fresh bacon and this spinach."

"Thank you, dear, but we ate not that long ago," Mercy replies in a jolly voice. "But we did bring you some fresh breakfast rolls."

Nellie Jane gives me a tour of her garden, describing her plans for the upcoming season. A half hour passes before we walk back to the house. The moments feel extraordinary for their normalcy.

This is life. This is the real life.

"How long will you be staying with us?" Nellie Jane asks me.

I am ready to stay forever in this moment of comfort and reverie. It was like this—calm, warm, whole—when I was a child. And I say so.

"Forever, if you'll have me," I say with a smile.

Yet Mercy is abrupt, ignoring me to address Nellie Jane directly, as though I am not present to hear. "Ned will be arriving soon. We'll have a late lunch, and then they will go home." She gives me no opening to object. "Ned's sister died last week. Ellen must spend some time with him for comfort. They have both lost so much."

"I'm so sorry about your mother, dear." Nellie Jane speaks with heartfelt compassion.

I feel dread crawl in my belly. I don't know how to read Mercy's brush off. After all we shared last night, now nothing but "Be on your way, girl"? I am mortified, flung back into the shadows of fear and uncertainty. I feel sick.

"Oh, and I do want to thank you for all the driving you did to get us to and from the funeral." Nellie Jane looks lovingly at Mercy and touches her hand.

"You're welcome, Nellie Jane." My reply is forced and doesn't sound right in my head. I'm angry with Mercy but need to let it go for now. "I was happy to do it. I have to say, though, that I'm not ready to go just yet. Ned will want to see you."

Nellie Jane's eyes crinkle at the corners with pleasure, matching her smile.

"And I want to show Ned the family farmland Aunt Mercy told me about last night."

Mercy shows me a fierce look that sends a clear signal to be quiet. I promptly stop speaking. A cloud passes over Nellie Jane's face—a small cloud, not a thunderhead like the one I see on Mercy. Something is wrong. Something is off.

Nellie Jane abruptly excuses herself to use the bathroom. Mercy excuses herself from me as well. In short order, I can hear them avidly discussing something at the back of the house. They keep their voices low so I can't catch the words, but they are upset. I can tell that.

Nellie Jane is first to return to the table. "I think Mercy needs to rest, Ellen. The loss of her brother has taken quite a toll. And the farm is nothing more than scrub land now. I think it's owned by a hunter from Duluth. I doubt there's anything to see. We haven't given the place much thought since the store moved into town, decades ago."

Absolutely sure that the ladies are in cahoots over something and trying in the kindest possible way to shoo me away from their secret, I dig in my heels.

"Regardless," I dismiss her comments, "Ned will be here soon and will want to see both of you. After lunch, Nellie Jane—we'll stop in to see you before we leave."

"Fine, dear. That will be fine."

I wish I knew what the old girls were colluding about. Their lame attempt at a cover up annoys me. I get Mercy home and leave her to rest.

"I'm going out for a walk, Aunt Mercy. Ned may arrive before I get back."

"I look forward to seeing him." She yawns a goodbye.

I get in my car and drive to the local tavern to ask questions about the McInnis family farm. The old barkeep tells me where to find the place. He tells me it's down the road from here, on County 2, about four miles.

CHAPTER 13

Just beyond the mile marker, I park by the side of a recently plowed gravel road. I pick my way through the deep snow-covered grasses to a clearing. It is scrubland typical of the area, sporting tamarack, dense brush, and pine.

I feel a surge of miracle tugging at my Achilles tendon. I could have tipped right over like a fainting goat from the power of my imagination moving so fast that the rest of me cannot follow. I am overwhelmed.

I have roots here, roots that extend beyond William the Terrible, my father. Yes, real family roots. They twine and claw beneath my toes. There is an urgency to rid myself of my boots, to let my feet, my toes feel that life deep in me through the frozen ground. These roots are the living past of Matty McInnis but Flora too, my grandmother, beautiful and soft and ever hopeful, as Mercy reflected.

It is a forgettable place. There is nothing significant to mark the ground, to set it apart from any other rough meadow and wood. For Mercy, it hangs in memory like a dimming star in a once-upon-a-time heaven of Flora and Eleanora and hellish madness. Maybe that is it, really. Maybe that is the fuss between Mercy and Nellie Jane. Maybe she simply doesn't want the dust of hell tracked back to her, through her house, to find her.

Let the dead bury the dead.

The still-warm sun on my face and the wild scents and silence from snowfall soothe me. For a few minutes, I forget about relaxing and simply let myself loose to wander the ground. I feel amazed, I suppose, that this place is, in some sense, mine. I've never had a home of my own. Not really. Ned came to be my family later in life. Our family of two is not rooted, not like how blood and cells from ancestors beyond memory can anchor a soul. Ned is safe and sure He is my good fortune. But he is not my home.

This land is your land. This land is my land. The tune rings through my mind, and my memory jiggles a little. Do I know this place? Have I been here? I think hard, standing in one spot for a long time.

I think about how this place turned my father into a monster. But of course, the place didn't make him that way. He was born to kill his own sister and brutalize his own daughter. I shudder.

I want to buy this land. I want to make it live again. I want to dream of life on the farm with Ned and good, loving family and friends nearby. I wonder if Ned will agree to this extravagant impulse.

A subtle movement, a mild shift, and I realize something is changing around me—something in the air. Maybe the dead relatives have spotted me and are beginning to stir. I shiver from a sudden chill. It must be close to three o'clock. An early evening breeze brings a cooling. I am in a place where cougars roam and timber wolves are on the hunt for dinner at this time of day. It's time for me to head back to Mercy's and tell Ned everything.

Ned's car is in the driveway, so I park on the grass. I find him where I like him best, in the kitchen cooking. He and Mercy are chatting away. She looks happy and refreshed. They watch me as I enter the room.

"Hello, dear," Mercy greets me. "Did you have a nice walk?"

Apparently, she hadn't noticed I'd taken my car.

"I did." I snuggle up to Ned and kiss him and hug him while I snatch a crust of garlic bread. "Hi, sweetie. You must have arrived not long after I left."

Mercy interrupts. "Nellie Jane will not be able to join us for dinner. She asks that you make a plate and take it to her when we're finished. She would like to see Ned before you leave."

She's still hard on my exit. Even in front of Ned. *Nice to see you. Now go home.* I can't figure it out.

When I have Ned to myself, we'll talk about that and the farmland. It will be too dark to go back there tonight, but we can stay overnight in Twin Bays and return for a thorough hike of the property in the morning.

Ned serves up a goulash of fresh vegetables and homemade pasta. Crunchy garlic toast is sliced from his home-baked French bread, steamy hot on the breadboard.

But I'm not at all hungry and want the meal to be over. Mercy is getting on my raw nerves. She shares nothing of her story with Ned. I'm impatient to tell him, but I hold my tongue. We finish off the meal with warm gingerbread, make a plate for Nellie Jane, and say goodbye to Mercy, but not before Ned and I clean the kitchen, leaving nothing but a sparkling shine behind.

"Thank you for everything, Aunt Mercy. You've given me a lot to think about. I can't express how much I appreciate that you opened up to me last night. I love you, you know."

I mean it. The long-standing love and appreciation I feel for her nearly equals my temporary annoyance.

"Yes, dear." She gives me a long, heartfelt hug and a kiss on the cheek. "You're welcome back anytime."

I know to take her at her word. Maybe I imagined an earlier brush off.

Besides, now I'm eager to leave. I'm excited to be alone with Ned to talk this out. On the walk to Nellie Jane's, I tell him we have lots to talk about.

"Let's stay in Twin Bays tonight, and I'll tell you everything. Then I want to come back tomorrow. Not to Mercy's, but there's a place I want to show you just outside of Capitol."

We knock on Nellie Jane's door. She calls for us to come in. We leave our coats and boots at the door, bring in her food, and set a place for her at the table.

"Ned, how wonderful to see you." Nellie Jane receives a bear hug from Ned. She is beaming. "Sit down. Sit down. Thank you for bringing me my dinner."

She eats only after first preparing a spirit plate. She is quiet and deliberate in her selection of foods, adding tobacco and coffee. She sets the plate on the counter beneath a small window adorned with a four-directions sun catcher.

Ned made her the sun catcher three years ago, when she was taken with pneumonia and hospitalized in Twin Bays. It broke our hearts to hear her fight for every breath and to exhaust herself with relentless coughing. Mercy would not leave her side at the hospital and was beginning to fail from the exertion.

Ned strung the sun catcher on some fishing line, making a loop to secure it to a suction cup which he stuck on her window. The colored glasses spilled their light onto Nellie Jane's chest at the height of mid-morning. She was delighted and claimed that the medicine wheel not only lightened her spirit but put breath back into her lungs. She was released from the hospital within the week.

Nellie Jane makes her prayer to the spirits as she sets the plate on the counter. This is her ritual before every meal. Even when eating a berry from the garden, she will share and speak to the spirits as though they are with her, knives and forks at the ready for a feast.

She savors her meal. Ned pours her a glass of water.

"Thank you, dear." After swallowing a forkful of goulash, she speaks. "Ellen, the two of you are leaving today?"

"Yes. Mercy is quite insistent. Though I have to say, it's not like her to rush us off. We had an intense conversation last night about family history at the family farm. She told me some awful things about my father that I did not know. Maybe I wore her out." I touch Ned's arm. "I'll fill you in later."

Nellie Jane nods her head. "Her family past was hard, and she doesn't like to talk about it. I'm surprised the subject came up."

"Actually, I was the instigator," I tell her. "The conversation was upsetting for both of us, Nellie Jane. Since my parents are dead, there's no one but Mercy to answer questions about our family: how they came to be in Capitol, what made my father the man he was. I know nothing about her parents, my grandparents. She's shared with you, right? I'm not breaking a confidence?"

"You're fine." She nods. "She and I have talked throughout the years about family and the farm. I was raised with her in this place off and on, and then we spent our summers here throughout my married life. Hers is a tragic story. She's done the best with it that she can. Many impossible feats can be overcome with a will and a way—and I would add, with time may come honesty."

"After what I shared with her last night—my own history with my father and mother—she may need time to process it all. We covered a lot of personal history last night. Not only mine, but she told me about what happened at the farm. So terrible. Unthinkable."

Nellie Jane looks concerned. "Your story? What happened?"

"I don't think I've got it in me to say it all again. Not today. But since their deaths, I'm reliving the nightmare of my life with my parents—and it was a nightmare." I take a breath. "I told Aunt Mercy about my home life and my parents because she's my only living relative who I can speak to about these things. I have an uncle, Terry, who won't respond when I reach out to him. Mercy's the only one I've got to tie my life into my father's and hers and Terry's."

Nellie Jane is concerned. "I know your father was violent in his youth. Was he violent with you as well?"

"He was terrifying. And for now, I'll leave it at that," I reassure her. "But it's done. He's gone."

Ned remains quiet but reaches out to take my hand. He smiles at Nellie Jane. "It's been quite a night and day for them." He kisses my hand.

I pull my hand away as I remember what I came for, to tell her my vision story. "I went to my cabin in Ely for a couple of days, to get myself sorted out after their deaths. While I was there, I had a vision—I guess. It reminded me of things you and I used to talk about when I was a child. The little people."

"I remember." She nods.

"I'm having a hard time controlling my feelings about my parents. I keep having panic attacks."

"Grief can be like that, dear." She closes her eyes.

"I want to know if there's an insight you might glean from what I experienced."

I tell her about my first night in Ely, about making the spirit plate then waking up in the morning to see I had not made a plate at all.

"You didn't tell me about this," Ned says with a surprised tone.

"No," I speak with an edge to my voice. "I believe we were arguing." I shake my head.

One thing happens, then another. It's like ice piling up on shore when the lakes thaw. I feel exhaustion sweep through me.

"But anyway," I say, turning to Nellie Jane, "I thought of you. I thought it peculiar that I would unconsciously respond to my stress by borrowing the rituals you've shared with me."

Nellie Jane responds with warmth and interest. "You have a sensitive spirit, Ellen. Sensitives instinctively know what to do. Many people are highly insulated against responding to their inner connections to all living things. That insulation allows them to create havoc among the living, to destroy the earth without a thought or care. I'm not surprised at all that your trouble would bring you to the foot of the mountain."

How did she know about the mountain? "I haven't gotten to that part yet."

"Go on, then," she encourages.

I tell her the rest of the story about my dream—including the eagles.

"You said once that a vision should be held for twenty-eight days before being told to the elders. But I didn't set out with an intentional mind to vision quest. It just happened. You're the only person I know who might understand this. It was spooky."

"This is the crux of the problem with Western thinking. A set mind leads to nothing but nonsense. An intent spirit, however, a seeking spirit, will call to the ancient in us to speak. It is through these stories that have grown since the beginning of time that we are led to health and resolution." There is a tender smile brightening her face.

"Was it a dream, a hallucination? What do you think?"

Always a good Western thinker, I want a concrete answer that can be used to add two and two together to make a tidy sum of four. I don't want spirit mumbo jumbo talk.

"It's not what I make of it, Ellen. It's how you walk into it as you go now. You've been given an opening for birth. The Eagles have chewed you up and spit you out. They have sung your song from the bone in your hand, the instrument of creation. They have called the relatives together through your own bone. You are connected. You are connected." She repeats herself to drive home the point. "Now what will you do?" She gazes out the window. "If you're looking for acknowledgment, it was given. If you're looking for retribution, then that is a path you will walk alone."

I don't really understand what she's talking about, but it doesn't matter. I've heard what I want to hear: that I am acknowledged by the spirits of the Great Mystery—by someone, anyone. That's good enough for me. I learned as a child that for all the intrigue Nellie Jane can bring with her Indian ways, I am white and Western or Eastern European or whatever makes for stubborn and simple, through and through. I am a blockhead when it comes to circular, mystical logic.

I thank Nellie Jane for her time and patience with me. Ned and I say our goodbyes with hugs and kisses and leave her to nap after her meal.

As usual, I am confused by her words, but still, I feel good with a buoyed sense of validation. Maybe I haven't completely lost my mind. And I can't wait to show Ned the farm.

CHAPTER 14

As we walk back to Mercy's, I tell Ned we can take my car for our next outing, then track back for his before caravanning to Twin Bays for the night.

A couple of miles down the road, I pull into the local bar to have a beer and finally tell Ned about my conversation with Mercy the night before.

He is appropriately stunned and stricken. He grabs at my free hand, the one without the beer mug.

"Jesus, Ellen."

I manage a gulp of beer along with a nod. I sport wide eyes, my face flush from the alcohol and intrigue.

"And then I went out to the land where it all happened. Ned, it was exciting. Something about being there stimulated me. I felt connected." My spine tingles, and my shoulders quiver with adrenaline. "I want you to look at the place. I want you to consider moving here, fixing the old place up, and maybe starting a hobby farm. I know this sounds like madness. But what I felt when I stood on that ground—it was like a welcome, a command to come. I don't know."

Ned laughs and puts down his beer. "That's quick, even for you! Could it be that you're looking for a distraction from your grief, pain, everything you're feeling?"

He's thoughtful in his consideration of the idea. I find myself crossing my fingers and holding my breath.

"If we were in our twenties, I could say yes in a flash," he says. "We're not. How would you work from here? There are so many things to consider."

I interrupt. "Yes, I'm sure this is a sidetrack keeping me from dealing with the past and the present crap running around in my head. I know. But we're not doing anything much in Breeson, right? Just look at the place. See what you think. I know I'm a little crazy right now. It's okay to say so. But maybe we're due for a change. I don't know. With the windfall from my mother, we can afford to make some mistakes." I know I'm rambling. "We wouldn't have to stay here year-round—although we could, at least until Mercy passes. I don't know. Will you look at it?"

"You can stop selling. I'll look at it tomorrow."

We finish our beers, pick up Ned's car, and head for Twin Bays, about a half hour away. In the morning, I remind Ned to top off the gas tank. There won't be a station until Capitol.

Ned drives by my directions to the farmstead. I am aware of the isolation here. There is nothing but pine and marsh and tamarack along the way. Only a few road signs announce a town or a state or national forest. There are fewer billboards.

It's warm enough to have the windows rolled down a little. I find the sound of the tires beating against the pavement as we roar along soothing. Even when I lived in the city, I'd open the windows late at night and listen for the distant sounds of highway traffic—mostly truckers, tires pounding the pavement, off to destinations unknown to me. The sound evokes in me a wish to travel out west, where spaces are open and spirits litter the highways, looking for a lift with lonesome nomads.

I think about Nellie Jane's caution to me about singing my song, how it will define my way. The song of the roadway spurs an urge to move on. Maybe this is the song I've been orchestrating from my scavenger-ravaged bones. Move on. Move on. Move on.

I touch Ned on the knee and reach for his free hand. "I'm excited," I say.

He smiles, then suddenly hits the brakes, not so fast as to throw us in the ditch but fast enough to avoid making road kill. In the middle of the highway, in the middle of the morning, stands a lone coyote feasting off a deer carcass, an accident victim of a local drunk, I suppose.

"*Mitakyue oyasin*," I spout the words out loud on impulse. In my head ring more words: *Carrion's bones. More songs in Creation.*

The coyote saunters off into the underbrush. Ned picks up speed, and we're back on track to reach the family farm before noon.

We park the car on the side of the road. The driveway is blocked by a homemade tire-spike strip. Clearly, the owner is not a welcoming fellow and wants to discourage vehicles from entering—probably four-wheelers that will tear up the ground.

On foot, access is wide open through the snow-brushed tamarack and grasses. We make our way through the uneven terrain, up a slight incline to enter an expanse of meadow. The air is cold but no longer bitter. The sun is a heat lamp, bright and hot in contrast to the chill rising from the frozen ground. There is no breeze.

Ned walks away from me without a word for a solo tour of the land and buildings. He takes his time inspecting the old house and the vacant hunter's shack. He returns with a flush to his face, either from excitement or the cold.

"How many acres, did you say?"

"Ten."

"That's enough, I think." He has his project-planning look.

"For what?"

"If we can purchase this from the current owner, I'm on board. I've wanted to try some of the new options for gardening in the north. I think we can make something of the house. You could benefit from strengthening your relationship with Mercy before she passes on."

"Ned!" I look at him in amazement. "I've never known you to take action before contemplation. What's going on? Where's the research? Where are the spreadsheets?"

I tease him, but I have no idea about the gardening thing. Do we never talk to each other? Do I never listen?

"This checks off nearly every item left on my lifetime to-do list. I still want to travel to Scotland and Ireland, but other than that, this is it for me. I don't see a downside. What's to lose?"

I'm stunned. "I'm up for the challenge, as long as you're sure."

We stroll back to the car, both feeling happy for the first time in a while. I feel hopeful, for once. Ned keeps his thoughts to himself, so I force myself into silence too, allowing him room to muse.

As we head back to Breeson, I close my eyes and listen to the sound of the car on the road and the wind whistling through the open window. I am empty of thought or mood. No. I'm expectant, holding my breath. I force myself to breathe out, hard and long.

Relax, Ellen. Relax.

Ned does all the research to find the farm's current owner and work out a deal. The land has been sold and resold over the decades to hunters. The most recent owner, also a hunter, lost his driver's license twice and for good—a chronic DUI sort. He wants more than the place is worth but not so much that it stops us from striking a deal.

I've dug up an old bone abandoned by my father, by all of them. I feel as proud as any mongrel might with such a prize. I have roots here, roots that make me part of a family that might override Billy's influence. There could be something here for me that has been overlooked for too long. Ned and I can make a home. I can say, "I'm from here." For the first time in my life, I can avow with conviction, "I belong here."

Ned gets hard at work establishing a purpose for the land. His plans are ambitious: small animal outbuildings and areas to plow, to plant, and to fence.

I thank whatever energies move things around for Ned. He is a craftsman builder and thoughtful in his planning. He retired some years ago from a career as an architectural engineer. He loves his free time to putter and fish and read and cook dinners, his finest talent. But this farm idea takes over his attention and interest now. We eat a lot of takeout this spring. There's no time for cooking. I'm stuck with the washing up and the laundry and all tedious, hated household chores.

I didn't know that he'd wanted to farm, that it was his first choice of career when he was just a boy. His father, a successful banker, was horrified that his son wanted to be a pig farmer or cow wrangler, so he sent him off to a college far away from any agricultural nonsense. Even so, Ned managed to sneak in some agricultural classes along with botany and plant sciences. Now, with the passions of youth inflamed, he prepares for sixteen-hour days of hard labor and a myriad of unpredictable calamities.

The month of May arrives, and we are ready to take the first steps toward our move up north. It’s time to let Mercy know we’re moving to Capitol.

CHAPTER 15

The spring thaw forces the frost from the ground, and the roads are frost-free and dry. I drive to Capitol to tell Mercy about our plans. Nellie Jane is visiting with Mercy when I arrive. They greet me with hugs and kisses and invite me to lunch with them.

As we sit at the table over chicken salad sandwiches and garden tomato basil soup, Mercy tells me that two old men, brothers native to the town, passed away.

"Their funerals are this afternoon at three. You could help us set up at the church," she suggests.

Mercy inspects me briefly to decide if my appearance is appropriate to lend respect to the passing of the brothers as they are sent off by the locals. I'm glad I've chosen a fresh cotton striped blouse instead of the tattered Harley t-shirt I'd planned to wear. For once I'm grateful I spilled coffee on myself, forcing the change.

"There won't be a big crowd. Just a few of us old folks," Mercy says. "They were brother bachelors, so no children or grandchildren will be here to mourn them. It's sad to think about Leo and Fred, being sick with the flu and dying out there alone. I wish we'd known. But I suppose there wasn't much we could have done. They were both in their nineties and had a good run at life."

Nellie Jane adds that there might be a sister somewhere. "Beulah said they hadn't found a phone number or address. Maybe when the girls go to clean out the place, they'll find something."

"The girls" would be the other eighty-plus-year-old women who volunteer for such tasks. They will sort and share and clean and donate anything that can be recirculated for benefit of others in the surrounding communities. There will be no intrusion by the law except when it comes time to collect taxes after the land and house are auctioned off. Any proceeds will go to the auctioneer and will barely recover his costs.

We finish our lunch, and I clean up the kitchen while Mercy and Nellie Jane change into their funeral best. I drive the quarter mile to the Methodist church, a pre-fab pole shed adorned with a cross. Baked chicken, the last jar of dilled green beans, blueberry cobbler, and apple cider are packed in the back seat with Nellie Jane. Delicious smells inside the car make me a little dizzy with hunger. The other churchwomen will bring more food—a variety of potato dishes, cake, and coffee.

What a contrast to William's funeral. In all, there are fifteen old women, five timeworn, withered-up men, two teenagers and their mom in town visiting their grandma Beulah, and the minister.

The noise in the converted pole shed chapel is deafening. Two overhead heaters warm the room, and three standing fans circulate the heat. The noise from the whirring of the fans raises the level of noise from the mourners.

No one else seems bothered by the clamor. They aren't wasting a single moment on tears or grief. This funeral will be the last time one or more of these folks get together for a party outside of a coffin. They all know it and make the best of every minute.

The service is lively. The minister, well-known to this community, was brought in from Twin Bays. The regular pastor left for a two-week vacation to see his daughter in Florida. A few old men stand to speak briefly about the brothers, and the women are loud and nearly on key with their hymn singing.

There will be no burial until tomorrow. The backhoe is being repaired. So at the close of the ceremony, everyone shakes the hand of the visiting pastor as the men pull tables out from storage to set up for lunch. Chairs are put in place, table covers are laid out, and the food line forms at the back kitchen serving counter.

I'm surprised by the amount of food the old men eat and with such gusto. There isn't a frail or fading one in the bunch. This is hearty immigrant stock—many from Ireland or Scotland via Canada, from impoverished families who took to the seas with hopes and a vision for work and success ahead. Others are Scandinavian and German immigrants with dreams for better futures as well.

These men were miners, loggers, and railroad workers. Success for them is land ownership. I can't imagine any other benefit of the decades upon decades of hard labor behind them now. Some still put in a hard day's work, though maybe a shorter day now. But they still take care of themselves, knowing there is no one left to pick up the load.

I hear that old Benny Harvaald still chops his own wood. He's ninety-two. I whisk away the image of him chopping off a hand.

When everyone is fed, I sit with Mercy and Nellie Jane, who are taking a break from serving and fussing. I want to tell Mercy about our acquisition of the farmland. I don't know if public or private divulging is best. Yet I learned today that the present moment might be the only moment.

"Aunt Mercy," I speak with eagerness. "When you told me about the family farm—even though you tried your best to dissuade me—I had to see it. Ned and I drove out to visit the land before we left here back in March. We walked around in the snow, saw the hunter's shack and the old house, imagined what it might have been like when you were a child. I felt something when I was there, something moved in me, connected. I've never experienced anything like it before." I turn to Nellie Jane. "It reminded me of your story about a child's umbilical cord. I felt connected, wanted."

During one of Nellie Jane's instructions in her native ways, she shared with me the importance of the umbilical cord, the tie to the mother and how we were connected to both the mother and the earth by that cord. "You are born from water and blood," she told me that day. "This is your lifeline. We do not lose that connection. It is not possible."

I tell them about Ned's enthusiasm. "It is exciting to see Ned's passion for this. Turns out, he's always wanted to own a hobby farm. He's drawn up plans and ordered supplies. He's over the moon about moving to the farm. I had no idea he'd ever thought about such a thing."

Both women look uncomfortable, but I push forward.

"And we want to be closer to you. You're all the family I've got now." I clutch and squeeze Mercy's hand. "I want to learn from both of you. We both want to get out of the small-town isolation and experience real community like you have here."

I wait for some reaction, some word, a reaching out or a pulling away. The women look concerned but do not look at each other, not even at me. They pick at their food.

I keep talking. "Ned loves a project, and he's excited about this one. We want to live closer to you both. I don't want any more time to pass without you near. I want to be here, here where I have a loving family.

I want to live here and establish some roots for myself, even if only for a few years."

I know I'm talking too much and stop to give them a chance to respond.

Nellie Jane stands to speak. "All right then. *Wašté*. We will learn to see the place in a new way." She rests her hand on Mercy's shoulder. "Maybe you and Ned can bring it to life, the life it was intended to have. *Taŋyáŋ yahípi*. Welcome."

Mercy is reluctant to agree but nods her approval. "It will be good to have you both here."

"I hope you mean that." I say, "because we're planning to move in—at least to the old shack—by the end of the month."

Mercy's expression goes unchanged.

I touch her hand again. "Aunt Mercy, can I stay with you for a few weeks? Ned wants me out of his way while he packs up his stuff in the Breeson and gets us moved into the shack."

Mercy's reluctance does not obstruct her politeness. "Of course you can stay. I'll talk to Beulah to put together a welcome lunch here at the church. When did you say Ned would be here? And I'll talk to Jack Martin about helping him. Jack is an old school chum who's more than handy with a hammer."

For the next two weeks, Ned takes care of packing whatever we need in our new life. The rest is left to me to sell, donate, or toss. He goes back and forth to Capitol a few times to meet the area men, review his plans, walk the grounds, and collect samples from the soil and water.

I use this time to reacquaint myself with every place Missy and I explored during our pretend archaeological hunts. I remember finding rocks we were certain were skulls—and real skulls of small animals that made us run away shrieking in fear and disgust. We found snake skins and empty bird nests. Once we found a half-eaten rabbit carcass left for later by a red fox.

We hunted for ancient Indian burial mounds, which we never found. But we did find a child's cemetery on the east side of the town. When we told Mercy about it, she shared that long ago, an illness spread through the township, and many children died. The townspeople believed that the dead still carried the active disease, so the children were buried in a special place, never visited by family but remembered in prayer.

Ned calls to say everything is packed and ready. He'll arrive in Capitol in two days to start work on the farm. Once he arrives, that's my cue to go back to Breeson. I will close up the house, collect LuLu, arrange for cleaners and a real estate agent, and see to all the remaining details to end our residence there. I've already moved my office into a small space I rented in Twin Bays, though I've notified clients that I'll be unavailable, except for emergencies, for three weeks.

While I'm at the house, Patsy stops by to find me tagging the last of the household items for a garage sale Annie agreed to run. I promised Annie the profits as long as she gets rid of whatever is left after the sale. She will have access to the place for three more weeks, giving her plenty of time to set up the sale. I also put her in charge of overseeing the cleaning and repairs.

"I noticed the For Sale sign," Patsy says. She peers into the living room to see packing boxes taped shut and stacked high. "It won't stay on the market long. I'm sorry I couldn't get over sooner. Where are you going? Why are you going? And what can I do to stop you?"

I tell her all about the farm and Mercy and Nellie Jane's mysterious behavior around my interest in the place.

Pasty stares at me. "So you're moving into godforsaken Podunk to raise goats? Is your mind broken?"

I laugh and nod. "Maybe. Honestly, I need a distraction to get me back to normal rhythms. I can't obsess about my childhood and my parents forever. When my aunt told me the horrors of her young life with my father, it was enough to move me off—"

"What? What horrors?" Patsy interrupts. She sits on the floor and pats the space beside her. "Spill it all, now."

I sit down—marker in one hand, item tags in the other—and tell her the whole truth and nothing but.

Patsy closes her eyes and rocks slowly back and forth. She opens one eye and uses it to inspect my mood. "And you're okay." She opens both eyes. "You're not flipping out."

"I certainly did when she told me. I felt like I was being emotionally skinned. I still haven't processed everything. But for now, I can complete a sentence without a breakdown and get things done without dissolving into emotional chaos. It's a start."

"So you're numb." Patsy touches my hand and strokes my fingers.

"I don't think so. You know, there's an idea, fleeting, that's driving me. If we transform that land, bring it back to a good life, then Billy is erased forever, right?"

She arches an eyebrow. "I know I sound a bit manic, but I feel free for the first time ever. I can't get enough of this feeling!"

"And Ned's all over this farming thing? Impressive for a sixty-three-year-old man. This is a lot to take on."

"I know! He's more excited about this than I am. You think you know a person! And if it doesn't work out, we can walk away."

Patsy stretches flat out on the floor. "I'm not happy to lose you. You're not getting rid of me. I'll visit often, if you'll have me."

I poke her in the side. "You'd better come to see us."

CHAPTER 16

With the car packed and LuLu secured in the back, I'm ready to get going. The drive is easy. LuLu sticks her nose out the window, acquainting herself with north woods smells.

I pull into the rutted, makeshift road leading to the hunter's shack and park beside Ned's truck. I can hear men's voices coming from the direction of the old house. I let LuLu free to explore while I stand by my car to soak up the sun and fill my lungs with fresh spring country air.

Then panic begins to rise. What in the hell was I thinking?

We're too old to be taking on this kind of a project. Either one of us could keel over by noon tomorrow. We don't know anyone here except for Mercy and Nellie Jane, and they're older by nearly two decades. We're in the middle of godforsaken nowhere. Winter will be horrible and will last three weeks longer than it did in Breeson, and that is way too long for me.

I remind myself that Twin Bays and some culture are less than an hour's drive away. We don't have to be here all the time. This can be a summer home. We can get an apartment anywhere for the winter months. The persistent panic retreats. For a moment.

But who will care for the animals—that we don't have yet?

I try to shake off my concerns. I'll have time for worry later.

I scan the landscape that enchanted me not so long ago. I try to feel the connection I felt on the first visit. Now all I feel is an urge to run away. I involuntarily flash on my grandfather beating my grandmother to the floor. I shudder. A pronounced cold sweeps through my belly and into my arms.

The sun is too strong, though, and it beats back the panic. Its heat and the smells it draws out from new vegetation and the ground brings me back to the present moment. It nudges me forward to unload the car and get unpacked.

I hear LuLu woof in excitement and the men laugh. She found Ned.

With an armful of bags and coats and bedding, I take my first step into the hastily remodeled shack, our new temporary home. The kitchen is on the left of the front door entryway. Ned installed a wood block countertop and cabinets. The fumes from the varnish he used on the cabinets hang at the edge of the hallway.

To my right is the living room. The furniture is arranged around the wood stove centered on a red-brick hearth. It is a cozy and inviting space. I notice that Ned installed bookshelves against the wide-windowed wall, along with a bank of storage cupboards. I suspect there's already been some evening poker with his new friends.

I trot down to the only bedroom. The bathroom, on the opposite side of the hallway, smells of fresh paint. I drop my armful of belongings onto the bed and return to the car to finish unloading and start unpacking. I want wine and a rest in one of the old recliners Ned's cleaned well enough.

We will live in the hunter's shack for most of the summer while Ned and Jack Martin work on rehabbing the farmhouse. Jack, near eighty years old, was sent over by Mercy to help. Turns out he is a hard worker, knows this land, and is familiar with the old house. He lives on forty acres just down the road less than a quarter mile, across the railroad tracks. He has been in the area for over fifty years.

Mercy told us he'd been injured in a lumber accident when he was a young man, leaving him with a disfiguring scar on the right side of his face and blind in that eye as well. Jack never married, perhaps because he is a little slow in his thinking and speech. He has a full beard and mustache, white as white can be—which, we are told, he will trim only when invited to Mercy's for holiday and celebration gatherings.

Nellie Jane says he is her cousin, son of her Aunt Katey and Uncle Buster Martin on the reservation. She says he has a younger brother who moved to the city before he turned sixteen. He was called Little Boy because he was a big child.

Nellie Jane doesn't know what happened to Little Boy. She thinks he assimilated once he moved to the city. It doesn't often happen that an Indian truly leaves the reservation behind. Family ties across generations are strong, and they influence everything in a native's life. The white world is believed to be a shadow world and unsafe.

Jack is a good handyman, and he knows how to take care of animals and gardens and the land. We plan to hire him from spring to the last bit of fall harvest. He can help us learn how to get the most from what we have, while giving back to the soil what it needs for the growing season ahead.

We learn a lot from him. Jack teaches me how to amend the sandy, sometimes claylike soil and what to plant for fall vegetable harvest. He brings seedlings and seeds and shows me how to care for my first garden. He also brings perennial herbs and flowers to plant for culinary and medicinal use as well as for beauty. Jack has an eye for color and form. I can see the beginnings of beautiful and useful gardens taking shape.

Nellie Jane and Mercy contribute advice and plants during their frequent visits. I enjoy watching them and Jack work together. There is a closeness between them that I envy. After decades of learning by doing, there is much interest and discussion regarding the development of our gardens and animal safety and care. I am happy to have them do the work of it. Especially because summer brings a near overwhelming work schedule for me. I am often away or working in Twin Bays where the wireless connections are consistent.

With Jack's direction, Ned restores enough of the house for us to move in before the first hard frost, freeing up time to build secure and weather-worthy shelters for the goats and chickens And we find that we love every minute of being up north, regardless of the threat of winter always around the corner. We love the colors, the sounds, the movements nature reveals each moment. We are proud of our decision and are welcomed with enthusiasm by the community. We are bringing a good way of life back to the farm, as Nellie Jane had hoped. We are happy.

CHAPTER 17

Not long after we settle into the house, CiCi calls to say she's coming for a visit. She has been performing in Minneapolis and has decided to take a brief vacation tour of the North Shore before heading home—which means a meander to me and us.

This will be CiCi's first trip to the farm. She often visited in Breeson but has only heard stories of Capitol and the farmstead. She says she'll be here for a few days, if we're cool with that.

We are cool with it. The "we" includes LuLu, so happy now to be living a country lifestyle. She's known CiCi since she was a newly adopted pup and loves her like crazy.

"CiCi is coming!" I tell her. LuLu races to my side, then to the door.

Ned is delighted too. In his spare time, he's been working out in his new workshop on a stained glass window for CiCi's back porch. The glass is ready for polishing.

CiCi is coming. Lord, how I have missed CiCi. She makes everybody happy. It's all in the way she collects experience and spreads it over us like Nellie Jane's chokecherry jam thick on a warm buttered biscuit. She is always welcome. Her stories are always welcome.

I met CiCi at the park by my house when I was seven, after my first summer with Mercy in Capitol. I was home only one day from

Mercy's house in the north woods. It would be a couple of weeks before school would start. Second grade. Terrifying.

It was hot outside. It had been cool at Aunt Mercy's, except on the sandy beach by the lake. It was damp chilly under the jack pines.

"Damp chilly" was something Uncle Jasper said. Damp chilly. I liked the sound in my head. I said it out loud, over and over again, as I spun the merry-go-round. I wished for my cousin Missy, somebody to play with. For all the kids at the playground, none was a friend to me.

The steel bars on the self-propelled merry-go-round burned my fingers. I could smell the heat and feel the grime build up on my face and legs as I pushed the merry-go-round with my right foot, filling my pink sandals with sand, propelling it forward. My toes would burn right off if I lost a shoe. It was a risk I was willing to take.

Better to burn. I heard those words somewhere—something about hellfire and damnation, maybe. Better to burn up out there than go back to my house cooled by box fans and their whirring whispers.

When the merry-go-round was spinning fast, I pulled my leg back up onto the platform. As it slowed, I stuck my foot out into the hot sand again and pushed hard, harder, forcing the merry-go-round into a wild spin. The faster it moved, the louder it squealed with an unnerving sound of metal scraping on metal, emitting a high-pitched noise that could call an eagle out of its nest. I knew all about eagles because Nellie Jane taught me stuff like that.

I spun and twirled, letting my long brown curls loose into the breeze and humidity of the late August afternoon. My pink barrette, supposed to hold my hair in place, came loose, bobbing against my face as I spun. I clutched it in my hand while my thumb braced my grip on the merry-go-round bar.

Tired and bored, I stopped and listened with my eyes closed to the playground equipment and other kids. I heard children laughing, crying, yelling, and screeching. There was a faraway sound of calling from a mother to her child. But nearest to my ear was the loudest, happiest laughter I'd ever heard.

I opened my eyes and searched through the kids for the source of the incredible laugh. It was coming from a chubby girl in green shorts, laughing with her head thrown back as far as it would go while she pushed her glasses up on her nose, over and over again. Her close-clipped auburn curls stayed in place with the swing of her head. They had no movement of their own. Her arm moved up and down in a mechanical fashion, like a robot arm from *The Jetsons*. She kept on laughing and pushing up her glasses.

There were two smaller boys with her. I couldn't tell what any of them were doing or why they were laughing. Then she began to run. She ran with the abandon of a coyote pup after a mouse. She flailed and stumbled.

The smallest of the boys caught up to her, pushed her hard on her shoulder, and screamed, "You're it!"

He raced past her, but her stride outpaced him. When she tagged him, the slim boy, dwarfed by her size, went down into the sand with her, where they wrestled and laughed. The other boy gave up the game and went off to climb on the jungle gym, unnoticed by his friends. The girl's glasses flew off her face. I jumped off the merry-go-round and ran to save them. I didn't know her, but I knew she'd be in some kind of trouble if those glasses broke. They had to cost a lot of money.

By the time I reached them, the girl and boy were getting to their feet and brushing the sand out of their hair and off their faces. They were still laughing, more a giggle now.

I squatted next to the girl's glasses sticking out of the sand. With the utmost care, I retrieved them. I blew away the dirt with all the breath I'd been holding since I'd first heard the girl's laugh.

I made eye contact with her and reached out my hand, offering the glasses, no worse for the tumble.

"Thanks!" She spoke in a voice of honey, thick and lilting. She put on the glasses, then tagged me. "You're it!" She ran off with her friend lagging two leg lengths behind.

In a flash, I was on the run without thought or care for my white sun top and blue shorts. All I wanted was to tag that girl. My normal state of wariness and caution and my fear of consequences to come evaporated in a single moment of welcome to me from another child. We played until there was no play left in us.

"I'm CiCi," she announced as she jumped on her silver bike with colorful streamers dripping from the handlebar grips. Front and center was an empty wicker basket laced with plastic yellow flowers. She punched the bell perched at the top center of the handlebars. *Ting. Ting. Ting.* She looked at me with a wide, happy grin, exposing crooked bottom teeth. Her smile was perfect.

"I'm Ellen." I said my name as if it meant something, my voice echoing in my head. I felt a flush of shame crawl up my sunburned cheeks.

"Hey, I live over on Applewood Lane," she said. "You should come to my house sometime."

CiCi's pudgy legs, streaked with dirt, pumped her bike with fury. I watched her ride away from me until she turned the corner of my street and disappeared from sight.

I waited at the park for her every day until school started. We played. We talked. We laughed. I'd never been happy before. I'd never had a friend before. Ever. CiCi was a miracle. CiCi was everything to me.

She invited me for a sleepover after her birthday party. I could hear her parents arguing downstairs after we went to bed. CiCi snored right through the whole thing, while I shivered in fear under a summer-weight, freshly starched bedsheet. The argument didn't last long. I heard CiCi's mom cry a little, but then I heard laughter. I fell asleep and dreamt about a small, safe house with chickens and a dog named Mutt.

When I woke up the next morning, it was to CiCi shaking my shoulder.

"Get up! Mom's makin' pancakes! Get up!"

I studied CiCi when she wasn't looking. If CiCi was looking, we were playing. CiCi never once stopped moving, not even in her sleep.

Her mom cooed over her, sometimes snuggling close. Her father always greeted her with arms wide open. "Where's my princess?" He'd wink at me as he caught her hugs, as if he were letting me in on the secret of how much he loved his little girl. My jaw hurt from smiling all the time. I couldn't help it.

CiCi and I talked about almost everything. We explored the neighborhood, going places we weren't supposed to go to. We were partners in crime, famous adventurers, the best of friends.

When she asked if she could come to my house, I told her no. I lied to CiCi. I told her my dad didn't like noise in the house.

"I'll be quiet," she promised.

I told a bigger lie. I said my dad was sick sometimes. I wanted a perfect world with her, my one friend, and I couldn't risk ruining everything by letting her in my house. I had to lie.

"I don't like her spending time with that girl."

I heard my father's angry, disapproving voice from the living room. They thought I was asleep—or they didn't care if I heard. I cringed under my covers and pushed my face down, deep into my pillow. I wouldn't let them keep me from her.

Her mom fed me lunches and took us to a nearby lake for swimming. If Nellie Jane couldn't be my mom, maybe CiCi's parents would adopt me. Maybe if I told them about the things my father made me do, maybe they would take me away from him.

But I couldn't tell. I was afraid CiCi would hate me, that her parents would hate me if they knew the things I'd done.

Years later, we were in high school, talking about our plans for the future. I had to tell her why there was no college fund, why I needed to make a way into my future on my own.

All she did was hug me. That was it. Until she told her dad. That's how she changed the course of my life.

Love and friendship require a third leg of support to hold up over time. Even now, I can't imagine my life without CiCi in it.

CiCi, grown, is a large, bawdy broad. She wears too much makeup and exhibits dramatic, sweeping wardrobe choices that on her look great. She sparkles. She is sultry, salty, and spicy. Her singing voice is deep and rich, and it swings with her hips and thrusts with her breasts. She is a performer throwback to vaudeville. She is entertainment. She writes most of her own music. She likes soul—jazzy stuff.

I want her to write music for my country western songs. The older I get, the less able I am to get romantically enthused. Ned is fantastic. I do love him. But he doesn't put a twinkle in my eye the way a good ol' country wanna-love-ya-gotta-have-ya heartbreak ballad puts me right over my sexual edge. Ned likes to keep an old cowboy hat around and his boots polished, just in case I might want to engage him in a little bedroom two-step.

It was CiCi who convinced me to marry Ned.

One night at her apartment in the city, we were half in the bag.

She was classic CiCi, wrapped in a colorful African motif kaftan. She'd picked it up in some second-hand store on her last band tour. It was jewel toned in rich blues and greens with gold accents. Her toenails were painted in gold.

CiCi has no defined style or aesthetic. She surrounds herself with used furniture she refers to as "antiques." She also loves wall tapestries, mostly in mossy greens and browns, along with second-hand-store treasures of art and lamps. She is so proud of every object. Altogether, it shouts everything CiCi. It screams tacky kitsch, and I love all of it.

I was seated in a comfy tan linen chair that I gave her when I got my own place. CiCi lounged in a well-worn dark-purple plush fabric recliner she bought for $75.

She shared with me how she'd met this man named Ned while out to dinner with mutual friends. Ned told her all about a carpentry project he was working on. She said there was something about his enthusiasm that piqued her interest—made her think he and I would make a good match.

"And he's so good looking!" CiCi said with a laugh. "That sandy hair, those sexy eyes—God! He's so manly!"

CiCi said that when her friend left for the restroom, she moved into the empty chair next to Ned and started asking him questions. She was firing on all cylinders. She knew he was the one for me.

She was right. Ned and I hit it off. But after love, CiCi started pushing marriage. I told her I wasn't interested. Ned and I were fine the way we were together. I had no intention of marrying anyone. I'd done that already. The divorce nearly killed me. Why would I set myself up for that again? I knew I was no good at give-and-take. And I couldn't—no, I wouldn't—risk my heart on another cheater.

So I asked her why on earth I should marry Ned.

"Because he loves you and he's steady, and he's not weird, Ellen!" And then she added, "And because you need to learn how to live in a family and not be afraid."

That raised the hair on the back of my neck.

"You've been on the run since I've known you," she told me. "You're a mine field. You've stepped along in your life, blowing yourself up, rebuilding, only to blow yourself up again. You have to find some safe ground. And that's Ned, right?"

If anybody in this world knew how to live in a family, how to thrive in a family, it was CiCi.

"Okay," I said, nodding. "I'll say yes to Ned—should the subject ever come up."

She nodded back. "Good. Because he already asked me for your hand in marriage."

As it turned out, Ned and CiCi had gone out for burgers at a pub around the corner the night before, while I was at work.

"I want to spend the rest of my life with her, but I don't want to overwhelm her," he had confided, feeling his way through the idea of proposing marriage to me.

"You gotta jump in," she told him. "You're the best thing—next to me, of course—that's ever happened to that girl. She's getting old, and she needs you. I need her to be attached somewhere. She needs to be connected." CiCi was adamant.

"So, you approve?"

"Oh, hell yes, Ned. Please, get it done!"

The following Sunday morning, Ned and I met for brunch at the Mill House Inn. It was part of an old mill from the late 1800s, restored and renovated to appeal to young urban professionals. The inn was a riverfront destination for the art crowd and opera, orchestra, and theater patrons. Its interior stonework had been sandblasted to a soft, creamy wheat color. Some of the original small factory windows had been replaced with floor-to-ceiling windows that looked out over the river and its banks—where many, many homeless winos lived and died.

That night I was distracted by two old men who were sharing a bottle. I wondered at that life. I thought about karma. The word slipped from my lips.

"Karma?" Ned asked.

"I was thinking out loud."

I pointed out the two men on the river bank. One now appeared to be passed out. The other was taking a swig from his brown-paper-bag-wrapped bottle of hooch.

"It makes me wonder about that life, about my life, about karma, if karma is a thing."

"We've done this topic to death," Ned said. "We've agreed that karma is just another way for the little guy to feel better about his lot in life."

By this time, both of the drunks on the bank were passed out.

"What did those guys do to deserve this? I just can't buy into the whole 'deserve, punishment, payback' idea. I guess I don't want to, because then I'd have to ask myself—what's my story? I'm certain I wouldn't want to know."

We laughed. The waiter came, dressed in a black long-sleeved button-down shirt with crisp white flour sack apron tied at his small waist. He looked so young. I could hear the sound of a tray crashing back in the kitchen and a child crying at his mother's hand as his family took the table next to ours.

"Would you care for a beverage from the bar?"

Ned ordered a beer, and I ordered a mimosa. We took a moment with the elegant menus, decided on vegetable omelets, then set the menus to the side. Ned took my hand.

I love Ned, I thought. My body relaxed.

Then things got serious. "Ellen, I'm ready to retire. You know I can take an early retirement. I'd like to do some traveling, and I'd like to travel with you."

"Ned, this is not news." I felt cautious. "I'm the one who's been encouraging you to retire, am I not?"

Ned increased the pressure on my hand. "I know. But I want to travel with you as my wife, not my lover or girlfriend or sidekick. I want to start this chapter of my life with you firmly attached to me. I want to plan a future with you."

Our server interrupted with our drinks. I thanked him, pulled my hand from Ned's, and grasped my mimosa. I stopped myself from draining the glass in one chug. Ned did not look away, his hand still extended toward me.

"Okay," I said as I moved my hand off the mimosa and placed it back in Ned's open palm. "Okay. I hear you. Plus, you already know I have to say yes because you set me up with CiCi to say yes, and now I have no argument against it. However, I'm going to have to get used to it. I'm not going to swoon."

Ned nodded in agreement.

I smiled an impish smile. “And,” I continued, “I expect a ring.”

Ned laughed. “No swooning. I’ve got a ring.”

He pulled a velvet case from his pocket and flipped it open to show me his grandmother’s wedding ring from the late 1800s—maybe as old as this mill.

“I’ve been saving this for you since the day we met.”

I started to cry and stuck out my ring finger. “Engage me, baby.” I leaned in close to his face and softly whispered, “Marry me. I hope you never regret this.”

I pulled away from him, sat back to admire my ring, then looked him square in the eye.

“Don’t ever make me regret this.”

With that, Ned stood up, walked over to me, pulled me up out of my chair, and kissed me hard.

“Nope. No regrets, ever,” he said.

The waiter delivered our food, but our appetites were gone. We paid our bill and left to walk into the future together. Neither of us looked back at the winos.

I remember thinking that we were going to beat karma if karma was a thing we could beat. The memory leaves me misty-eyed.

And so we married, and things have been okay up until now. CiCi’s career has taken off. I’ve maintained an even keel. But now, it’s not about how I manage. It’s about how I can’t manage anymore. It’s about how I’m drowning and nobody gets it. Nobody can help.

CHAPTER 18

As I wait for CiCi, Ned arrives with Mercy and Nellie Jane in tow. They bring beef stew and biscuits and a fresh blueberry pie. They are excited for me and eager to meet my childhood friend.

We can see the dust spray from the dirt driveway the minute she pulls off the highway. And suddenly, here she is. LuLu goes wild.

"CiCi's here!" I shout.

She sweeps out of the car in that grand way she has of making an entrance anywhere. Ned is prompt with his greeting, hugs and kisses, then steps away to grab her luggage.

I can't get my arms around her fast enough. I bear-hug her, and she laughs her husky laugh as I knock her floppy straw hat to the ground. I step back and bend over to retrieve it, noticing her fuchsia toenails and thick-soled leather sandals.

Ned lets LuLu out of the house when he walks in with CiCi's bag and fiddle case. It's all frenzy and fur after that. LuLu pushes me away, nearly knocking CiCi off her feet. But CiCi knows how to control a dog and makes her sit. I think LuLu will explode out of her skin. CiCi crouches to pet her and tells her how pretty she is. Just then, a whiff of something more interesting catches LuLu up, and she races away from us, off on a hunt.

"Oh, my friend, it's wonderful to see you," I say as I wrap my arm around CiCi's waist and walk her into the house.

"You, too," she says. For a moment, she rests her head on my shoulder.

Hat in hand, all smiles, we join the others inside.

After a big meal and much chatter, Ned leaves to drive the ladies home. CiCi and I take our time sauntering down to the hunter's shack. I reach for her hand to hold.

At the shack, I give CiCi the tour, then I pop open a couple of beers while she makes herself comfortable in a recliner. We put our feet up with a small table between us so our beer bottles are within easy reach.

I give her every detail of the death saga and meltdowns and family history surprises that led Ned and me to the farm outside of Capitol. But I haven't got the courage to tell her about my confrontation with Virginia. The old fears of *she'll hate me if she knows who I really am* have taken over.

CiCi leans forward and lowers her voice a little. "I don't know if I ever told you this, but I had an uncle who was always feeling me up at family get-togethers. If I passed by, he'd reach for me and grab me around the chest, giving me a squeeze. It started when I was twelve. I had nice little breast buds, and he just had to have a feel." She winced. "Nobody seemed to notice, and no one would listen to my complaints. Typical grown-up bullshit."

She shakes her head and swallows a gulp of beer.

"But I took control of it. One afternoon, he was standing with my dad when he reached out and tweaked my buds. 'Honk, honk,' he said right out loud in front of him. My dad was gonna knock him out, but he didn't get a chance because I punched my uncle in the nuts. Then my dad followed with a smack to the back of his head. Laid him right out on the floor. He hollered for my mom, his sister, who made him crawl out to his car. It was a great day! I never saw him again."

I picture CiCi's assault on her uncle. "Good for you! Punch 'em in the nuts. Way to go! And good for your dad!"

She smiles and laughs a throaty, snide laugh. "In spite of him, I've always liked men, and I've always liked sex. I wasn't gonna let Uncle Asshole ruin it for me."

She takes another deep swig of beer. I wonder how she could still be sober.

"But your situation was different. I know that. And that's why I wanted you with Ned. I knew then and I know now, he'll take care of you. I know he will never ever hurt you. Ever."

CiCi and I are quiet, gazing out on the land we can see through the picture window. I imagine the previous owner sitting here, watching his deer stand and dreaming of his next hunt.

CiCi nods off, asleep, snoring. That girl can raise a roof. I throw a blanket over her and leave her to her dreams while I head to the house, where Ned is busy cleaning the kitchen.

"Honey, would you make up CiCi's bed?" I ask. "I forgot all about that."

I enter the guest room that will be initiated with CiCi and her snores. It is a lovely room. Ned did a superb job of restoring the house. He took care with the architectural details in each room—the chair rails and built-ins and bedsteads are all handcrafted.

He left the decorating to me, even though he knows it annoys me. While I have some natural talent, I don't enjoy it. I tried to imagine who our future guests might be. We have two additional rooms, one in the second story. I don't expect it will ever be used because we don't know that many people who will want to travel this far north or go up and down stairs in the night.

Patsy might. I should call Patsy.

The downstairs room is painted a soft mossy green. The oak woodwork has a natural stain. Into the wall next to the closet, Ned built a bookshelf-with-desk-and-dresser arrangement in natural oak with freshly painted white accents. The room looks clean and fresh. I can't imagine anyone not relishing their stay.

When CiCi makes her way back to the house, I show her to her room where I've stashed her bag and fiddle. She pulls a garish afghan from her bag and hands it to me.

"I've got a housewarming gift for you. I asked Julie to make it. I picked out the colors and the pattern. My mother has one just like it."

I hug her and thank her and suffer an invisible cringe at its extraordinary garishness. But it is CiCi. All CiCi. I am reminded of Nellie Jane's bizarre quilt compilations. I need to get over my aesthetic snobbery and remember how fortunate I am to have such remarkable women as guides in my life.

I smooth the afghan over the bed cover, and we sit on the bed together. I'm beginning to shiver. Anxiety tears through me. I can't stop it. I have to tell her. I have to get this demon truth about Virginia out of me.

"CiCi." I speak with my eyes downcast. "I have to tell you something, something about my mother."

She looks at me with puffy eyes, still groggy from her nap. I put my hand on her hand and tell her how I spurred Virginia on to suicide.

"It's my fault that she killed herself."

"Oh, for God's sake! Those people . . ." Her voice trails off while she works up a head of steam.

"No, CiCi. You have to listen."

"No, I don't. I don't care what you did. You did nothing to compare with what they did to you. Those people did only for themselves.

Always. You never made a dent in their emotions, their thoughts, their existence!"

Now she is yelling at me, her face contorted with fury. My teeth chatter with panic.

"You had every right to confront her. If she chose to chew pills to avoid bad press, that's got nothing to do with you!"

Ned races into the room. "What's going on?"

I am shaking so hard I can't speak. I try, but I can't make a syllable.

"Her goddamned parents," CiCi chimes in. "She told me she thinks she killed her mother—the fucking mother who let her husband fuck her child, beat her. Jesus!"

Ned is motionless. He is seeing, for the first time, the reality of what happened to me, through another's eyes, another's truth. He starts to cry.

"I . . ." His words drift away.

"Here!" CiCi barks at me as a sergeant might to a flailing recruit. She wraps me in the afghan, putting her arms around me, cradling me, rocking me gently until warmth creeps back into my body.

"Ned," CiCi coos. "Come here."

Dutifully, he sits on the bed and takes her place, holding me. I roll into him, into his body heat, and begin to sob.

"I didn't mean to do it." I choke out the words.

"You did nothing, honey. Nothing."

Ned holds me, soothing me, while CiCi leaves us to make some hot tea. I hear the kettle sing. It rouses me from panic. I smile at Ned and dab at my eyes. With the afghan secure about me, we go to the kitchen together to join CiCi for tea.

Much of the evening is spent consoling me, reassuring me, until I've had enough.

"I've got it. I really do." I sit back in my chair, realizing I'm hungry. "Are we going to eat anything tonight?" I look to Ned for service.

CiCi is relieved. "Thank God—reason settles in. Whatcha got, Ned? And where's the wine?"

Ned too is relieved that I've surfaced. He's happy to start dinner. "I've got pork chops and au gratin potatoes to reheat, a green salad. And CiCi, I've got a double-chocolate cake for you!"

I couldn't eat after the first bite, though. "Sorry, you two. I just can't eat this." I look up at Ned. "Not that it isn't delicious."

He smiles at me and turns to CiCi. "I'm glad you're here." He reaches for my hand and squeezes it tight. "We both need you."

The rest of our visit is comfortable and easy. CiCi takes naps between our many walks around the farm. She coddles the goats and collects eggs from the hens. She strolls alone with LuLu bouncing at her side. In the evenings, she plays her fiddle. She puts ground under my feet by reminding me how much she loves me. This is true. This is right. This is family.

My eyes smart from the sting of tears as I watch her drive away. "We have to take some time this summer to visit her—maybe see her in concert on an overnight," I say.

Ned agrees. He loves her music as much as he loves her. We are both sad to see her go.

LuLu will mope for a week.

CHAPTER 19

Once we're settled and the major projects are retired from Ned's do-list, our arrival in Capitol can be officially celebrated with a formal town hall reception. The reception is just an excuse for a community party. No one waited for the party to meet us.

From the minute the first delivery of lumber arrived on the land, locals appeared with home-cooked foods and curiosity. They wanted to see for themselves what was going on at the old homestead. There wasn't an old man or a young one who didn't manage a trip out to the McInnis farm to meet Ned and to inspect his plans and workmanship. The advice was never ending and, for the most part, useful.

It was Milo Rykaanen who started poker night. He walked into the shack, inspected every inch, then proclaimed, "Poker."

Ned makes friends easily. It is his affable, unguarded personality that invites people in. I envy him his ease with strangers.

For me, friendships are tricky. I seldom trust anyone and don't like small talk. I have no babies to swoon about, and all my relatives except for Mercy and Terry are dead. I have nothing to bring to the table for discussion.

Besides, most of the women who live in the area are seventy years and on up. That's not to say older women can't make good friends, but I can't see how it might happen. I have nothing to offer. None of them know a thing about marketing trends, nor would they care. What else do I have to talk about? I can imagine my receiving a lot of wisdom, advice, and foodstuffs for Ned. I suppose that if I relaxed enough to consider the simple pleasures of their company, I could make friends easily, too. That's Ned's way, not mine.

Ned is in a social heaven. He quickly made friends of Milo and with Scotty, the Irish railroad worker who came to Capitol with his family in the '40s. Ned tells me that Scotty had his eye on Eleanora when they were kids, before she was murdered. He never married, never wanted to. Mercy claims the loss of Eleanora ruined him for anyone else.

"How could that be, if they were only children? There are plenty of women here who would have taken him for a husband." I am quizzical.

"No," said Mercy. "No, he was infatuated once and for all with Eleanora. He still lays flowers on her grave on holidays. Maybe he does that on other days too. I don't know. I've never looked."

The welcoming reception is set for the third October Sunday after church. We will gather in the township hall, built to establish a neutral, nonreligious site from which to conduct political business—even though nearly everybody is Methodist or Lutheran and gets on just fine. It is the largest gathering spot in the near area, discounting numerous pole barns that are often cleared for wedding dances.

Mike Patterson arrives with a case of beer. He's Ned's same age and new best friend. Mike is a reader, thinker, and planner. He knows construction and is a farmer at heart. He could have been Ned's twin.

In physical appearance, they are similar. Both men have kept a full head of hair. Their bodies are trim from hard physical work. And they both carry themselves with a casual confidence, making them extremely attractive to women of all ages. The one feature that most distinguishes the two is Mike's laugh, a Santa Claus "Ho, ho, ho." If he had a white beard and big belly, he could, hands down, pass for St. Nick.

Many of Mercy's friends are in attendance as well. There is Nellie Jane, of course, and Beulah, Shirley Janson, Cindy Parker, and Geraldine Small Dog. Her sister Winnie stayed home to care for a cousin who is recovering from pneumonia.

We fill two 12-foot-long tables with food and drink and bodies alive in conversation and laughter. Many of the old timers' sons and daughters are here with their children and their grandchildren. The town hall is packed to capacity.

The old men stand outside to smoke pipes and cigarettes, though mostly to keep away from the women, who are too fussy for their tastes. Ned joins them for a time. He comes back reeking of smoke and happy. He gives me a hug and swings me around. I can smell the beer alongside the cigarettes.

"Having a good time?" I ask as he sways with me in his arms.

He kisses me on the cheek, then heads outdoors again to rejoin the other men.

Our welcome is genuine. We are now part of an old community hungry for new and younger life.

I head to the kitchen to help Nellie Jane.

"Sit. I can do this," I tell her.

Nellie Jane sits. I can tell she's tired. It doesn't matter, I've learned, if one is a sturdy eighty-year-old—fatigue can still be quick to come and is not to be ignored. One of Mercy's dearest friends thought she could fight off the weariness, but fell, hit her head, and died after a long week. It was upsetting to everyone.

I worry about Jack, the handyman, and all the work he's doing for us. Ned insists that Jack take frequent breaks and drink lots of water. Jack does not mask his impatience—always with a shake of the head and grunt—but it looks to me like he enjoys the attention and concern.

Sometimes we spot him in town and wonder if he walked. Although Mike says he has Jack on a short leash, driving him anywhere he wants to go when he isn't with us at the farm.

Nellie Jane gets to her feet and insists she can handle the rest of the cleanup, so I go sit with the resting women at one of the tables. The room is much quieter since the men removed themselves to the Capitol store backroom for whiskey.

A streaked-blond, heavily-scented grandmotherly type with sun-leathered skin and layers of gold strands at her neck sits across from me at the table. Her three grandchildren, all preteen girls, pile in beside her. She extends her ring-encrusted fingers toward me, offering a handshake greeting.

"Hi, Ellen, I'm Beulah's daughter Sylvie."

Before I can reach out to shake her hand, two of the girls start a fight over whatever it is girls fight about.

"Hush now! If I have to separate you girls one more time, we're leaving!"

"Can we? Can we please?"

Sylvie ignores them and turns back to me. "Mom tells me you're a farmer."

I laugh, choking on my apple juice, sputtering juice on the table. "Not exactly. My grandparents once had farmland here, and we were able to buy it back from the hunter who owned it. We thought we'd try our hand at living rural for a few years before we settle permanently into a senior condo in the city."

But she's distracted by her girls. "Girls! I told you to stop!"

With her head turned and away and rising from her seat, she makes her goodbye. She turns back to look at me, shakes her head, and apologizes with a wide, insincere smile.

"I'm sorry. It was lovely to meet you." She extends her hand again. "Maybe I'll see you the next time we're up to see Mom."

And with that, she and her three girls are up and away out the door.

I sit at the end of a row of elderly women left at the table. They intrigue me with their talk of canning and quilting and church doings. I do not hear one word of disparagement of a neighbor or any gossip. These women represent the heart of community to me. They show me, simply by being, how complete we can be, we humans, if we let ourselves attend to what's at hand and care for that well. I feel inspired. I hope their children—excluding Sylvie, perhaps—will demonstrate to me the same communal bond that I witness with their mothers.

My thoughts are interrupted by Nellie Jane, who takes Sylvie's vacant spot across the table from me.

"Dear, we have finished cleaning up and are ready to go home. Would you like to join us at my house?"

"No—thank you for everything, but I think I'll collect Ned, and we'll head back home. I like your friends. I look forward to getting to know them better."

"Thank you, dear. I hope you had a good time."

I follow the line of old women out of the building, helping them carry empty dishes, utensils, and towels. Back in my car, I drive to the old town store, where I find Ned a little drunk in the backroom drinking parlor—although, it looks like some the old men are just getting warmed up.

When he sees me, his smile is broad, and his arms sweep me up in a gleeful embrace.

I accept his affection, then urge him toward the door. “Come on, honey. Let’s go.”

He nestles his flushed face into my neck and exudes hot fumes of whiskey.

“To Ned’s pretty wife!” someone hollers, and they all toast me.

I want a whiskey too but ignore the desire to join in. Instead, I try to shuffle Ned toward the door. The room is smoky, and there is a sickening smell of old man sweat and unwashed coveralls. This may be nirvana for men, I think, but my stomach tumbles and churns.

Ned kisses me on the cheek and mumbles, “In a minute, sweetie.”

I can’t take another minute of the stench. “I’ll meet you outside,” I tell him and rush the exit.

I cross the street and sit in one of the old wooden rockers on the storefront porch. I can look over to Mercy’s house and up toward Nellie Jane’s. It is quiet. The women are in their homes either napping or putting things away or preparing a meal for later. The stillness is beautiful. I imagine people in small towns across the world live like this. Since the beginning of cooked meat and stored food and fermented grains, they’ve lived together in community.

On the way home with a happy Ned in tow, I feel good. I feel deeply grounded inside, for once. Though not safe. I know that ground can shift and erupt out from under me at any moment, like the thief in the night who steals the family fortune from beneath his sleeping victims. Inherently suspicious, I enjoy the moment of good feeling while stifling the nudge from my ever-persistent fears.

CHAPTER 20

Summer was good for us, as was harvest season. But now we are left with a bitter winter. Winters in the north are frigid. Many weeks in a row can hold minus temperatures with winds that cut and freeze tender skin in minutes. Local natives say winter is dreamtime—time for storytelling and time for waiting. Nellie Jane would say winter is no time to start anything new.

We find ourselves in a rhythm at the farm. I spend more time than I want in my office in Twin Bays, but on the days I don't work, I help with farm tasks. The goats need milking, and the eggs need collecting, though there's far less laying in the winter.

We keep the goats and chickens inside most days. But on sunny, windless days, even if the temperatures are still bitter, we let the goats run a bit in the outdoor pen. We add our vegetable scraps to the chicken feed, and I toss a whole cabbage into the chicken coop once a week to keep them busy. Jack tells me chickens like toys as well as any domesticated dog or cat. They roll the cabbage and peck at it instead of each other.

Ned continues working on plans for expansion and builds shelves and storage bins for the animal shelters and the barn. He gives his Tuesdays to stained-glass projects. The weekly poker game in the shack is always well attended.

Jack comes for dinner almost every night. He seems to like working with Ned, who picks him up at the crack of dawn on the days he helps us at the farm. Often, after dinner, Jack slips away before Ned can get him in the truck to go home. No matter the weather, Jack at eighty, prefers to walk himself home. We make a game of who will be first to catch him before he gets out the door. Ned starts pulling the truck up to the back door when they come in for the evening meal.

This January morning, I watch the chickadees flit on and away, up to the branches of a small birch and an arrangement of feeders supplied with hulled sunflower seeds, peanuts, and corn. I've also set out a suet log packed with animal fat soaked in maple syrup and honey.

I see a female sapsucker that failed to migrate south. She feeds at the suet each day even when the temperature registers less than minus 20 degrees. I try to save her.

Nellie Jane shakes her head and mumbles, "Saving the ghost." She believes that living things out of their natural place and order are shadows, ghosts, echoes. The real or original life—that is, the pure life before the first injury, whether to body, soul, or mind—is gone. I always felt that who I was died at the first moment of violation by my father, that I live in the shadow of what my life could have been.

I should let the bird go, let her die her natural death. But I can't. The poor thing suffers cold and fights to stay alive longer because of me. I have forced her to outlive her pure life.

Then comes the day the sapsucker doesn't make it to the feeder. I watch for three days for her to return before accepting that the poor thing's suffering is over. It is the beginning of suffering for us. Spring nudges its way into winter, bringing unimaginable loss.

LuLu is killed on an icy township road when she is hit by a slip-sliding RV. Ned wraps her in an old blanket, where she lies frozen in the shed until we can bury her after the thaw. I know she's out there. I want her to get up and play, whine for her Milk Bones.

I suppose I should know to read the sign when LuLu is killed. But I don't think that way, Nellie Jane's way. "Watch carefully," she would tell me. "An animal will take the first death." So it follows that Nellie Jane is the second RV road sacrifice that week.

Ned and I are visiting with Mercy when the bell rings out, calling everyone to the town hall. The roads are so muddy that we take the car, passing many hurrying on foot to learn what trouble has come.

The sheriff and his wife are the first to greet us at the door. The sheriff—a short, stocky man with an unkempt beard and suspenders holding up his trousers and badge—is wiping his eyes with an orange bandana, probably a Christmas present from a grandchild. He waits until the room is filled with a murmuring crowd of locals before delivering the news about Nellie Jane.

"There's no easy way to tell you this, so I'll just say it." He wipes his eyes again and blows his nose. "Our friend and neighbor, Nellie Jane Makala, was struck by an RV about two hours ago. She might have been going to the store or a neighbor's house when old Syd—you know he just don't see that well anymore—hit her square on. Killed her right then."

He turns to his wife, helpless to continue. She approaches him, takes his arm, and between tears of her own, tells us that the local hospital has been called to collect Nellie Jane's body from where it now lies at the doctor's office.

Ned instinctively reaches out to Mercy, but she holds up her hands, gesturing him away. I watch her take this bullet as if she is wearing some magical armor.

And then I lose track of her and everyone else. Maybe I take the bullet for her, because I am the one who collapses to the floor. There are no tears, only shock and paralysis. My mind is empty. I sit on the cold, wet, muddy floor until Ned brings me to my feet. I feel his tears on my neck and pull him close. He cries, and I hold him until he is cried out.

Mercy is surrounded by her friends and neighbors. They all know what to do. There is another funeral to plan and a burial to complete. Ned and I leave her and head home to grieve with each other.

LuLu. Nellie Jane. What next?

The next morning, when the phone rings, I think it will be Aunt Mercy. But it is CiCi, calling to tell me she is sick again and will die soon. Ten years back, she had her first bout with breast cancer and survived with chemo and radiation treatments. But now her cancer has come back, found in her liver, and it's going to kill her.

Even though winter is dreamtime, and I don't want to start anything, the call from CiCi has me caught between the space of desire to move and emotional paralysis. I pull on my big boots and tromp through the heavy snow to visit the old grandfather Who Rock, on guard, just beyond the deer fence near the edge of the pine wood. I learned from Nellie Jane that some rocks have a spirit and I should ask, *Who are you?* if I feel a presence speaking. This rock, this Grandfather Rock, has a traveling spirit. He was collected from a South Dakota buffalo pasture, where I noticed him and listened as he nudged me to *Take me with you.*

I call on all my relatives, the spirits of all things unseen, lifting tobacco to them to honor them. I sprinkle all of it over the grandfather Who Rock as Nellie Jane taught me when I was little and felt alone and afraid. I speak out loud to all the relatives I can see gathering.

"I know it is winter. I'm not here to start anything," I begin.

I'm concerned I've called them at the wrong time, in dreamtime, but I need them. I need them to know about CiCi. At first, I apologize if I'm doing this wrong, and then I thank them for the life of Nellie Jane, who was so good to me and everyone. And I thank them for LuLu, who we loved with all our hearts. I imagine her following or leading Nellie Jane wherever they might be now. I hear a woof and laughter and the soft sound of Nellie Jane's rattle. I take a moment to feel what I hear, clutching more tobacco from the pouch in my hand, trying not to cry.

A pileated woodpecker calls. I look up to see it perched on the tallest branch of a green ash tree, a leafless skeleton—not where one might generally be seen. I have not heard a cry or a call from a pileated for months.

I know then that we are all in agreement, the relatives and me. The pileated shows me that yes, we are out of place, but we are together, that our eyes are open, and our souls are awake. Like a bear gives birth in the depths of a frozen den in the dark, and the tiny cubs feed from her, we are together in this moment in that way.

I give the tobacco with my heart and my prayers for CiCi. I acknowledge the relatives, then walk back into the house. The pileated flies past me straight to the grandfather rock, then veers off to the west. I am awed by this acknowledgement of all things worked up into a pattern and progression of agreement.

Nellie Jane's funeral is like every other funeral in Capitol—there are fewer old folks in attendance each time. But it is beautiful because it is for her.

I grieve for Mercy and her loss. She is inconsolable, deep in grief without Nellie Jane. I can't tell her about CiCi. Not now. There will be time for all of us to grieve CiCi.

After the funeral, I sit with Mercy in her living room. Nellie Jane is gone, but I feel her not far off. With Mercy beside me, we hear the spirit drums and singing. Though distant, it is a steady, pervasive sound. We know the sounds are not real in the way Mercy's rocking chair creaks and taps against the floorboards. Nonetheless, the sounds are real enough and keep a beat in us.

Mercy sways in rhythm with an inner prayer. I burn sage and sweet grass to honor Nellie Jane. I hope to scrub out the loss of her with the smoke. I wish to rid us both of all present and future grief.

I slide into shock, consumed by the iciness of a great void split open in my mind. I feel hewn as a giant oak felled. I am scattered throughout a vast abyss.

"This is grief," I tell myself. The words, their sounds, are more distant than the drumming.

My mentor, my guide, the one who should have been my mother has left me alone to face the passing of my great friend, my one and only anchor to this life.

This is not grief. This is abject terror.

Mercy tells me Nellie Jane left her belongings to me. There isn't much. She didn't like to accumulate things.

I can't shed light on why Nellie Jane made this decision. "What about her family?" I ask. "Doesn't she have relatives? What about the tribe? Couldn't they make use of her things?"

Mercy shakes her head. "I don't know who is left, if anyone."

With that, she stands and leaves me to go to bed, to put her grief to sleep for a while.

I go to Nellie Jane's house, no longer a home. It is silence and cold. I sit motionless for a long time in Nellie Jane's rocking chair—

absorbing her, feeling her, immersing myself in everything I can remember about her.

A chill sears up my spine, forcing me from my chair to search for a blanket. On my way to the hallway closet, I raise the thermostat to seventy from the fifty-two-degree standard set by Nellie Jane.

I open the closet door to find not one but piles of Nellie Jane's quilts. Each quilt is individualized with a name stitched along the border in black embroidery floss. I know these are death robes. Nellie Jane knew to open up her hoop for another soul and honored each one with a hand-sewn quilt built from scraps harvested by the churchwomen and salvaged from other sewing through the year.

"Travelers," she called them, the ones who she knew were dying. "Travelers and ghosts."

Mabel's daughter's quilt lies on top of the heap. It is a small quilt, infant sized. Mabel is due to deliver in less than a month. I prepare myself for one more loss.

The quilts feel alive to me, as if the souls of the intended are preparing themselves for passing. I feel connected to them. And now I am responsible for them.

The house is finally warm enough so that I can stay here for the night. Sleep brings bad dreams. I wake and pace on the chilly floor. The responsibility for Nellie Jane's house and her things has me in a grip of indecision and anxiety.

As I did at the cabin, I do now—only for real this time. I make a spirit plate from odds and ends left behind in the house. I set the plate outside.

"It is done. Wašté," I speak to the night air and to the unseen worlds. "Thank you. Thank you."

I turn back into the house for sleep, hoping for no dreams. In the morning, with a bright sun warming my face, I hear the faintest sound of singers and drummers singing away the last bit of a calming dream.

CHAPTER 21

The next day, back at the farm, I'm itching and scratching at the hives I've developed from worry. There's low-level noise in the henhouse from mumbling to myself, out loud, like a possessed woman off her meds. I try and fail to navigate the cascading thoughts of what to do and what I don't know and how much I need a drink. The chickens are eager for the feed I toss to them. They peck and coo, disinterested in my present state of bother.

"Excuse me, ma'am."

I jump in my work boots, startled and embarrassed.

First at my back and now in front of me stands a middle-aged woman, perfectly fit, crowned with gorgeous auburn hair. For just one minute, I stop breathing.

"My name is Lydia Campbell."

"Campbell. Scottish. That explains the red hair." Then I realize I'm thinking out loud and stop talking.

"I'm looking for the town of Capitol. I thought I had the right directions, but I've been driving for an hour, and I honestly don't know where I am."

She looks around, as if that will help her locate the small town, too small to have seen as she passed through it.

"I saw your sign for fresh eggs and turned in here. Maybe you can point me toward Capitol? I'm looking more specifically for the home of Mrs. Miles, Mercy Miles."

I stare at the woman, my mouth agape, chickens clucking and cawing around our ankles. I watch her step back from a Rhode Island Red who is interested in a shoelace exposing itself from the side of an ankle-high walking boot.

Who the hell is she?

"Come with me." I speak with head down.

The chicken follows until I shoo it back from the coop door. I listen for the click of the latch, assured they are secure and safe from predators.

I walk the woman back to the house, where Ned is working on dinner. Thank God he isn't off with Jack somewhere. He distracts her with his charming ways while I phone Mercy to ask what I should do.

"Who?" Mercy asks me to repeat myself.

"Lydia Campbell." I say the name slowly and softly as if speaking to a child just learning the language.

"Oh, well…" Mercy's voice trails off, thoughtful, then decisive. "Put her on the phone, Ellen. Please."

I beckon to Ned, who is watching me from the farthest edge of his line of vision. He leads the woman back to the phone.

"Mercy would like to speak with you." My words are polite, but they could scorch a horse hide.

She takes the phone from my extended hand. Ned and I both listen intently, but nothing is said on our side that provides information we can use to satisfy our curiosity.

Why would someone be traveling from who-knows-where into the middle of god-forsaken nowhere to talk to Mercy? Could something have happened to Missy? No. That makes no sense. Nobody would come all the way out here when a phone call would do.

Lydia Campbell replaces the handset in its cradle on the wall, thanks us graciously, and in a puff of fairy dust—I swear—she is gone.

"What the hell?" I look at Ned with alarm and impatience.

"What?" He looks amused.

"There's something about that woman that sets my teeth on edge."

Ned smiles. "She seemed harmless to me."

I ignore him. "There must be something we need at the Co-op. Let's go, then we can stop in at Mercy's just to be sure everything is okay."

"You don't think that's a little obvious?" Ned grins.

"Don't care, Ned. Don't care. That woman gives me the willies, and I want to know why. Let's go."

I'm impatient to get moving and annoyed with Ned to boot. Maybe I am too nosy. So what?

We stop at the Co-op. As I head inside, Ned heads over to Jack, who is outfitted in an old parka and settled in one of the aging wooden porch chairs. He's enjoying the late January afternoon sun—despite the brutal cold. When I come out, I find them sitting side by side in silence, like contented cats.

"Jack." I smile at him on my way down the steps. "Do you want to keep him, or should I take him with me?" I ask, referring to Ned.

Jack looks puzzled for a moment, then replies, "You take him."

"All right then. Come with me, Ned. We're heading over to Mercy's. See you later, Jack."

I stash my unnecessary purchases, except for a can of coffee intended for Mercy, in the car. Across the road, I can see the Campbell woman's car parked in the driveway.

"Are you going to just barge in?" Ned asks as I power my way up to the door.

Impatient, I knock. Muffled voices sound from the kitchen. After barely a second, I announce us, then walk boldly in, kicking off my boots in the entryway. Ned catches the outside door before it can smack him in the face.

Mercy and Lydia sit across from each other at the kitchen table. Coffee mugs and a raisin pie sit between them. Raisin pie is my favorite. The sight of it nearly disarms me and but not to the point of forgetting my mission to learn what this stranger wants with my aunt.

"Hello, dear." Mercy rises from her chair to greet us. "Ned, it's good to see you."

She gives him a peck on the cheek. He towers over her. He has a long way to lean down to receive her greeting.

"Can I get you some coffee and pie?" Mercy asks.

She fills cups of coffee and reaches for two more plates and forks, putting everything on the table while I stand like a statue staring at the stranger who stares back, mute.

"Sit down. Sit down." Mercy gestures. "I would like you to meet Lydia Campbell."

"We've met, Aunt Mercy. She stopped at the farm. I called you, remember?" My tone is rude and abrupt. I set the can of coffee on the table.

"Yes, of course." Mercy picks up the coffee can and places it on the counter behind her. "Thank you, Ellen." Her voice is lilting and happy.

She serves the pie. The pie is on my fork and in my mouth in a flash, faster than I can sit myself down properly in the kitchen chair. I haven't bothered to remove my coat.

"Lydia is the daughter of someone I went to school with here in Capitol. That was back in the thirties."

I can feel myself begin to relax, melting with the butter-rich pastry flakes in my mouth. "Oh," I say. "What was your mother's name?" I ask, tensing up again but trying to be polite—and failing. I can hear my tone is razor sharp.

"It wasn't my mother," Lydia explains in a condescending, teacher-correcting-student manner. "It was my father, Carl Farnsday."

"Oh," I repeat. "Sorry." Not really.

"No, that's fine. My father often speaks of this place, how wild it was when he was a boy and what good people lived here back then. He made it sound so—oh, I don't know—pure, pristine, that I wanted to see the place for myself. I'm thinking of buying a bit of property for family vacations—make it a surprise for dad."

As the woman speaks, Mercy is glowing and gooey, which makes me even more nervous and defensive.

"I told her about Nellie Jane's house, dear," Mercy says.

I almost choke on the last bite of pie.

Ned is happy I have a fork in my mouth, as it keeps me from blurting some atrocious nonsense. He knows me so well.

While my mouth is full, he gently pushes for more information from the Campbell woman. "Tell us a little bit about your family and what you're looking for in a property."

Ned is not at all put off by this interloper. *Interloper? What's wrong with me?* I push my pie plate away.

The woman unfurls her life story. She has a sister and a brother. She's been married to Bryce Campbell for twenty-six years. They have one daughter, Elizabeth, twenty-one, married to Allan Carter. The whole family would like to acquire a vacation home. They live south of Minneapolis now, but see Capitol as a destination for future retirement.

"Nellie Jane's house isn't on a lake. It's right here in town. And it's small, tiny. There's only one bedroom. Your family would never fit in there." I sound like a petulant child, brat, bratty.

"We don't need lakeshore, just lake access or public access for fishing. And Mercy tells me there's room to build on. The lot is two acres, did you say?"

Mercy nods assent.

"What we really want is the community feel," the woman continues. "Most of us enjoy camping, and with the state forest nearby, the location is perfect, especially for Dad. He's about to turn eighty, and we'd like to bring him back home for a while."

Mercy has been quiet throughout the conversation, although she looks like she could squeeze Campbell like a new puppy. She stands up, clears the table, and turns to the sink.

With her back to me, she speaks with authority, "You should consider this, dear. Nellie Jane would have liked this very much."

I'm not convinced. Not even interested. But I say, "I'd like to think about it. I'll be in touch."

Lydia Campbell leaves.

I feel washed through by soul stifling fatigue. Can I let Nellie Jane go this soon? I know it's too soon to make decisions about her house. What about her tribal family? I remember the prayer from the night before.

"Honey," I finally ask Ned, "would you mind if I stay at Nellie Jane's again tonight? I have to think this over. And then we should talk."

"Sure, as long as you take me home first. While we're at it, let's check on Jack, see if he's still around and needs a lift home."

"Deal."

We both hug Mercy goodbye. “Before I go to Nellie Jane’s, I’ll be back for supper so we can talk about this too, if that’s okay?”

“Yes. That will be fine.” She agrees a bit too eagerly.

On our way to the car, we see Jack still sitting on the porch at the store. We offer a ride.

“No,” he says in his gruff yet gentle—even contemplative—voice.

So we leave, confident someone will collect him and get him home.

At home, I run in just long enough to pack an overnight bag. Then I slide into the driver’s seat of the still-warm car. I feel like lead. The weight of heartache is measurable.

During the ten-minute drive back to Mercy’s, I try to settle my mind and emotions. I keep replaying Mercy’s words: “Nellie Jane would have liked this very much.” Why the hell would she care?
Jesus, help me.

“Goddamn it!”

The car, lacking a cognizant pilot, is aiming for a porcupine lumbering to its feet after a good tumble from an overhanging branch. With a lurch to press my full force of body onto the brake pedal, I miss the creature and give my neck a good wrench.

I remain stopped on the empty roadway until I’m ready to focus on making it to Mercy’s house in one piece. The porcupine ambles off, as is its right, while I recover my senses.

CHAPTER 22

Mercy is not a cautious person, which often gives me cause to worry. I'm concerned and confused about her readiness to concede Nellie Jane's legacy to a total stranger, based solely on Lydia's story, which may or may not be true.

But why would it not be true? And wouldn't having an old schoolmate back in town be good for the old timers?

But Lydia Campbell is simply too good-looking, too Scottish, too something I can't put my finger on directly but can feel squiggling beneath the weight of my worry.

"What is my issue with this woman?" I wonder aloud.

I know it's not just Lydia, it's her timing. How did she manage to show up so soon after Nellie Jane's death? Maybe her father has some other old school friend who told him about Nellie Jane's passing. But then, why wouldn't he come with Lydia? And why not attend the funeral?

This is the work of Iktomi—the eight-legged trickster. Nellie Jane dies, and this Lydia Campbell shows up. And with how many others in tow? Who will I find on the other legs? My brain hurts from too much speculation. I am sure of one thing only—I don't like Lydia and never will.

When I arrive at Mercy's, I see Jack walking out the back door. I call and wave. He does not respond nor look my way. He continues walking on his way home, I imagine, four miles, past our farm, at twilight.

"Jack! Do you want a ride?" I call out again.

He does not break his step to reply. I think about going after him but remember he's been handling his own life without my help for a long time. *He's eighty, for God's sake, Ellen!*

But I know I can't let him go alone. I stay in the car and drive to meet him on the road. He's smiling from ear to ear on his frosty four-mile stroll.

"Get in, Jack. Where are you headed?"

He looks surprised to see me. "Home."

"Then get in. I'll take you. It's too cold and too late for you to be taking such a long walk."

Jack says nothing.

"How'd you get into town anyway?"

"I come with Mike sometimes." Jack speaks in his standard monotone.

I nod. "I saw you leaving Mercy's house. Did you have dinner with her?"

"Too early."

Jack is wordless for the rest of the ride. I drop him off, turn around, and head back to Capitol. My attention is undivided. It's almost sunset. Deer leaping from the woods onto the roadway is common at this time of day. I've had one near miss already and don't feel lucky enough to play the roadkill lottery again.

Back at Mercy's, I park the car and enter the house, removing my boots and hanging up my parka. This is the northern winter litany, practiced like a religion—boots and coats and hats and mittens, all on and off, off and on, all a winter's day long.

"Mercy?" I call out to her from the hallway.

She doesn't respond. She's not in the kitchen.

"Aunt Mercy?" I call out a second time, then make my way through the small house, toward her bedroom.

"I'll be right out, dear."

I sigh, realizing I've been holding my breath. Did I think something had happened to her in the space of time to travel eight miles?

Back in the kitchen, I open the refrigerator door to find beef barley soup and some excellent aged sharp cheddar cheese.

Grilled cheese, I think. *Fats and carbs. That will settle me down.*

With kettle in hand for reheating the soup and a frying pan heating for the sandwiches, I slice the cheese, butter the bread, and start the butter to sizzle in the ages-old cast iron skillet used for nearly every meal. In moments, the soup is simmering, filling the room with fragrance punctuated by mouth-watering smells of melting cheese and burnt butter rising from the skillet. I pour myself a glass of iced mint tea—the mint from Nellie Jane's was harvested and dried last fall—and sit down at the table to wait for Mercy and hot food.

She appears in the doorway to the kitchen. She has dark circles under her eyes, as though she's not been sleeping well.

"You look tired, Aunt Mercy. Are you all right?"

"I am tired." She nods and smiles. "It's been a busy day."

I accept her explanation, though I'm worried. I stand, stir the soup, flip the sandwiches, fill her glass with tea, then sit down next to her to study her face. She and Jack hold a strong resemblance, as do most old folks. From the stark white wavy hair to the way they sit in a chair—straight with a look of readiness for the next task. Generational training, maybe. To younger people, the aged take on a look that unifies them as a group of their own, distinctly different from the young and even the middle-aged.

I will look much the same when I'm eighty.

So many in this community—well into their eighties, even nineties—will soon pass on. It frightens me a little.

Why am I here in Capitol? Will I leave when they all die?

I serve up the meal, then immediately start quizzing Mercy about Lydia Campbell. The soup is too hot to eat anyway.

"So, Mercy, what were you thinking when you brought up Nellie Jane's house to that Campbell woman, a stranger?"

Mercy takes her time answering my question. "Nellie Jane's house is empty, and a new family is willing to fill its spaces." She pauses. "It's not often that we get new people here."

"Well, that's not entirely accurate, Mercy," I object. "Things are changing in rural areas. Did you know that Capitol and Maysburg, which is an even smaller township than Capitol, are now considered to be first-tier bedroom communities for Twin Bays? That's why the new development is going up on Border Road. That's why Mattson's Grocery opened up a new store in Cray's Bay. That's why there was a 4K Fun Race last summer. Don't you remember how Lumber Main 12 was blocked off that Saturday when we tried to get over to Beulah's?"

Mercy doesn't react to my community growth and development report. Clearly, her mind is fixed on something else.

"I remember Carl Farnsday. I would like to have him and his young family here with us. I would like to see children playing in Nellie Jane's yard and have activity there at holidays. You and Ned have done so much to bring life back to the old farm. This old town could use more of the excitement new people can bring. Good people."

Why is she so quick to label Lydia and her bunch "good people?" How can she know that someone she hasn't seen in seventy years is "good people?" I know that Lydia makes me feel creepy, as though she were a monster clawing from behind my bedroom closet door.

Mercy takes my hand. "I'm not saying it's time to let Nellie Jane go. We have suffered a great deal of loss in the last months, and I think we should remember that when making decisions. Emotions are at high tide, and currents are running strong. Until they recede, we can let go of nothing."

Mercy is right. There's been too much loss. And there is more to come. CiCi will soon be gone too. I wonder how long it will take for the tide of loss to recede. I still haven't told Mercy about CiCi. As far as I'm concerned, she can be surprised. Why spend any more time on grief than is necessary?

The conversation takes on a lighter tone as we talk about reworking Mercy's flower gardens. I feel a wave of deep sadness, imagining a summer without Nellie Jane in her garden. The bears will get all the berries this summer. Maybe the fence should come down.

Mercy says she will not have a vegetable garden this year since Ned and I produce plenty for all of us. There will be enough and more to feed some of the isolated old folks and families tucked away deep in the forests outside of Capitol.

This is Ned's dream for the place, to find people to feed. Last season, he made a weekly trip to Cherry Lake, a small town forty miles northwest of Capitol. He delivered bushels and boxes of vegetables to a small group of Episcopal churchwomen there. They canned and dried whatever he gave them, then distributed the goods to rural folks as far as seventy miles away in all directions. Many of the churchwomen were in their seventies and eighties, yet they went after this daunting task like worker bees keeping the hive alive.

This mission work has been in place for as long as the women's grandparents have populated the region. The men are woodcutters and trappers, for the most part. Some found wives among the natives, who taught them tanning and drying techniques. Ned told me that the women managed to recruit some boys and girls from county schools to learn the skill of food preservation that will keep northern families fed long after the elder women have passed on.

He's so proud of his contribution. I'm proud of him, and I tell him so often. Sometimes I brush off his cowboy hat and demonstrate how proud I am. Not that he needs encouraging.

Mercy and I finish our meal and clean up the kitchen. She yawns. I know it's time to leave. I hug her goodnight and savor the moment.

"Sleep well. I'll bring rolls in the morning." In the hallway, I put on my coat and boots and leave.

I walk in the dark through snow troughs to Nellie Jane's house. There's no moon tonight. The flashlight helps me navigate the rutted road. There are only a few houses to intersect with the paths created by nature's own creatures, be it by a swoop or a slither or a rustle or a stomp.

The nightlife is wild, out and about with me, going this way or that. I can easily become a meal for an individual of tooth and claw that I will never see or hear before feeling the weight of a pounce or the cut from a chomp on my arm. I'm anxious to cover the short distance to Nellie Jane's.

At the door, I stop to soak in the history of the house and balk at the changes I imagine the future might bring. I have not lived in this community for long. Will I be able to allow other lives in this space—living, laughing, playing, sleeping, being a family?

Being a family. That might be what I have against the Campbell woman. She is part of a family, a hostile condition that can promote arrogance and entitlement that comes from belonging.

I should stop thinking of her as hostile. I know nothing about her. And being a family. What do I know of family? Billy and Virginia were parents by their ability to procreate.

Virginia did nothing to stop Billy from hurting me. She had family that could have sheltered us, loved us, but she never told them what life was like in the McInnis household. I hardly knew her parents, my grandparents. They lived in New Jersey and never once visited their daughter in Minnesota. On special holidays, they would call, and I would be put on the phone to pretend a polite exchange.

Uncle Terry is a fleeting figure in my life. I don't know him. I know he's depressed. He has good reason to be depressed. If I were wheelchair-bound for sixty or more years, living estranged from my unforgiving family, I'd be depressed too.

I need to get off this porch, out of the cold. I enter the house to stand in the dark, shivering, thinking dark thoughts about my mother. Virginia lived in a fantasy world of icy elitism and perpetual disdain that covered her own wounds well. Billy tortured and terrified me. Family should mean safety, but to me, family equals a horror movie, a slasher flick. I can't understand a family that would want to live together, vacation together, and retire together.

I flip the switch that lights up the kitchen and sit at the table. My boots keep my feet warm on the cold, cold floor. Chunks of snow mixed with dirt release from the boot treads onto the floor to melt. Nellie Jane would have reprimanded me over my carelessness. But then, if she were here, I wouldn't have been so lax in care of her space. Now my space. Is this an act of defiance at her absence? *There! See what a mess we are without you?*

The inside air is cold and stale. I crack open a window but promptly shut it again. Too cold. I track my dirt into the living room, settle into her rocker, and cry. I sob. I nearly choke but silently. I do not want my wailing to be heard by anyone. I feel completely alone and want it that way.

My bellyaching cry is interrupted when I realize how freezing cold it is in the house. I turn the thermostat up to eighty. If I'm ever going to sleep here tonight, I'll have to blast heat into the floors and walls. The house even smells cold.

I think about how a person's life can take a space and make it warm. I imagine Nellie Jane at work in her kitchen. I loved her kitchen, when she was here. It was the warmest place on earth for any soul. Always an empty chair appeared when needed. And always something wonderful came from the woodstove cooktop. I can smell Nellie Jane's fresh-baked apple crisp cooling on the wood slab countertop. I can taste hot coffee. Feel a mug in my hands and its steam on my face, in my nose. I feel heaven move in me.

I remember sitting in her kitchen after Billy died, listening to Mercy and Nellie Jane talk about him in the hospital. I was surprised to hear that she'd been to see Billy. Virginia seemed to think she didn't know he was sick or dead. She lied to me again, I suppose. Any opportunity.

This was one of a few times they had much to say—in front of me, at least—about my father. Mercy was by Billy's hospital bed in his last hours. It sounded as though she was kind to him that day. She told him to let it all go.

"Let it go, William. Let it go," she told him.

He snarled as best he could manage and told her to get out.

"I didn't expect anything from him, Nellie Jane," she said that day at Nellie Jane's table. "I didn't go for myself. I was there for him."

"Mercy, take your own advice." Nellie Jane's tone was sharp. "Let it go."

I didn't go to the hospital. I hated that man as much as a daughter can hate a father. No matter what they do, the idea of father to a child trumps the truth of the man. No, I did not go to see him try to beat back death. I was afraid he might succeed.

I remember trying to unhear their conversation. Lost in vague, groundless thoughts, I watched through the kitchen window as a few leaves skipped and twirled on top of the ice-crusted snow drifts, four feet deep in some places. The winds of March would come and tear through the few remaining red oaks, releasing the last of their leaves. This would be the first herald of spring.

I could see at a distance the edge of the frosted marsh. In the spring, beaming rich in color, stands of red willow would beckon to Nellie Jane. It would be time for her to harvest, peel, core, then shred the sacred heart of the *cansasa* for pipe smoking. Prayers of the People, Nellie Jane taught me, are not like white people's prayers. She meant no disrespect to white people or to me at all.

"Prayers of the People—they come from the heart of the mother, from the things that grow from her. The heart of the *cansasa*, fresh in the earliest spring with new life, is shred into the smallest bits. Burning in our pipes, we pull the spirit from its embers into our mouths and gently puff the smoke out to our relatives of every kind. That is how our prayers heal. We do not pray for cars and the right man and satisfaction, not even for peace, as people like to say when they see our pipes. No, we pray—oh, let's say, for the swirl, like the Milky

Way. In the midst of nothing is everything alive. And that is the prayer, the honoring, that we make."

But there would be no harvest this year. Not by Nellie Jane.

It's hard to believe that nearly a year has passed since Billy and Virginia died. So much has happened—good and bad alike. Now that Campbell woman is here and might want this house and bit of land.

Maybe I will let her have it.

I will wait the four days to give the ancestors time to answer. Nellie Jane will have to dissuade me from her grave if she has a different idea about what should become of her property. I will take her advice to Mercy to let go, and I'll let go. Lydia is present. Mercy is happy. That will be good enough. Besides, I don't need to have anything to do with Lydia. She can be somebody else's problem.

Feeling settled about the matter of this house, I turn the heat down to fifty-five and walk out the door to go home, home to my husband. Maybe I'll polish up those cowboy boots tonight.

CHAPTER 23

At the front of the house, I see another vehicle parked in my spot. I do not recognize the SUV. My frisky mood vanishes. It has to be close to midnight.

Who would be here this late?

I park directly behind the SUV, step out of my car, and walk with intense deliberation. Very few lights are on inside. I feel panicky. I realize I'm shaking as I try to open the door.

In the kitchen, I find empty beer bottles on the counter. Five beer bottles. Empty. A woman's purse sits on the kitchen table. I'm in full-blown panic now. I can't imagine Ned ever cheating, but what else could this mean?

Walking out of the kitchen, I peer into the darkened living room, then head down the hallway that leads to the bathroom and bedrooms. There is a light illuminating the doorsill of the guest room. I am holding my breath. I don't think I've breathed since I first saw the stranger's car in the driveway. I let free the air in my lungs—enough to have blown that bedroom door down—and lightly knock.

"Wait a minute, Ned." A woman's voice, soft, undisturbed is speaking my husband's name, as if she thinks it's him knocking at her door. As if she's been expecting him to knock at her door.

With every bit of drama alive in me now, I barge into the room. There is a war whoop screaming in my head—and then I see her.

"Jesus Christ, Missy! What in the hell?"

"Shhhh!" She giggles and gestures me into the room. "Don't wake up Ned!"

"Screw Ned. Why are you here? Why didn't he call me?"

"I stopped here to say hi before heading over to Mom's. Then Ned and I got to talking, and it got too late. He told me you were staying at Nellie Jane's house. I decided to stay here. I didn't want to wake Mom, and I didn't want to disturb you."

Missy has lived in France long enough to have obtained a slight accent. I almost laugh at her as if we were kids again, playing a game of make-believe.

"What brings you home?"

"You."

"Why?"

"Mom called and said you're having a rough time. She's worried. She asked me to come home and 'be cousins' with you."

"That's ridiculous!" I snap. "Not that I'm unhappy you're here, but we're not little girls anymore. I don't understand. She probably needs you for herself. Losing her best friend at her age is a very big deal."

"I thought so too," she said. "It's not like you to need me and I can't Skype. I could have called you or texted, but she was clear that I should not tell you I was coming home." She paused. "Something's going on. I thought maybe she was sick and needed me to be with her, only she didn't want to say so over the phone. She sounded so, so urgent or intense. Something is not right. So I dropped everything to jump on a plane to get here."

Missy's face clouds. "Ned told me about your parents dying. I'm so sorry. I should have called. Mom told me you had moved here. I have to admit, I don't get it. Ned said something about this being an old family farm, but I wasn't following. Jet lag, I suppose."

Missy hugs me hard. I can tell that Ned spared her the whole ugly story.

"Let's get some sleep, and in the morning, we can roust Mom, have breakfast, and find out what's going on with her. Then you and I can have a long, overdue talk."

I get into bed without waking Ned, forgetting all about country lovemaking. My sleep is fitful. My mind, whirling.

Why would Missy travel all the way from France for me? Maybe Mercy does need her. Maybe Mercy is worried that I will—what? Collapse under the emotional stress of selling Nellie Jane's house? The churning dread in my gut has become a chronic condition. Could she be sick? Oh, God, not that on top of CiCi. It is really too much.

The next morning, Ned is the first up, and that isn't until 8:30. He throws himself out of bed when he realizes how late it was. He expects the chickens and goats to be complaining loudly about missing breakfast. But when he makes it out to the sheds, he finds that Jack has already been there. The animals are fed, watered, and content.

"I swear, that man is as much of a snoop as you are," he says to me once I'm up. "I bet he saw Missy's car in the driveway and sprinted over here!"

"Should we invite him along? I'm sure he would enjoy seeing Missy again."

"Let's not do that today. Mercy doesn't even know she's here yet. Let's wait, okay?"

By eleven-thirty, we call Mercy to let her know we're on our way. The two cars make a short parade into town. Missy parks at Mercy's and goes on in while we walk over to the co-op. I want some of Delia

Morrison's sticky buns—a Saturday morning tradition. Of course, they're gone. Eleven-thirty is too late in the day to try for the best-baked goods in the county.

On the way in and out, we walk by Jack sitting on the porch and nod to him. He's silent but returns the nod. Ned thanks him for helping out this morning. And off we walk to see Mercy love up her darling Missy, my cousin, from across the pond.

It's too late for breakfast, so I pull some crackers and cheeses out from storage and also a chicken to roast for later. There is still some coffee I pour into a carafe, then I make a fresh pot.

The visit starts out warm and friendly. Mercy glows with delight to have her daughter within reach. It's good to hear of Missy's adventures and of her husband's success. She loves France. They would like to retire in Spain. We say she should come home more often—she says maybe she will.

After a couple of hours of this, I stand up to start making an early dinner. I listen to the others while peeling potatoes and carrots. I thaw the chicken in the microwave—a wonderful invention—then season it and load it into the oven to roast. A freshly made and untouched cherry cake sits on the counter.

A simple meal for simple people, I think. Suddenly, I flash on Lydia and imagine her here with us. A quiet *fuck you* flashes in my head.

Once the chicken is in the oven, I return to the table. As soon as I do, Mercy reaches a hand out to me over the top of the table, cupping my fingers in her soft, papery skin.

"I have something to tell you. I probably should have told you this a long time ago."

My hand arcs away from her touch in an involuntary retreat. It takes so little to frighten me, and this doesn't sound like a small thing. Missy is here. Nothing good will come from this. I can feel the punch coming. I feel sick, panicky. My lower lip quivers with that now too familiar cold from shock.

As Mercy speaks to me directly, with a flushed face and teary eyes, I realize why Missy has been called home. I can see Mercy's lips move, and I can hear her words, but they fall off her face like bits of food to be sponged up and rinsed down the drain. I comprehend but stop actively listening after the first strike.

"I couldn't tell you until William was dead and we were certain that Terry couldn't hurt anyone ever again. I too saw him at the funeral, you know. I couldn't tell you until I knew it was absolutely safe for Eleanora. I couldn't tell anyone. It wasn't just you." She looks at me, shamed. "You see, Terry didn't know about Eleanora. So when he saw her at the funeral—well, we had to wait to see what he might do. We couldn't tell him. We couldn't. We were so afraid."

"Eleanora?" I repeat. "What do you mean, Eleanora? Who?"

I know what she is about to say, but it is incomprehensible.

"Nellie Jane, dear. We gave her a new name." Mercy is done in. She's exposed. She looks so small and tired.

"I've carried this for so long." She begins to cry softly. "All these years, as I've protected my baby sister, I've known that Jesus might not be forgiving of my sins. I have lived this lie and carried such fear." She looks at me, defeated. "I know I've hurt you, dear. I didn't know what to do. The Mikkelsons were quite clear that we needed to keep all the children safe from William and from Terry. Then once Millie and Jake were gone, it was my duty to protect the children. I was the only one who could."

I want to run, but I'm paralyzed. I am a fireball consuming itself.

They've all been lying, all this time. I trusted them. I trusted them with me. I trusted Mercy. I trusted Nellie Jane.

I don't remember my first hurt, wound, heartbreak, betrayal. It's all the same after a while. Each is a storyteller's dream—dramatic, juicy, mean through and through. And here's another one. I'm such a fool. Such a dupe.

I thought I meant something to these people. They allowed me to have expectations. I felt a part of them. Smoke and mirrors. All smoke and mirrors, staged to protect the innocent from the monster who was my father. I am merely collateral damage in their war.

After all I told her about what he did to me! How could she continue this farce, knowing how he broke me?

Was it worth it, bitch? Was your fear worth the price I paid?

Ned has his arm around me, holding my body. He doesn't know I've been decimated by landmines set for me with intention.

Missy's mouth is agape. She stares at her mother. She too has been left outside the circle of truth. But it doesn't hurt her, the truth. It just causes her pain to see her mother in pain. She cries and kisses her mother, wraps her arms around Mercy's shoulders and gently caresses her cheek. This is the testament to the power of love. Missy can feel for her mother because she was raised in love.

I can feel nothing but rage because I was raised in rage.

Then all the alarms sound in me. It's like there's a damned air raid siren going off in my ears.

"Who the fuck is Lydia?" Her name spits from me like fire and venom. I'm on the attack because I'm facing my enemy.

Ned's arms tighten around me. He knows this is not the time to ask me to censor my words.

Mercy nods, tears streaming, flowing over Missy's arms. "Carl's daughter."

She cries harder, coughing up phlegm building from emotion.

"The boys I told you were lost that night at the farm? They were not lost. We've kept them hidden too. With Eleanora's passing, Carl is ready to be home."

The noise of her words plays like a trumpet in a high school band. Out of tune. Lacking melody.

"And the other boy?"

"Jack."

I hear the scream coming from my mouth. I hear the obscenities from way across the room, in a corner where I crouch low, as far away from the explosion of Ellen McInnis as I can get.

The sickness in me is now an entity, a demon. I am possessed. I have no will nor mind nor thought of my own. I want to kill her. I want to take her sharpest knife and slice her soft face into shreds of parchment, then write the word *bitch* on each scrap in her blood. My rage descends as a trickle to swell as a tsunami displacing every cell and particle that makes me, pushing forward the black void that is my father's legacy.

Ned holds my head in one arm and my body in the other. We remain as statues like this for a long time, me screaming. My screams blow Mercy out of the kitchen to hide in her bedroom.

"She was mine too!" I screech, doubling over, gasping from hysteria. "*She was mine!*"

Somehow I break free from Ned, pick up a chair, and send it sailing across the room, breaking through the picture window, letting the outside in. Fitting. I feel the fresh, cold air of the real world brush my face, chill my temper.

Ned grabs my arms, pinning them to my sides.

CHAPTER 24

Ned leaves food for me. I don't eat. I don't drink. And then he threatens me.

"You have a choice. Eat and drink or go to the hospital. I don't care which. It's up to you."

I eat a little, drink a little, and start to move a little, but I cannot speak. I cannot speak. It will be weeks before I can speak. *Weeks*. My tongue is paralyzed in the desert of my mouth. Any words that form in the devil's den that has become my mind are too vile, too violent, too lonely for a common human to survive the hearing.

I sit in a wooden-backed chair in our bedroom. I sit in the dark, alone, while images of my grandmother's children and their love for one another, their care for each other's safety throughout decades, flood past memories of Billy destroying every strand of my being with each heave of his body inside mine.

I believed, all this time, that it was my fault for not telling. That's why no one helped me. Every one of them could have helped me. They could have pulled me in under their protective cloak and kept me safe. But they did not. By choice, they did not interfere or try to rescue me.

I longed for Nellie Jane to be a mother to me, and she could have been just that. But she lied. Every single moment of every day for almost sixty years, she lied to me. She hid herself from me. We've all been in hiding from each other for too long.

I should be hearing the trumpet of glory, the gates of heaven opening to the let the children loose upon the earth, free from fear. But I am too angry. I am so alone. The realization of how little I matter is great in me. I cannot come out from under its weight. I am nothing to them, any of them.

Lydia, Mercy—they matter to each other in a way I will never matter. Their fathers are not Billy McInnis. They are not the devil's child. No one can see the individual me, the victim me, the family member, the lost child. They can't see past the filth and violence of my father.

I imagine the McInnis children in the aftermath of the bloodbath that was their family. I see them huddled under the nurturing, comforting cloak of Millie Mikkelson, hiding them away until she and Jake could get them settled, well out of harm's way. The Mikkelsons could have stepped in and helped me too. Anybody could have helped me. But no one could see the child in the darkness behind the monster that was my father.

How could they not care what my life might be like in his hands? They sacrificed me to their fear of their brothers. They sacrificed me to a magician's illusion to throw Billy and Terry off the truth that Eleanora lived.

I won't see Missy. I won't see anyone. Missy has to go back to France. She tries to tell me she didn't know either. I don't care.

The hole I'm in is cavernous and dim. Much of the time, I choke on my own breath. I feel as if I've been buried alive. Every way I have ever been abandoned and tortured has now been heaved up, exposed again.

All my years of trying to heal have been wasted. In that one moment, Mercy ripped my wounds wide open. She was like the eagle in my vision, feeding on my flesh. I can't stop the rush of fear and pain and despair. And so I've collapsed.

There is no answer to the question of what I did to deserve the devouring flames of this hell. I was a *child*! Questions and justifications make no difference. I am consumed by—and that's when the word *discouragement* pops up like a jester. I am consumed by discouragement.

I laugh. The laughter begins as a quiver in my lip and turns raucous in a flash.

No expectations. No disappointments.

I begin a quick crawl out of the rabbit hole I've fallen into. I can feel the light of day in my soul. There is just no keeping a dead Billy's daughter down. Never again.

CHAPTER 25

I walk out of my room and into a shower. I am disgusting. The room I stewed in needs fumigation.

Poor Ned. I wonder if he's still here. I would have left me.

Hearing a car pull into the driveway, I lift the bathroom blind, clear the steam building from my shower on the window glass, and peer out. I can see Ned. The car is familiar.

It's CiCi's.

I can't get dressed fast enough. I hear Ned walk CiCi into the house. I hear low rumbles of their voices together.

For a moment, I don't know what to do. That damned afghan is stashed out of sight somewhere. Where?

Where's the goddamned afghan?

My mind is on high-speed search and rescue. It knocks over the boulders of entrenched thoughts and kicks through the piles of fetid, fuming debris that has been my state of mind for weeks.

Where the hell is that afghan?

I run back upstairs, remembering that I stored it under the bed. I drop to my belly and slither an arm under the bed frame. I grip the heavy plastic zip bag that stores extra throws. And there it is! I drag it out, fling it open, and race down the hall to CiCi's room.

I throw open the door to find CiCi unpacking. I sweep her reduced heft up into my arms, wrap her with the afghan, and lie.

"I just pulled this out of the dryer. Perfect timing!"

I can't stop hugging her. I thought our next visit would be over her urn.

Ned's jaw drops to the floorboards when he sees me. He wouldn't have called CiCi if I'd shown any sign of life.

But then as suddenly as I awoke from the bowels of Hades, I begin to decline. The adrenaline rush subsides and leaves me limp in mind, body, and soul. I wonder what day it is, and then I decide I don't care. I force myself back from CiCi. I've been clinging and sobbing.

CiCi laughs. "You'll be okay, Ellen. I need to use the bathroom."

I wobble my way into the kitchen to face Ned. Before we can speak, CiCi hollers out for a beer. She's lost a significant amount of weight. I feel the spill of panic in every muscle. I sit down, heart pounding.

She meets us in the kitchen, and we all sit down together. Ned holds my hand with a look of both relief and frustration.

CiCi speaks first. "Ned called me."

"I figured. You picked the right day, girl. I just finished the wash. I must have known you were coming."

CiCi doesn't look like herself anymore, physically. But she is here, like she always is, to shore me up, give me feet. Ned, still speechless, listens to me blunder and lie my way through this wash, all right. White wash.

"I suppose Ned filled you in about the latest twist in the family story, the one that excludes me from the truth about my father and his siblings?" I try to speak with control, but my voice quivers.

"Yes. I'm so sorry." CiCi shakes her head. "You hit the motherlode of drama with this crew."

I sigh. "Who would believe...? And Ned, I'm sorry I've put you through so much. I'm just sorry." I give him a loving, encouraging, smile.

Ned squeezes my hand. "It's all right. It's all right."

I squeeze his hand in reply. He's still dazed but not letting on how extraordinary it is to have me sitting at this table right now, chatting away as though I hadn't just crawled out from under a fallen log in a soul-sucking swamp.

Then for an hour, Ned drones on, catching both me and CiCi up on the latest twist in my current nightmare. While I was on my fainting couch, Ned talked with Mercy, trying to understand all the details and motivations behind this massive family cover up. He knew that at some point, I'd want to know.

"Mercy explained to me how she and Nellie—Eleanora—became other people's children with other people's family names. Eleanora, barely ten years old, was taken in by Millie's sister Annette and her husband, Rudy Tropwell. She was renamed Nellie Jane. And Carl, Lydia's father—"

"Who's Lydia?" CiCi interrupts.

I groan. "The devil's spawn. She and Carl moved to Capitol recently. It's their story and Mercy's story that…oh, hell. She's awful.

Ned waits for me to finish. I nod and close my eyes, except for an occasional peek at CiCi. I'm fragile, and I know it. I don't want to start screaming again. I can feel the demon's screech still clawing at the back of my throat. Ned continues with the story he got from Mercy.

"Lydia's father, Carl, just nine years old, was nicknamed Big Boy. Marty was renamed Jack Martin. He was only eight, but wounded too, grazed by the last shot." Ned turns to me. "That's how his face was disfigured. Not a lumbering accident at all."

Ned leans back in his chair, thoughtful for a moment, as if imagining Jack as a little boy accepting his wounds along with the bloodshed all around him.

"They were taken in by Millie's other sister Katey and her husband, Buster Martin. They all lived on the reservation. It was easy to keep secrets there. Law enforcement didn't interfere."

CiCi has tears streaming down her sunken cheeks.

"The sheriff helped keep this quiet from everyone. He was more worried than the rest of them about Billy and Terry coming back and killing Eleanora if they learned she was alive. Everyone took his fears to heart and carried them forward through the decades, through this masquerade."

Ned pauses, then asks CiCi if she wants a beer.

"Please!" She nods, staring at him with mouth agape, on edge.

I shake my head, no. He grabs two bottles from the refrigerator. He pops open the caps and sits back down to continue telling the story of Eleanora.

"Of course, the sheriff had his own badge to consider. He worked with the doctor to fake Eleanora's death certificate. Billy and Terry were charged and punished for a murder they did not commit. I suppose if they'd been older, things would have gone a different way." He stops to look at me. "You okay with this?

I nod encouragement for him to keep talking, not letting on to CiCi that she and I are both hearing about his conversation with Mercy for the first time.

"When Mercy told me all this, she begged me for understanding. She kept saying, 'We needed them away.' She even cried out, 'Oh, Jesus, help me!' and sobbed. It broke my heart to see her in that state. Keeping the secret has been her life's mission. But to continue lying, she has trusted the power of her fear over her faith in God to protect. Now her greatest fear is that she will never be forgiven by God."

I am furious. "Seriously, Ned? This is your takeaway?"

"Oh, honey, no. I'm merely trying to color the whole picture, as she did for me. Lives can be lost in more ways than physical death. You are well aware."

I interrupt. "When she told us about Eleanora, you think I didn't see her fear, her suffering? I didn't care. And Jack. Jack is in my house every day, never letting on, lying to me too. I thought he was a nice old guy helping out, except that he's my uncle. He is my family. Only I am not to be trusted with this precious information. I am not allowed to the family hearth because of my monstrous father. How much more can that man take from me? How much more?"

Ned nods, eyes on me. "Mercy and Nellie Jane had one mission, and that was to keep all the children safe from your father and your uncle Terry." He sits forward and takes my hand. "I'm not minimizing your experience—honestly. But I am trying to drive home the fact that all of you are survivors of your father. This is no longer your horror story alone."

"But they left me alone in it, didn't they? I didn't lie to Mercy. *I* didn't lie. She took *family* from me. Couldn't she see me as a child, too, in need of protection from a known murderer?" I shake my head no. "I have no feeling for her right now."

"No wonder you pulled the plug for a while." CiCi's voice is soft and raspy. "How could you possibly process a thing like that?"

I knew she would understand. How will I go on without her? I can feel the crush in my brain and the weight in my chest.

"I can't think logically about this. There is no logic. There's just pain. My mind won't take in anything else. Feeling has blown every circuit in my brain."

In my mind, I stand as an observer, witnessing the violent scene that nearly took Mercy's sister's life. A little girl in terror watches as her mother is beaten to death by her father, the man who swooped her up in loving arms to spin her into giggles. She watches her brother, my father, attempt to kill her little sister in a fever of murderous excitement that could easily have led to the death of them all.

"I can almost see how the secret safety of Eleanora and the boys might bring focus, purpose to the mind-bending grief and terror caused by the violence that night." I'm speaking my thoughts out loud, though still perceiving as a detached observer. "I can almost understand why they did so little about me. They were handling so much and hadn't counted on one more child in need popping up."

My mind won't let me go much further. I can feel the blackout clouds rolling in at the edges.

"Violence and tragedy also happened to you." CiCi hasn't much of a forgiving nature either. "It happened to you regardless of what happened to anybody else. Do you remember when we lived on Park Road in Minneapolis? Do you remember that little girl who was shot in the eye—the drive-by? That happened to her. Nothing will ever change that. It doesn't matter that other children didn't get shot in the eye. Lydia didn't get shot in the eye. She got to cover for her father, a victim. Her father was in hiding from your father. They could embrace Lydia with ease because she was complicit in their deception. She has nothing to do with you."

I am flush with realization now that my hatred of Lydia has foundation. I feel her superior air because that's exactly how she feels about me. No wonder she comes off as a know-it-all. She does know it all.

"I know. Maybe you're right. But there has to be some way to . . . oh, I don't know. I can't think it through."

My mind is almost entirely shut in darkness now. I feel faint and want to let go. But I catch my breath, breathe deeply, and get back on Lydia.

"But here's the thing. Lydia. They didn't have a problem including Lydia. She wasn't kept in the dark. Her father wasn't the monster. He was the victim. For all of them, I am an extension of Billy's threat of violence."

Rage is collapsing into defeat. "I see who I am now. Keep your friends close but your enemies closer. Right? I am no friend or family. I am a suspect in a generational crime, and I have no say."

The weight of the truth levels my spirit, already flattened by so many other truths. "They don't know me. They only know what they suspect may be me. They are afraid of me. They don't know me. They didn't even try to know me.

I stand to pace, back and forth, like I rocked myself to sleep as a child. More muttering to myself than speaking to Ned and CiCi, I hear the sounds of fact stumbling from my lips. "Their love for me was a cover."

If I could see myself in this moment, look into my own eyes, I think I would see the loss of light, my spirit bundled—like one of Nellie Jane's prayers, made with tobacco, wrapped in cloth—ready to give to *Tankashala*. Here, take this offering of my great pain.

I wish I could take myself up on a hill and toss my spirit to the four directions. But of course, now, all that is a lie, too. No one will take me. No one wants me.

CiCi asks me to sit down. I can barely hear her voice but it's like a magnet and compels me to sit. There is silence in the room. I hear the refrigerator's steady hum. I witness layers of dust casually floating through the air on light that fills the room from outside, not inside. Inside, my inside, has no light. I look at CiCi and am reminded by her sagging skin, that she is dying. This is an awful day.

"CiCi. I know you will be leaving me sometime soon." I grab her hand and cry. "But you're not leaving to do something to me. You're leaving because that's your life story. My life story is that I had you, and then I didn't have you. But I had you."

CiCi looks pained. She looks unwell. This conversation is a nightmare for all of us.

"Yes," she says.

I stand and go to her, kiss her on the head, my arms wrapped around her shoulders.

"I don't think I will ever love anyone the way I love you. You are the absolute best thing that ever happened to me." I hold her that way for a long time.

"Before you go to bed, CiCi," Ned speaks, "I want you to know that I have for long accepted my place as second in Ellen's heart."

I interrupt him. "No, Ned. It's not the same thing. I couldn't have survived without CiCi or thrived without you!"

He smiles. "I love you for saying that." He turns to CiCi again. "But CiCi, I want you to know that I've never stopped being grateful to you for sharing Ellen with me. Never."

CiCi hugs and kisses Ned and heads off to bed. For the first time in weeks, I climb into bed beside Ned, who lets me smother him with need.

"Thank you," I whisper into his chest.

Sleep is healing. Yesterday was painful. Today is a new day. Up and dressed, I see morning light filtered through the bare limbed trees. I feel heavy and empty. Ned hands me a cup of coffee. We stand, shoulder to shoulder, facing the window, staring at nothing in particular. I can see Jack out by the goat shed.

"Jack. Crap," I say. "He's such a dear old man. But I'm mad at him too. I can see why they did what they did. I'm fighting against the urge to care. But I want them all to understand what they took from me. I want them to know how they hurt me."

"What if they can't understand?" Ned blurts. "What if they can't understand the magnitude of impact on you? What if they can't take one more ounce of guilt on themselves?"

I sigh and look away. Ned grips my shoulders and forces me to face him.

"Ellen, for most of your life, you've struggled to gain a foothold. You thought you had achieved a certain balance. And now your elderly aunts and uncles took that away by reinforcing the fact that your position in the family is one of neglect and abandonment. Am I right so far?"

I wince as if he slapped me. I can feel imaginary blood of the sucker punch run down my face. It tastes salty, like tears as it floods my mouth. My lungs scream for the air he took at contact. This is hell, has to be. Reason applied as a tourniquet accomplishes nothing, yet the patient lives.

"What do you think they can do with that information? They've lived in fear all their lives. Some of that fear was irrational, probably. But fear becomes a habit, right?"

I want him to shut up. I struggle to pull away. The need to run and scream and burrow deep in the earth is punished by his deepening clasp on my body.

"Ellen." His voice strengthens in power against me. "Do you think there is any likelihood that you could turn their attention onto you when they have only now discovered each other free from fear?"

I am screaming at him in my head, but only his words make true noise in the room. Perhaps I have died. Perhaps I have split in two and left a shadow for him to plead his case against. I almost laugh. I'm too far gone. I feel myself dissolve into a graphic display of black and white pointillism. He thinks his earthly sense-making will have an effect. He doesn't know my demon.

"This is the first time with each other with no terror of Billy, no concern about Terry, no fear. And even if you could get their attention, do you really want to blame them for excluding you from their place of fear? How much more can they carry? Do you think they could have stopped their suffering to think about you? Could *you*? Have *you* done that for them?"

And now I'm back together in a whole person, working up a head of steam.

"Let's review. I was fine. For years. Then my effing father died. He tore up all my safe routes away from him. The flashbacks started. The panic came back. Then Virginia killed herself, leaving me without a culprit to pin the crimes on—which matters somehow. Then Mercy and I shared our history together. I felt safe and connected, like when I was a child. Oh, but wait—that was another layer of lies. But so what? They have pain. So I'm to be the martyr—continue to suffer because I don't want to bring more suffering to them? Is there no other choice? Can't I want something for myself?"

"Of course you can want it, sweetie. But you aren't likely to get it. Not now, if ever. If you try to get them to acknowledge your pain, then they have to take responsibility. How are they supposed to do that?"

I can tell Ned thinks he has made headway with me. He thinks he has my attention. I'm finished with this conversation. Almost.

"Fuck you! Fuck you for having a straight line through life. Fuck you for thinking you have any idea what you're asking. Fuck you! Nobody ever left your bloodied, beaten, baby-body as a mess for your ice queen mama to clean up. Ned, fuck you!"

CiCi arrives in the kitchen, dressed and ready for coffee. "What did I miss in the last 10 hours while I slept? Sounds like you're still in the same paragraph."

"See this?" I circle my face with my finger. "This is a sneer. No, not the same paragraph. This is the next scene, different day. Note the sun is out today. Here." I hand her a mug of coffee.

"Wow! Good morning to you too." CiCi takes the mug and gives Ned a kiss on the cheek. "So what did I miss?"

"Ned seems to think that my father's siblings have greater rights to a happily ever after than I do."

Ned shakes his head and scowls. "That's not what I meant."

"Yeah, it kind of is. You think—you suggest—that my claim to pain will fall on deaf ears because of the joyful sibling homecoming celebration in progress. You suggest that I do nothing, say nothing, because they can't hear me right now for all of their joyful noisemaking with each other."

The urge to hurl the room through the center of the universe takes me to the brink of a rage blackout. I sit. The sound of my foot tapping is annoying. My body shuffles in the chair. I feel blood banging in my head.

Release me.

I reach for CiCi's hand and stare at her dying face. My life on a land mine, I blow to bits and smithereens.

Ned leaves the house while CiCi calms me. We're two hours into another crappy day. I want this to end. I want to be done.

Later that afternoon, CiCi asks me to take a walk with her outside. I wonder how much physical activity she can stand these days. I'm so afraid of her death.

"Since the chemo diet, I'm more a walker than ever. Donald plowed a path down to the creek so I could walk the dog every day this winter. The neuropathy gets in the way sometimes, but I manage."

"How is Donald? Gosh, I haven't seen him since your dad's funeral."

"He's good. He's more supportive than I dreamed possible. He puts up a fuss when I take off for gigs. He thinks I should be home and act the invalid."

I laugh at that. When CiCi and Donald met, I could tell they were a great match. He hovered over her as her mom used to, and she ate up every bit of attention. After fifteen years, it sounds like not much has changed.

We decide to visit the old cemetery, the one Missy and I used to explore as children. It's about three-quarters of a mile down Lumber Road 9, a poorly maintained logging trail cleared annually by hunters for four wheelers. Once paved, now the road is a mix of gravel, dirt, and broken tar. I get the car and drive us so CiCi can ride and save her energy for walking among the headstones. Ned flags me down as I pull out of the drive. I reluctantly let him in the car.

"We're going to the cemetery."

I can hear a pileated calling from outside my partially rolled down window. I think it might be calling out to CiCi. I think of Nellie Jane, who taught me about the connectedness of all things. I feel gratitude to have CiCi and Ned with me, even though I'm furious with him. And I feel sick from disappointment throughout my body. It will be good to walk it off.

The cemetery is beautiful. I feel the force of sound made by a deer scattering through the brush as we approach. The north woods are at an arms-length away in any direction.

The grave markers are all shapes and sizes with eroded family names making a faded claim to the land. They rise out of deep grasses and shrubs still hanging on to clusters of snow and ice. As we walk along, Ned brushes the snow off headstones.

We pick through the markers, reading dates and names. Baby names and dates inspire flashes of hard life and hard birth and bloody or disease-causing death.

I can imagine Nellie Jane, now at rest here, eagerly pushing her way through the summer grass and brush, like a child late for tea. I can almost hear her young girl's gleeful voice calling, "Mama! Papa!" as though life was always good as it should be for a child. I shake the images from my mind.

This is the world of spirits that Nellie Jane taught me about. I can hear her remind me to stay grounded, to not be fooled by tricksters, who will occupy a place like this, especially while I am so vulnerable. I can feel her world like a cape or shroud over my head and shoulders. I think it strange that her way still haunts and urges me, even after learning she was no Indian.

We find the headstones of my grandparents. One reads *Matthew Elias McInnis—b. abt. 1902 d. August 7, 1940*. And the other reads

Flora Eleanora McIntyre McInnis, Most Beloved Mother—b. abt. 1907 d. August 7, 1940.

There is a third headstone, smaller than the other two, which reads *Eleanora Janet McInnis. Born May 12, 1930. Died August 7, 1940. Beloved daughter*. Its message too is somewhat obscured by wear of weather and time. Above the words are an engraved angel of feathery wings and outstretched arms. The headstone has been toppled and lies on its back, gracefully accepting its inevitable decay along with the dead of the place. I wonder who placed the family markers.

Off to one side of Eleanora's angel-embellished headstone is a small, set-into-the-ground marker. *Eleanora Janet McInnis Makala. Born May 12, 1930. Died April 9, 2012. Beloved daughter, wife, and sister.*

"Look," I say to Ned and point. "Look." I point to Eleanora Janet's name and cry hard out loud while Ned holds onto me. "The truth was here, for how long?"

The shocks to my heart and soul should land more softly after all these years. But no. They still land with force.

CHAPTER 26

CiCi leaves, and I am in hiding for weeks. I am simmering in my own grief stew. I want to cook my goose alone. I am tired of letting everyone else off the hook. I am exhausted from the inside out.

I'm stuck between what I want, which is fantasy, and what I can have, which is reality. I want a fantasy where everyone apologizes, even the dead, for what I could have had with Eleanora. I could have been loved by my aunt. I could have had her to love as someone "to me." Instead, I loved her in a most apologetic way, as if I was intruding on her relationship with Mercy.

I felt guilty all the time, the guilt of a thief—for stealing the Indian truths to use for my own comfort, for stealing time from her and from the others, the liars. They lied to me. It is the one thing I cannot tolerate. A lie, to me, demonstrates an unforgivable indifference. It is irrelevant to me that they suffered.

Ned often holds my hand and consoles me. I thank him for being such a good man—faithful, understanding, and generous. He has his own story from Vietnam, where he saw enough death and devastation. He lives aware that this is a moment and just one moment.

He told me once that if we think about eternity, we can imagine there won't be any pain. "You'd have to take a pretty big punch to feel it across the span of ever after."

But he knows I can't let go, not yet.

Ned and Jack keep the place going while I struggle to square myself within and without. Just as it took time to snap out of the shock, it will take so much more to come to grips, to accept, to proceed. I wonder how many other land mines my family has strewn about my path.

Spring and summer seasons pass by me. Autumn nudges its way into the air and soil. It's a sunny day, nearly warm enough to sit outside on the porch. From the window, I can see that most of the leaves have fallen. I haven't put the gardens to rest for winter. I will have to finish tilling before the ground freezes.

Tilling. Planting winter cover crops. Mulching.

A stirring of interest in a new day begins in my belly. I feel a loose control of my thoughts and emotions. I may survive this round.

And why the hell not?

It's that span of ever after, I guess. Time outlasts pain. Not fear, though. I know that's the truth.

I need a shower. I strip my bed and throw the sheets in the wash. I feel better. I cook a meal of roasted potatoes, carrots, and casserole-style chicken pot pie.

I walk out to the shed, where I can hear Ned and Jack working. They both look up in surprise to see me.

"Come on in and eat with me," I say.

I scratch one of the goat's ears on the way out, smiling for the first time in a long while. It's a weak smile. I know that. But it's real.

Ned and Jack come in about twenty minutes later, wash up, and sit down. Ned pours his apple cider for us. I serve the meal, and we all eat together as if the last few months had not happened.

Jack is not one to mince words. He is not a complicated thinker. Direct, blunt, always.

"She was my sister, too."

"I know that Jack, and I'm sorry. But you had her. You had your sister. You had her."

Ned gives me a sharp look.

I look back, quizzical. "What?"

"I didn't know." Jack speaks deliberately, eyes averted from me.

"Oh, for God's sake! Does this crap never end? Do you mean they didn't even tell *you*?"

"Mercy never told me. Eleanora never told me."

I look at Ned in horror, then I look back at Jack. "Why would they keep that from you?"

I feel despair shoot another round of panic through my system. The screaming starts up in my head, like this is my battle.

The old man Jack is the same little boy Jack who ran away into the dark night, fleeing the murder of his mother and sister. The trauma of all he witnessed, coupled with his wounds and fear and running away and being adopted and shielded from the truth of history would have forced away any memory of Eleanora. Of course, he would not have remembered her.

I know Jack may have already used up his word quota for the day. I hope Ned will step in, but he is silent.

"They didn't want me to know," Jack says. "I was little. I was hurt. I was Martin's son. Carl left. I didn't know anything else. I forgot that was my life before. I forgot that we had run away."

I reach out to touch his hand. "I'm so sorry, Jack. I can't tell you how sorry I am."

Jack looks up, beaming a stunning smile. "I'm happy. I have my brother *and* my sister right here. I'm happy."

I envy Jack. How can he gain and lose so much yet remain even? I can see in him how far away lies sanity for me.

"I need to get out of here. Out of town. Jack, if Ned comes with me away somewhere, will you oversee things here? We'll get somebody to feed the animals."

"I'll do it."

I'm full of warmth and compassion for Jack, my uncle. What he suffered is unimaginable, yet he's happy with the outcome. What is so wrong with me that I cannot?

Because Billy broke me. And nobody turned me over to people who would love me. Nope. They left me out in the scariness to survive on my own. They did it with intention to save themselves. I have to find a way through this hair-trigger truth.

"Ned, you'll ask Mike to help out, too?" With that, I add, "Pumpkin pie anyone?"

I make reservations for a three-night stay in Chicago. CiCi has booked a gig at a renowned blues club. I imagine this will be her last big show. During our drive to the airport in Minneapolis, Ned continues to encourage me to make peace with the family story.

"Sweetie, there just might come a day, and not far off, that you realize you have been handed a family. Maybe in a backhand way, but still, a family. And just your kind of family. They're a bit quirky from being jostled around and banged up and confused all their lives. Does any of that sound familiar? You might want to embrace this tribe of misfits and make something of it."

I know he's right. I daydreamed of family—family love, nurturing, and safety. But this family has been beaten and shot at and raped and scattered. There is no way to put it back together again.

I see a big old fat Humpty Dumpty smashed in pieces on the ground as the end of the story. There are no king's horses or king's men to put us to rights. We didn't just fall, somebody pushed us. And with that comes another level of drama so complex I doubt we can find our way through.

But it's only me, really, whose pieces are rubble. The rest of them are fine with their lot. And it's not registering with them that I'm still in shards at the bottom of their wall.

Ned holds my hand as he drives into the city to catch our flight. It is a beautiful day, fifty-six degrees and sunny with that feel and smell and texture of autumn. I breathe deeply, often. I want to enjoy these last sensations of fall before winter slides under the door.

Part of me, a lot of me, feels untethered for leaving home, for leaving the earth and animal sounds and smells, for leaving real living behind. I hope distance can provide perspective. Maybe not a comfortable truth, but a twist to the view.

"Ned, before we go to the airport, I want to stop at Terry's. I know he won't answer, but I want to tell him what I know. If they didn't tell Jack, they surely did not tell Terry. From what Mercy said to me, Terry tried to kill himself because of his guilt for helping to kill Eleanora."

Ned is clearly worried about this idea. "We have time. You can give it a try. But I beg you, for your sanity and mine, don't be disappointed if he doesn't respond. Please."

"I *will* be disappointed. I want him to know. I need for him to know. It's strange, I suppose, but I feel closer to Terry—not knowing him at all—because of his suffering. I know that kind of crazy. It's my kind."

"No. You've got that wrong! You pushed out into the world. He collapsed into himself. You have tried everything, everything to survive the damage done to you."

I'm hot to defend my decision. "The difference is that I've always been clear that something was done to me. I had a reason to fight. Terry did the bad thing. He's the one who brought pain to others. He has no one to blame but himself—or so he thinks. Yes, he was out of control, but he tried to atone for that by taking the punishment on himself. The rest of the family was too cowardly to give him a break—although Mercy did say she tried her best with him."

We pull up to Terry's assisted-living care facility. I knock on the door to his room. There is no answer. The door is not locked, so I let myself into the room.

"Uncle Terry?"

His wheelchair faces a window. He does not turn around. "What?" His tone is gruff.

"Terry, it's your niece Ellen."

"Get out."

"Terry, we should talk about Eleanora. Aunt Mercy says you saw her alive at my father's funeral. She told me everything."

"Get out."

"Terry, this is important—to you it's important."

"Get out."

I stand in front of him as he turns his wheelchair around. He looks awful. He's shaved and clean, but his eyes are sunken and bruised. He is severely underweight. His eyes, half-closed, burn hot behind the lids.

I fight a fear that edges up my spine, but I pull up a chair up to sit and face him.

"Terry." I reach for his hand.

He pulls back.

"Terry, look—I don't know much about you. Nothing but the little bit Mercy has told me. But I know they all left you in the dark about things you should have known."

He shuts his eyes. I cannot tell if he's listening.

"When you were young, you thought you killed your sister."

His eyes flash open with unmitigated contempt. "You know nothing! Now get out!"

"But—"

"Get out!"

I rise to my feet to walk away. "I'm sorry, Terry. I'm sorry this all happened to you. I know what it is to fight the past every minute of your life."

I leave his room with a little bit of hope. At least I've seen him face to face. Though the exchange was vile, it's an improvement over silence.

"I don't think he'll live much longer," I say as Ned pulls out of the lot and we head for the airport. "I wonder if I should do more, try harder."

"Haven't you had this discussion with Mercy and with Jack? Could it be that everything that can be done has been done?"

"I suppose I'm trying to wring out the last bit of potential from this mess. Terry will die in pain when they could have let him off the cross of shame. They could have."

Ned turns briefly to face me. "Ellen, Terry is not an innocent victim. He was cut from the same cloth as your father and grandfather.

He has always been angry. Maybe he would have been violent again had he not been paralyzed. Maybe he is exactly where he needs to be. Maybe you can't save him for yourself."

"Jesus, Ned! Is that what you think I'm doing?"

"I don't know. I don't know what you're doing. But I do know that he is not emotionally or mentally stable, regardless of the reasons. He's unpredictable. I don't feel he's a safe person for you to be around. He's been clear about not wanting to see you or know you. He seems to be lost in his own hell, and you can't visit him there. You can continue to try, but you'll never make it to those depths. Would you even want to?"

But I do want to. I believe through and through that Uncle Terry and I can help each other heal. I want him to have a chance. I want a chance with him.

CHAPTER 27

We arrive at our hotel around 3 p.m. Ned steps out to pick up a tourist guide brochure and to ask the concierge about how to get to the blues bar where CiCi will be performing. Back in our room, he finds me in his cowboy hat and boots and my near-sixty-year-old altogether. Ned is a very lucky man.

Chicago is called the Windy City for good reason. When we arrived, there was a breeze, but now, night has turned on us and brought a hard-biting, gritty wind that would be considered respectable even in the northern Minnesota wilds. We have only a two-block walk to the bar with our heads into that wind. I want to throw my head back and laugh in its blustery face, but I need my furry hat to stay on my head. So I keep my head down, my nose buried in a fluffy silver-sparkled black and gray scarf Mercy gave me.

Ned pulls open the bar's ancient oak door. The smell of stale booze and fried food whisks by in the entryway, then pauses and stalls for a beat before big brother wind hurls it up and above and away. Inside, it is like any music bar or honky tonk from any era. Quick-as-lightning bartenders, now known now as mixologists, pour and sprinkle and adorn a miscellany of alcoholic wonders in a variety of glassware shapes and sizes. They push the concoctions toward a swirl of wait staff, aimed at a steady flow of cash rewards to be garnered from tipsy patrons.

We are escorted to a table by a healthy-looking waiter with both front teeth glittering of gold. In this economy, he could lose those assets in a homebound stroll. I wonder if there are bras for these grills, just as there are bras to protect sports cars' grills from hurtling rocks. In this case, it would be to protect from thugs.

We are seated, our menus are in hand, and our first drink orders are placed. We kiss in celebration. A young couple bumps into the back of my chair without so much as an *oops* or a *sorry*. They're snapping selfies and laughing, yelling over our heads to friends three tables away. Ned is oblivious. He's consuming the bar's ambiance, feeling its history.

"Ned, there's CiCi!"

CiCi's once full breasts and wealthy hips still command attention. She walks across the bar room as though she means to move it, push it before her, out of her way. Her lips are wide and red. Her smile is genuine and warm as she greets even strangers.

Dressing for stage is her great passion. Tonight, her head is wrapped in a gold lamé turban. Her earrings are big, bold, glittery danglers that swing in a hail to her audience. Her breasts are confined in a black lace teddy under a knee-length open tunic-style shirt of multi-colored metallic thread that flounces and puffs away from her body, offering a voyeur's peek at her once exceptional cleavage. Flared polyester lounge pants, cranberry red in hue, shine beneath the fringed edges of her shirt, finishing with silver sequined flats. Her neuropathy must be worse than she lets on, or she'd be wearing a chunky platform heel.

She is, as always, accessorized with a plenitude of antique-store sparkling bangles and oversized rings. CiCi's first love is performing, second is music, and third is a good second-hand store. If it weren't for used clothing, CiCi would be naked, and we would all be out a good show.

I hate seeing her diminished form. She's disappearing in front of my eyes, though patrons see only her lively showcase of gaudy glitz. A bold-faced lie masks death's understudy status in the wings, waiting behind the curtain for its upcoming performance.

"Yeah, Domi—get me water with some lemon, would you?" she speaks to our gold-toothed escort. She sits down with us.

"Get up!" I order.

We rise from our chairs, and I hug her hard. I hold her back from me for a thorough inspection.

"Okay," I say.

We take our seats. She's lost at least forty pounds. I can't bear that she's dying.

"Give me your hand. I want you to have this." She peels a ring of diamonds and pearls from her index finger and puts it in place on my middle finger. "You'll have to get it resized." She nods. "My father gave this to my mother, and she gave it to me. I want you to carry it with you as much as you can. Then we can always, the whole family of us, be together forever."

She abruptly stands before I can say anything. She sways her way through tables to meet and greet her public.

Ned and I make small talk through the first round of drinks, both feeling the impact of CiCi's gift. We're here to celebrate her life, not write her eulogy. I fiddle with the ring before securing it in my bag.

We order ribs, slaw, and popovers. We drink sodas with dinner and save Jack Daniels for later, a nightcap before going back to the hotel.

CiCi takes the stage while Ned and I enjoy our meal. For two sets, she hammers the room with her smooth bellowing vocals. A waiter removes dishes from our table and replaces them with our last call of Jack Daniels.

I feel a surge of deep, soothing wellness of being spill into my thoughts. My limbs relax. The force in CiCi's voice, the bluesiness of the room, brings me to my soul-home. I didn't expect to ever feel this at ease again. I know I can survive anything now.

Near my left ear, I hear a man's voice speaking, "*Hau, Kola.*" "Hello, friend."

I look up, but there's no one near me.

Lost in my thoughts, I open to the unseen. I should not have had that second shot of whiskey.

"*Mitákuye oyás'iŋ*," I whisper, feeling guilty that I speak the words while under the influence.

Then my ease evaporates along with the alcohol as it is attacked by adrenaline. A rerun of Nellie Jane's collapse at my father's funeral plays out on the stage. The clatter of drumsticks hitting the floor accentuates the pause in all other noise.

CiCi is down.

CHAPTER 28

I planned on my first marriage to be one and done. We divorced after seven years of arguing. First came love, then came marriage, then came divorce followed by depression. I thought divorce would be good for me, to get away from daily clashes. I was wrong. It wasn't an either/or situation.

Divorce illuminated a new rip in my psyche—I couldn't be alone. I quit eating. I attempted suicide by running my car off the road. I hit a ditch before my target, which was an overpass support column for the highway overhead. AAA called a tow truck to pull the car out of the ditch. I was in no way dead—at least not in body. But I hurt like hell for the next week and a half. I'd hit that embankment hard as a bullet into steel.

It was CiCi who tried to console me. She was on the road, touring. She'd left the month before on her first regional tour. She was always a good listener and advisor to me but had less personal time as her career pushed her ever closer to fame. Every gig moved her forward. She could see, straight ahead, the horizon of her big moment.

CiCi reassured me that I'd be okay. She'd be home within a week, and we could figure things out.

"Hang tight," she said.

I considered how tight I might hang. In the end, she saved me again. And now, *now*, she's dead.

I watch people moving in response to the crisis of a dead singer on stage. I can't move. I can't stop the flashes of memory.

Oh my God, CiCi. You weren't actually supposed to go.

I feel the familiar spiral of panic rise to high tide through blood and bone and gut. I reach for Ned. But he's up on stage, holding my friend, my dead, dead friend. I drift.

CiCi, who could belt the blues in a downtown bar, did not like city living. She would drive three hours or more to a city gig from her sprawling forty acres of western prairie and return the same night if at all possible. Her friends were farmers and sustainability types. She practiced pagan arts. She loved folky festivals as long as she was asked to perform. She was fiercely loyal to friends—the more downtrodden, the better. She housed a small cache of stray cats. She had a big personality and ego to match. She was unique in a legendary way. And I loved her. And Ned loved her. Everyone loved her.

CiCi—who could not get enough of what life offered, the being in it, the trying all of it on for size—is gone. She—who would spring from sleep to pet a cat on her way out the door to stroll through prairie grasses on her way to strip down naked for a dip in the spring-fed creek—is gone.

CiCi was a pot smoker. She smoked to enjoy its naturally sourced pleasures. We laughed about the legal objections to marijuana use. Tell a cow not to eat grass. Grass exists for cows to eat. Tell a human not to enjoy the delights of the world. He'll enjoy them to the fullest if he can get 'em.

CiCi volunteered at the local used-goods store to keep a ready eye on what deals she might score from old ladies' attics and basements. She was the first at an estate sale, gobbling up the left-behinds from those who had moved on with no more need of things. Her house and furnishings were an eclectic dreamscape.

Her gardens were fat with produce and perennials. She carefully explained her design logic to me, but there was no design—CiCi was aesthetically illiterate. Her gardens responded by letting nature override her intentions—explosions of color amidst pounds of tomatoes falling over gigantic bell peppers climbed on by cucumber vines curling through the masses of basil and cilantro. Magnificence defined CiCi.

I am with her, here in Chicago, where the winds of death swirl around her on stage, like her death is an act in an awful play. I can hear the ever-creating universe gasp in a whoosh to absorb her. It knocks the wind out of me in its passing. *Hau, kola.* My good friend, hello and goodbye.

And it is done.

Ned and I fly back to Minneapolis with her coffin, then drive out to CiCi's hometown for her funeral. Her memorial service could have been bested only by a funeral procession in the heart of New Orleans. Everybody cries and sings their hearts out. Bands play. There are hundreds of us in mourning. She would have loved that. She lived her life well, and life said goodbye with a big bang of a send-off.

Born Cecilia Isabelle Nobels, she is buried as CiCi, beloved wife of Donald Jasperson. Loved by many, but more she loved her life, loved it completely. Donald is a trooper through the service, surrounded by local friends and co-workers. We know he'll be okay. And we tell him so.

He just smiles. "She was my queen, you know." We do know.

Her mother is here, looking frail. I stay with her throughout her ordeal of this day.

“I’m so sorry,” I tell her.

I cannot imagine her grief. My own grief is staggering. I look over the amassing crowd of mourners in the room. There is hardly a place to walk. The music is loud and carried by every voice and instrument.

“How will we ever live without her?” I speak the words aloud.

Her mother collapses in tears on my arm. I throw my other arm around her, cradling her, giving her refuge. I hug her to me and cry softly into her thinning, white hair. Yes, how will any of us survive our lives without CiCi’s boundless spirit to carry us?

That night we say goodbye to the best thing that ever happened to me. Many others claim she is now in the arms of Jesus the Savior. I think instead of how she was my savior. That day on the playground, so long ago, when she became my friend—it was because of her that Billy stopped hurting me. It was because of her that I could leave home and never have to look back. It was because of her parents, who lived to love her, that I knew kind and normal family love and that I should expect to have it and be it for others.

I cry harder as I hold her mother, then sit her down in a chair offered by a middle-aged pot-bellied man.

“Thanks,” I say to him. My hand rests on her shoulder. “Ned is getting the car. We’ll drive you back to the hotel.”

CiCi’s mother nods. It’s too noisy in the packed town hall building to bother trying to speak.

We settle her into her room and leave our number on the bedside table. I kiss her and hug her and wish her pain away as I tuck the flimsy motel blanket around her.

We left her niece at the town hall. She will come later, when the reception is over, to stay with her aunt and return to Minneapolis in the morning, when the weather and roads improve. There's a snowstorm, the first of the season. Donald will spend the day with them at the motel.

It has been a time of great loss for them all.

Ned drives us home through the snowstorm. The roads are beginning to ice up. The winds were once gusty, creating a whiteout, but they're relaxing now. Snow, in hypnotic bursts, spins across narrow beams cast by the headlights. I can't see through the flurry of white stuff mixed with sleet.

I close my eyes and fall into thoughts staved off by shock, grief, and the funeral excitement. My heart is broken. I fight off despair. I remind myself of the time we had together since we knew she was dying.

There is nothing ahead but a blank canvas of possibility, nothing now but to go forward. I want to see my animals, to shovel a path through the fresh snow to the barn, to peruse seed catalogs, to sleep without dreaming. Nellie Jane—Eleanora—would have told me to let the dreams come. I swear that in the deep dark of my thoughts, I hear a pileated call, flying into the winds and woods, carrying everything that ever was of CiCi.

What will I do when Ned is gone? What will I do when everyone else is gone? Who am I without them?

I realize I don't know who I am without my relationships with others. All my life I felt alone, yet I have not been alone since the minute I handed CiCi her glasses saved from the sand at the neighborhood park.

I try to sleep, but I can't stop the panic. I begin to hyperventilate. Ned pulls the car to the side of the road and stops. He digs into my luggage for my medication.

"Here." He hands me a pill and a water bottle.

Within twenty minutes, the pounding in my chest subsides. I am more than ready to be home. I wonder if I will need to call my therapist. I'm not sure I can get through this on my own.

"At least," I say out loud, "there's no one else to lose."

I sigh and cry and pity myself.

Ned had called Jack the night before to let him know when we'd be heading out. The house is warm and welcoming when we arrive. Jack must have called Mercy, because our mail and a fresh coffee cake lie in welcome on the kitchen counter.

I'm glad to be home, but the mail can wait. The cake will keep in the freezer. I don't have the heart or mind for anything but Ned and sleep. Although it's early, we both crawl into bed. Ned is exhausted from the treacherous drive. I'm tired from doing a backstroke in purgatory. I want to let go and drown in sleep.

CHAPTER 29

Sounds of happy people in our house wake me from delirium. I can see that it is morning by the light nudging at the bedroom curtain's edge. The smell of frying bacon hangs in our room against a backdrop of giggling and a "Woof!"

I nudge Ned, who barely stirs. "Did we come to the wrong house last night?"

We lumber out of bed, slow as sloths, dress in what's handy, and stagger into the day to face a blast of sunlight and strangers in our kitchen. Temperatures had plummeted overnight with the lifting of snow clouds, opening the heavens to a bright and blinding sun.

"Get down, Charlie! Get down!" An unfamiliar voice reprimands a dog in my house.

Charlie—a beautiful young golden retriever, buoyant, untrained, and bouncing with glee—is leaping around the two of us.

"Get down!" The voice calls out again.

Ned grabs Charlie's collar and moves him into a sitting position. "Down," says Ned calmly. "Good dog."

Ned lets loose of the collar. Like a jack-in-the-box, that dog is up again. Ned repeats the action. After three tries, Charlie responds obediently to Ned's command and ignores everyone else.

"Charlie?" I ask. "And who are you all?"

A handsome young couple is seated at the table with a child, a girl maybe six years old. Mercy is pulling basted eggs from the oven. Jack walks through the back door with an arm full of wood for the front room fireplace. He tracks snow across the floors. But on his way out again, he cleans it up with a towel he carries around his neck.

Mercy comes around from the stove and table to hug me. "Happy birthday, dear." She adds with a whisper, "I'm so sorry about CiCi. Heartbreaking."

"Hmm." I forgot my birthday.

On edge, I leave the group to take another chill pill. I stare at my unwashed, bare face in the bathroom mirror. Fifty-eight? Fifty-nine? Sixty? I can't remember my age. To CiCi, I'm ageless, because I'm still here. Or is it the other way around? The cold-water wash on my face feels fresh. I dab at my swollen eyelids with the cool cloth.

"Woof! Woof!" sounds in the other room.

My father's sneering face confronts my reflection. I want to scream an eternal scream. The bathroom floor tile is cold on my bare feet. I need to put on shoes. I need to. I *need.*

The anxiety medication begins to charm my nerves off the ledge of insanity. I head back to the kitchen and stand next to Ned.

The little girl walks right up to us, stares hard for a moment, then introduces herself. "Hello. My name is Judy. This is my dog, Charlie. Do you like dogs? Is that your cake?"

The cake now on the counter is a layer cake. It appears to be lemon, judging by the lemon-colored glacé. And next to that, a raisin pie.

My arms are snuggled around Ned's warm waist, my head at rest against his arm. I can feel him love me. I can feel the medication. This is a survivable moment. He's smiling at the little girl named Judy. I see her through my medicated eyes and am able to respond as any human would—with a pleasant tone and not the scratch-your-eyes-out, rip-your-throat-out puma lunge I felt earlier.

"Well, I don't think that is my cake. I think that's everybody's cake. I know that's my pie, though, because it's my birthday."

The little girl looks satisfied. I look for coffee. Ned finishes his first cup and puts the mug aside, telling the room he's going out to help Jack in the barn.

"And the rest of you?" I ask once again. "Who are you? I don't mean to sound rude, but we just got home last night from burying one of my best friends, and I don't know you or why you're in my house."

Clearly, I need a second pill, but the words are out of my changeling's mouth.

Mercy strokes my arm, softly speaking dangerous words. "These are your cousins, dear. Lydia's family."

Fucking Lydia! Jesus Christ! There are more? In my house! Jesus!

"I'm Lydia Campbell's daughter, Elizabeth, and this is my husband, Allan, and his niece, Judy. You've met her dog, Charlie." She smiles like the Cheshire Cat.

"Really, Mercy, really?" *Fucking Lydia!* "Can't you just leave us alone? You keep shoving this joyous reunion of yours down my throat. Now it's in my house. I don't want it. Jesus!"

"Take it up with Jack if you're upset," she replies with an uncharacteristic bristle. "This is his idea. It's your birthday, the first one he's been able to celebrate as your uncle. These are your cousins, who came to stay with me for a week. They do not need your permission to be here."

"In Capitol, maybe. But in *my* house? That requires an invitation."

I know I'm out of control, but they don't need to be here. Not today. Not now. Goddamnit.

"We can go," Allan offers.

"No," I snap. "No one but me is going anywhere. I'm taking a shower."

"I'm scared of her," I hear Judy say as I walk out of the kitchen.

You should be scared, kid.

The steamy, warm, cascading water slithers down my skin, a skin I should shed like the viperous snake I am. The hairdryer drowns out sounds of others in my house. I don't want to hear them talk about me.

I take another pill, then dress in a cotton turtleneck covered by a heavy wool pullover. I pull on wool socks and head to the kitchen to get my parka, snow boots, winter scarf, and the warmest hat and gloves I own. I throw on my winter gear in full view of all the others, who pretend there's absolutely nothing wrong.

"Does Judy have warm clothes?" I ask without a glance at my family members gathered to celebrate my birthday.

She's by my side in a flash, throwing on all her winter clothing piled in a heap on the entryway bench.

So much for fear.

Charlie crowds us with barking and bulk in the small space. I open the door, and he bounds free into the wilds of the backyard.

I eye-to-eye Judy with an intense, steady, unflinching stare. "Do you know how to do any work?"

"No," she replies.

"Fine," I say. "We'll start by learning to work in the goat barn."

The child is out the back door and halfway to the goat shed before I can lift my first boot for a first step onto the porch. On her tear to the shed she meets up with Ned, who tosses a shovel full of snow at her. Charlie leaps in the air, braying like a hound. Judy releases a giggly screech more bone-chilling than a cougar's scream. She falls into the snow, laughing. Charlie dances all around her, kicking up snow sprays caught up in windy swirls.

"Come on," I say as I walk past her pink parka in the snow.

We enter the shed together. Charlie stays outside with Ned and Jack. Someone will have to watch that dog whenever he's loose outside. He'd make an easy meal for a variety of predators.

I make introductions. "This is Miranda, and this is Misty, and this is Belinda."

The goats stand a bit taller than Judy, and each one tries to grab her stocking cap.

"Don't!" she scolds them.

"That won't work with goats."

I pull out an extra scarf, tie it over her cap and under her chin, pull up her parka hood to cover the lot. then secure it tightly under her chin as well.

"Will this work with goats?" she asks.

"No," I say. "This will."

I take her hand, lead her away from the girls, and sit her down on a stack of hay bales to make her taller. Then I bring the goats to her, one by one.

"The first thing to know about goats is this—they will eat almost anything, including your hat."

She giggles.

"The second thing to know about goats is this—they will follow you around, want to be with you, the same way Charlie wants to be with you. And the third thing to know about goats—and this is very important—you can never let a goat out of the shed unless you are with it and *you* are with an adult. Here in the north woods, other animals will eat the goats. You must watch the girls all the time when they're outside of the shed. That goes for Charlie, too. And the chickens."

Judy takes in the lesson as if it were the most important information she'd ever receive. Her face is angelic and sincere. But she's a kid, with the attention span of a minute or two. She'll forget the second we're on our way to something else.

I show her how to feed the goats and tell her if she's up early enough in the morning she can help milk them. We stop in at the chicken coop, see the rabbits in the barn, and finally meet up with Jack and Ned in the workshop.

Jack is all smiles when he sees her. He hands her a highly polished wooden dog he's carved from a piece of diamond willow. It's lovely.

She strokes the dog, mutters "Charlie Two," and puts it in her pocket, but not before stretching her arms up to him for a lift to kiss him on the cheek.

I feel there might be a heaven. Maybe. This is it, if it's real.

Judy and I walk back to the house. Inside, we remove our coats and boots. She runs to her uncle, chattering her excitement.

"I fed the rabbits some carrots. They were hungry. They have to eat breakfast too. And I can help milk the goats."

"Come wash your hands, Judy." I lead her into the bathroom, where we scrub up as if preparing for surgery. "You want to make sure your hands are very, very clean after handling the animals."

"I know. My hands stink when I pet Charlie."

There's that intense look of knowledge and wisdom again. Kids.

"That's right." I like her honesty.

It's only nine thirty in the morning, and I'm already exhausted.

"Would you all excuse me? I need to take care of some things," I lie.

I'm desperate for some private time. I head into the den. I moved Nellie Jane's . . . Eleanora Janet's . . . oh hell, Nellie Jane's platform rocker from her house to mine. As I settle in, ignoring the noisy kitchen people, I contemplate the universe, me in it, and a spider on the wall.

I fall asleep, then wake up feeling groggy and ill-tempered. Again, kitchen smells hang in the room. I hear talking, laughing, and an occasional "Woof."

They're still here.

I would call CiCi to clear my head, but she's dead. She's been dead for eight days. Dead. Unavailable.

I force myself from the chair, letting CiCi's afghan fall to the floor. As I collect it to fold, I feel the warmth from my body held in its threads. Like fingers, it grasps at my heart.

The tears come, and I let them escape. As though they are a separate other under my command, I will their flow. So they stop, of course. The afghan is placed on the guestroom bed.

Ned must be tired too. I head for the kitchen to give him a break from his role as host. Ned will always step up, but he has done enough.

Mercy is the first to spot me. "Hello, dear."

Charlie is occupied with a rawhide bone.

"I can see you've started dinner. But honestly, everyone—I have to ask you to leave. We're tired. We need some privacy. It's been a long, awful week."

Without protest this time, Mercy puts the food away. Alan offers to take Jack home.

They are unquiet people. They trample and stomp with their words and their boots and the rustle of their parkas as they prepare to leave. They offer us hugs and kisses and condolences. The door shuts, but still I can hear them. Judy laughs at a lunging Charlie. Car doors slam, and the engine comes to life.

I watch them in my mind drive off. I hope to God I never see any of them again.

CHAPTER 30

The winter months drag by. It is a snowier-than-usual winter, cold and windy. We manage to keep all the animals alive. In early March, the kids begin to drop. Each of the girls has twins, and every one of them survives.

Keeping the wolves from the door is no monetary metaphor here. Wolves are a real threat to our animals—as are the coyotes, weasels, pine martens, foxes. Nearly every four-legged creature considers our small farm a convenience store—milk, eggs, meat.

We keep to ourselves for the most part. Of course, Jack is present every day to help with the farm tasks that never end and always present new challenges. I can't help but warm to Jack as my uncle. My respect for him deepens. He is no longer to me just a steady helper, though a bit slow and limited. Now I see his strength, determination, and his gentle, fair-minded nature. I wonder if these are traits received from my grandmother Flora.

Ned shows signs of stress I've not seen in him before. He misses his sister. He misses time with his family.

"Why don't you bring them up here?" I offer.

But he won't do it. He says they'll never come in the winter. Never.

I urge him to go to Texas for a visit, but he refuses. He says he can't leave me right now—too much has happened.

I know he's right, but I hate that I'm the weak link in us. I can't seem to get my green light to work, but I should not be his red light. I make him go.

"Go. Go for a week, at least. Please. I've already talked to Mike about taking you to the airport, and he's offered to help out here while you're gone. He'll bring Jack every day."

"Are you sure?" Ned looks less hesitant.

"Jesus, Ned! Yes!"

While he's gone, I take advantage of the time alone to heal in my way without interruption.

The crystalline shimmer of snow cascading from the windswept treetops, the color-rich sunrises and sunsets through tamarack and pine, the wildlife tracks in deep snow, the otters at play by the riverbank—they can't dislodge the logjam of hurt. It is not until I take notice of the first bright red in the willow that I feel the grief lessen. A shift into the expansive openings of a new spring stir inside me.

I have my last breakdown and cry session. Nellie Jane and CiCi and LuLu and my youth and everything good that had gone from my life—I let it all fly the coop. I take tobacco to the grandfather Who Rock and cry out into the wind.

"*Wašté.*" It is done. "*Wopilah.*" Thank you.

Ned has been back for a week. I'm heartily glad to see him lighter of mood—light enough to engage in a bit of cowboy-on-cowgirl action. This morning, we've fed the animals, and Jack is bringing in a load of wood. I start breakfast and sit while the ham sizzles.

"So Ned, I've been thinking."

Ned refills his coffee mug and sits next to me.

"I would like to offer Nellie Jane's place to Uncle Terry. What do you think?"

As usual, Ned takes his time to reply, waiting to see if there is more coming from me before speaking.

"I think he's in assisted living for a reason," he finally says. "Didn't you say his health is poor?"

"He's frail. But maybe I should still make the offer, not that he'd take it. I don't know."

The pull I feel toward Terry is confusing. I've tried calling him many times since our last visit. I've left messages, but he hasn't responded.

"I don't know what else to do to draw him out. Everybody else has surfaced but Terry. I get his feeling of betrayal. I'm the only one who can begin to appreciate how he must have felt when he saw Nellie—Eleanora—at Billy's funeral. How do I get through to him?"

Jack is coming through the door with the wood. As always, he leaves tracks of snow in his wake. And as always, he wipes up the tracks on his way back through. I ask him to stay for breakfast—he always does, but he never once assumes the invitation.

As we're eating, Ned glances at Jack, then at me. "Perhaps you should run your idea past Jack," he suggests.

I explain my idea of offering Nellie Jane's place to Terry. When I'm through, I ask quietly, "So what do you think, Jack?"

He is hard at his meal, a forkful of eggs entering his mouth. He chews, swallows, then washes it down with orange juice before he replies.

"Leave him alone," Jack grunts without looking up from his meal.

"Why? Shouldn't he be given a chance to come together with everybody else?"

"Leave him alone."

Of course, I'm not satisfied with his answer. I want an answer that is a better match to my idea.

"Help me understand why, Jack." My request is sincere.

Jack thinks for a few minutes, then speaks. "You've seen a dog in a bear trap? That's why."

I don't know what Jack means—not entirely. It seems to me that a dog in a bear trap might need help getting out of the trap, help from someone to heal. That seems in line with my idea.

But Nellie Jane would have told me this logic is Iktomi, a trickster, at work. She would have said the dog is bait for the trap. The dog is a helper for the People, but he is caught in that trap—Iktomi's web. If you free the dog, will he be grateful, accept help to heal, and become a lifelong companion? Or will he snarl and snap and attack from fear and hurt?

I collect plates and silverware for washing up and leave the table without a word. Through the window above the kitchen sink, I look out to see three coyotes near the goat shed.

"Coyotes!" I shout.

The men jump to their feet, then to the window. The coyotes have disappeared.

I shake my head and wonder what Nellie Jane would have said about these phantom tricksters appearing at the edge of the change of seasons. I remind myself to remain vigilant until the earth once again slips out of dreamtime with the spring melt. And then I feel stupid. Why do I keep falling for the lure of Nellie Jane's worldview and life practice? She's not here. I'm not Lakota. She wasn't Lakota. I feel a burn of rage deep in my gut, but to my surprise, it does not take root to fester.

Spring is early. The snowmelt is rapid, but the ground is not thawed enough to absorb the runoff. The river overflows its banks, nourishing the marshland and washing clean the decay from autumn. It pulls the debris downstream to deposit the muck, with its cache of seeds, in new places.

Terrestrial life is beginning to stir—we are beginning to stir. I can feel excitement all around me now. The winter dreamtime has passed.

I am awake and in ways refreshed. I feel I may have been asleep my entire life. I've been waiting all this time for an apology or justification or resolution. Or maybe for truth. This year of grief has cleansed me of resentment and anger. The exhaustion in my core is lifted by the enthusiasm of renewed curiosity.

A dog in a bear trap, I muse.

It could be wise to consider that Terry might be the bait for a bear. Mercy, maybe? Paybacks are hell, right? I decide to leave the story to tell itself in its own way, without my interference. I hope I'm doing the right thing.

CHAPTER 31

We are invited to Jack's house for a family gathering to welcome Carl home to Capitol. I'm nervous about being confined with people I detest but excited to be in Jack's house.

We've never been invited to Jack's home. Ned's been to Jack's outbuildings a few times to help load tools or a piece of equipment for hauling here and there—most often to our place. That's it.

Unlike his wife, Ned is not curious a bit about what Jack's house will look like on the inside. Jack is always clean when he comes to us and careful to not leave evidence of where he's been. I don't know if that's a raised-Indian thing, or if he's a cleanliness is next to Godliness guy. Will his house be the same? Or will he need to ask Mercy to come over and clean before the big day? I think of bachelor housekeepers and cringe.

On occasion, I've visited the homes of some of the old bachelors and widowers in the area. These visits always involved Mercy and birthday pies and cakes, soups built from long-simmered stocks and home-grown vegetables, and sometimes complete pot roast meals. Nothing says love, care, and concern louder than Aunt Mercy's knock at an old codger's door.

One old guy had lost his wife ten years before and I swear hadn't cleaned a room since she departed. He did have a large poster of a World War II pinup girl positioned in front of piles of books and newspapers. It made me sad for his wife, who probably kept a spotless Finnish home, cooked and baked for him, and bore and raised his children to do better than this.

I like to ride along for these deliveries because I love seeing the inside of other people's houses. I grew up in a dustless, smudge- and spill-free zone, a place where dirt, grime, and jellied fingerprints were found unacceptable and punished with fierce scorn.

Virginia kept an immaculate house filled with fine, delicate, valuable objects—many smashed to smithereens during Billy's rages. I watched Virginia closely for any sign of despair or unhappiness when Billy destroyed the things she seemed to treasure. I say *seemed to* since those were the individuals in her life who received her care. I never saw her flinch. Not one time. She had something to prove to Billy, I guess—maybe that he couldn't break her, even when he broke her treasures and her bones.

While I'm sincerely eager to see Jack's home, I realize it's a convenient distraction. I'm ambivalent about Carl. I don't know much about him except that he ran away with Jack, then ran away again, this time without Jack. Carl left his adopted family as soon as he could and made his own way in the world—as a mortician, of all things.

He stared death in the face from the beginning. He stared at the barrel of the gun that killed his father, who murdered his mother, who lay dying in the same room as their dead—so reported—darling Eleanora. So how could he have left Jack, the more vulnerable of the two, to fend for himself? They were boys, only boys, who experienced crushing loss, leaving them suspended, alone, mid-childhood.

Carl, I decide, must be like Billy to have run off like that, to have seen to himself and his wants first and only. I know I won't like him. I feel a rise of loyalty to Jack, to protect the younger brother.

I know I should feel happy for Carl, that he's able to come home. For God's sake, he was a little boy when the family was ripped apart. Mercy and Jack and Carl all there for each other now because they've shared tragedy. But I have no siblings to share in my suffering. I'm alone in my pain.

And unlike Carl and Lydia and her bunch, I'm not counted as a member of the family. Not really. It makes me jealous. I'm hurt. I want to scream at them to let me in. Perhaps if I'd killed my father, I would have been welcomed into the fold, embraced as a hero.

I tell Mercy how I feel when I help her prepare food for the family event at Jack's.

Mercy sighs and shakes her head. "I know, dear, that you suffered. And I'm sorry that things worked out the way they did. It breaks my heart that you suffered so. I pray every day and night that you will heal and find comfort and some measure of peace. It is how I love you, because I can't fix what my brother did to you."

She reaches up to hold my face in her hands.

"But Ellen, I can't let you take this from us. We've waited so long to come home to each other. Can you let us have this time for ourselves?"

I cannot, but I say nothing. I hug her as if her words have meaning and can change anything. My tantrum can wait, maybe, for another time.

I am angry with Carl McInnis Farnsday. The boy ran away, and the man came back to feast on the fatted calf with his adoring and grateful siblings. They don't know him, not one thing about him, except that he sired a gorgeous, flaming-redheaded daughter who looks and feels to me like the devil's own spawn.

"You know," Mercy begins, "Carl arranged for carpenters and materials to arrive on Jack's land twenty-five years ago—without notice and without asking. Jack was living on the reservation in an old hunting shack with no running water before that. How Carl learned of this or why he responded to Jack's need for a house, no one knows. I suspect his tribal family sent the message that Jack needed much help."

I pull a roasted turkey from the oven and set it on the counter to cool before slicing. Mercy loads up the oven with a pan of sweet potatoes and one of apple pie squares. The kitchen table is covered in fresh salad ingredients.

I order Mercy to sit down and refresh herself with a glass of iced tea. It's been a long day of cooking, and I can see her begin to tire. I'm not tired, fueled by anger that has no real target.

"He built Jack a comfortable two-bedroom home with lots of light and storage areas as well as a mid-size barn and two large storage sheds," she continues, emphasizing the details of his generosity. "A new well was dug, and even some moderate landscaping was added. A new and sturdy fence line was installed as well. It would have held a herd of bison.

"When the construction was complete, the carpenters left without a word to anyone. I knew it was Carl's doing, even though he didn't reach out to me. All Jack knew was that he had a house. Once he moved in, we saw each other nearly every day around town, but I couldn't say anything about him being our brother." She casts an uncharacteristic glare. "I know what you're thinking—one more lie. It's the way it had to be until your father and Terry were no longer threats."

"No longer a threat? Did it ever once occur to you that Billy was taking his rage out on his wife and child? What would make us off limits to him? Nothing." I'm starting to get worked up again. "Never mind, Mercy. Never mind."

She lets it go, but I can see I hit my target. She's hurt now. I've wounded her. I broke through the fog of delusion that anyone in this family was ever safe. But I feel worse, not better. I took a potshot at Bambi and lamed her. There is no good end to this. I don't know what to do. Justice remains a mirage.

I will try to overlook the occasion of Carl's homecoming. Lydia Campbell and all her family will be there too. We will gather to celebrate the old man's return home on his eightieth birthday.

Mercy cannot mask her joy, even as she wears herself down to exhaustion. When we arrive on the day of the party to collect her, along with all that food, I find her napping.

As we pull into Jack's driveway, I do some fierce jaw-setting in preparation for the trouble that will certainly rise up today. But then it all washes away the minute I step inside the house.

The entryway is spotless. A closet in the entry opens to a well-organized space with plenty of available hangers and a large boot tray on the floor. A shelf above the closet pole holds neatly stacked scarves, knit hats, and gloves. Above that is another shelf, which holds canning jars—dozens of them packed in tightly, leaving not one inch of wiggle room. Each jar is labeled with the date it was canned and its contents, written in Mercy's hand.

After hanging our coats and shedding our boots, Ned and I make our way through the entry directly into the kitchen, where we offload all of Mercy's meal makings. The smell of a turkey roasting, mingled with other cooking odors, fills my nostrils and causes my stomach to growl.

From there, we walk through a short hallway to a large living room with an oversized hand-laid river stone fireplace. There are two old sofas—one blue floral and the other orange and green plaid—plus a couple of worn recliners. The walls are lined with shelves overflowing with books and magazines. A painting of lambs hangs above the fireplace. It looks to have been rescued from somebody's yard sale.

And there is the redhead, her father, and a blurred ball of other bodies. I frame, focus, and zoom in on Carl, the spitting image, though somewhat taller and more solidly built, of the now-quite-dead Billy McInnis. Ned, in anticipation of an eruption from me, circles his arm around my shoulder and presses my arm.

No one notices us. Jack hovers over Carl. Mercy comes behind Carl and reaches her arms around to embrace him. He does not bother to raise himself out of the recliner.

"Oh!" I hear Mercy exclaim as she kisses him and kisses him again on his cheek. "Oh!"

"Hello, Mercy," he speaks without making any effort to see her face. "Now, get off me."

Not to be rebuffed, Mercy moves to face him, then hands him a bag of homemade caramels. "I remember these are your favorite."

Carl takes the bag and sets it on the table beside his chair. "Hmm. You got any more Scotch there, brother?"

Jack smiles a smile of adoration. "Sure, Carl. Sure."

I can hear Lydia—oh God, Lydia—clucking. "Let me help you with that, Dad."

This is a waking nightmare. Lydia is the breadcrumb trail that takes me to this man, this man who is my father's brother, only bigger.

There is a shriveling at work inside me, in my brain, in my groin, in my knees that have gone wobbly. I feel that I might disintegrate, like a wicked witch melts when attacked full-on by a bucket full of water.

I can hear the happy sounds I always imagined good families might make when gathered together for a celebration. But more, I hear the sound of my heart beating. I am flushed, like a grouse roused from the serenity of its meadow home. I feel the bird busting through the underbrush, out into the open, where the hunters will surely shoot it and their dogs will tear it apart, wing from wing.

How much does Carl know? Fear of exposure will do me in.

I've got to get a grip. Carl is not Billy. I push my wilting body into Ned's side. He kisses my head and leads me back into the kitchen, where we are alone.

"What do you want to do?" he asks, as if he thinks I know what I want to do.

I'm paralyzed. Every sensory memory is whipped up into impending catastrophe. The flashes are not merely visual. I feel them, and my mind breaks. Pieces. Chunks.

"Take me home." I lean against his chest. "Take me home."

I don't want to start screaming or crying here.

"No, wait," I suddenly say. "Give me a moment."

My mind is quick to recover from the shock—it's used to these assaults, I suppose. Recover or retreat into insanity, these are my choices.

"I don't know how to explain this to you," I say.

"You don't have to. But,"—he presses my head into his chest, "I am getting you a glass of wine."

I smile the smile of an all-knowing and forgiving God. "Do that. Even Jesus had a little wine with his betrayal."

Ned makes his way to the living room, where I hear Mercy's voice. "Oh, Ned, dear! Where's Ellen?"

I look out into the room, unobserved by the others.

"She's doing something in the kitchen," he replies. "I came to get some wine, if you have any."

"Oh, yes. I will get a couple of glasses for you. But first . . ."

Mercy's arm then slips around Ned's arm, and she leads him to Carl's throne. Of course that's what's happening.

"Carl." Her voice is tender as she speaks to him. "This is your niece Ellen's husband, Ned."

And then I hear words from Carl I cannot believe. "We've met."

What the fuck?

After Mercy hands him two wine glasses, Ned returns to the kitchen a traitor, not a savior. Adrenaline beats his return, though. My fight-face is on, fists are clenched.

"You've *met*?"

He puts the glasses down between us but remains standing. "Yes. I met him when he first arrived. Jack asked me to help get Carl's things into Nellie Jane's house. We were at the store, about to head home. Have I committed a crime?"

"Why didn't you tell me?"

He pauses for a beat. "You want the truth?"

"Yes."

"I forgot about it."

"You know your married life exists in a mine field, right?" I feel he needs reminding. "All the mines are invisible but lit up. Any misstep will quite literally blow my mind."

Ned chuckles and sits. "I know. I know. And there's absolutely nothing I can do about it except hope I don't detonate anything."

He takes my hand. His hand feels good in mine.

"I'm sorry," I say.

"Don't be," he says as he reaches for the bottle of wine and pours us each a glass. "This is hard. And I'll admit I don't understand most of it, but I'm here. We've had a lot of years together before this, so we know each other. We know our bottom line. You'll be okay. You're a fighter. Maybe your opponents of late have knocked the wind out of you at every go. But honey, you're still on your feet."

I point toward the living room. "Did you ever think Billy could be bigger? Spitting image, but bigger."

"Is that what happened? He looks like your father?"

"That's right. You never met him." I stare through the wall as though my eyes could shoot a spear into Carl right through the plasterboard. "He can't be badder, though. As annoying as Lydia can be, she doesn't seem to be, well, like me. She likes her father. Dotes on him."

My wine glass now drained, I straighten myself for a move to the living room.

"But," I add in a near whisper, "there is something wrong with her, and I'd bet money Carl's the source."

I announce myself to Carl with the command of a general and an outstretched hand. "I'm Ellen, Carl—your brother Billy's one and only."

He ignores my hand and finishes his drink without a look up at my face. This, of course, pisses me off.

"How's the whiskey, Uncle? Gettin' enough?"

"Ellen!" Mercy is horrified.

The redhead glares.

Ned is quiet, waiting to see what I might do next.

The children ignore the grownups and continue to play with some rabbit pelts they found somewhere in the house.

Jack reaches for Carl's glass to get him a refill. He won't look at me either. He looks sad. Moments before, he was an elderly man who held his height and showed his strength maintained through daily work with the land and animals. Now he appears shrunken and stooped, his inner light dimmed.

I watch Mercy croon around Carl and softly pat Jack, her back to me. I am the one who ruined this reunion for them. I couldn't wait for the whiskey to do it.

Mercy speaks, still turned from me. "Dear, please, not today."

She is interrupted by Lydia, who comes at me with fire in her belly. "You will not speak to my father that way, Ellen. You know nothing of him or us or anything. Shut up!"

And there it is, family as I've always known it. Let the brawl begin.

I take Ned's hand and walk us both back into the kitchen. "Knowing this family's history with alcohol, you'd think . . ."

I let the words trail. Nobody was thinking about alcohol, only about Carl.

Ned focuses a steady gaze over my head. I can tell he's conflicted.

"A couple of drinks don't make a Billy, Ellen. Take some time with these people before you jump in and lose control. I'd like to see what good can happen in this family. I'm curious. And one more thing, what's about to happen in that room and on ahead is not about you, not one bit."

"Oh, I'm sure there will be bright, sunny days ahead for the McInnis clan reunited."

I'm snarky but in control. I know Ned doesn't mean to challenge me. He's trying to share his thoughts for consideration. He thinks we can be rational about Carl and Lydia and the lot of them. He thinks we're both like him. He's forgotten everything we talked about not fifteen minutes earlier in this room.

He is right, though, about the center of the universe for these old people. It isn't me. It is never me. I can feel my loving family connection with Mercy, what I've ached for all my life, being usurped by Carl. Actually, he is not taking it from me. It has always been his to take back. That hurts me worse than anything. I do not exist for them.

"I can never understand what this must be like for them," I begin.

I'm trying my best to be thoughtful, to approach my emotional distress with rational talk about them as the *other*.

"They're like old soldiers who survived a gruesome battle. They're done. They've served their time. But they can't see that the war rages on. I'm still in it, and they don't care. They don't. They can't see me as collateral damage. They don't know about the minefield established by Billy and Virginia, set to explode at the slightest touch or provocation. But Mercy does," I add.

Panic surges again. I can't let this take me down.

We return to the living room, where I keep a watchful distance from the family. I notice a slight smile of pride returning to Jack's face. I have to capitulate for him, an old man living his dream. Jack is happy. Jack's happiness means more to me than my urge to fight with the rest of them. Today is a day to let things be.

The roomful of relatives reads like something from the Bible. I thought I was nearly alone in the world, and now I see my place in the list of McInnis family begats. Carl's son, Max, and his wife, Annabelle, and their kids, Joe and Stephie, ten and eight years respectively, are in attendance. Lydia's children, Elizabeth Janet and her husband, Allan, with his niece, Judy, and Charlie the golden retriever of course, have also come for the reunion. There is also her sister Madeline with her husband, Freddie. If not for Carl, there would be no other children to take this family forward.

I watch Lydia carefully and find her to be fair and pleasant, although a little too accommodating of her father for my taste. And the hairs still bristle at the nape of my neck whenever I stumble into her because, of course, she is always underfoot. And then there's always Carl, who looks too much like Billy and drinks a lot of Scotch.

I can feel a headache building. I want to go home.

CHAPTER 32

I'm ready for Lydia's call the following Tuesday. She asks if we can meet. I know she wants to purchase Nellie Jane's cabin. She hopes she's charmed me enough with the weekend display of harmonious family life.

Mercy is ready for everyone to come home before she dies. I know she's lonely for Nellie Jane. I can't shut the door on her brothers and nieces and nephews, can I? Jack's the one who sold me, though. He perked up the minute I was nice to Carl. I realize I hold power over him. I don't like the feeling or the responsibility.

If Lydia hadn't called me, I would have called her. Within the week, the deal is made. The cabin is sold. *Come on, summer. Come on, Carl.* I'm ready for him, for all of them.

I make Lydia pay through the nose. Nellie Jane often talked about feeding the people. It's a way to give back, she'd say. So I give the sale money to Ned's churchwomen to reach more families with fresh food.

Mercy and I are cleaning Nellie Jane's house. I don't want a single thing of hers to be passed on to her brother's family—my choice to make since Nellie Jane left this place to me at her death.

"Aunt Mercy, I remember how stressed I was about why Nellie Jane would leave the house to me. It seems a million lives ago."

Mercy does not reply. She's picking through dishware and cookware and kitchen towels.

"Why can't we leave these things for Carl's family?"

"I don't want to. I want to see them with their own stuff, not mixed with memories of Nellie Jane. I don't want to see Nellie Jane's favorite quilt wrapped around a toddler and have my feelings for her trapped into a little person I don't know."

"But I think she would have liked to see her things with her family."

"Here's a news flash for you, Mercy. I am her family. You don't seem to recognize that. When I was a child, you saw in me what you wanted to see. The mere fact that my mother would drop me off at your house and drive away without a word should have raised a question or two, but you didn't want to know."

I'm pacing, fidgeting, fighting against myself to tell her the truth of how I feel about her.

"Clearly you discussed concerns with Nellie Jane. She acted on those concerns in the only way she was allowed—after her death. I wasn't so much as an empty frame to your family story. Nellie Jane is the one who painted me into the family portrait by leaving me her things. I struggle with this, Mercy.

"You convinced me that Nellie Jane knew about Carl's family, but still, she left these things for me. She actually saw me, felt me, cared for me enough to show consideration for my wellbeing and my future. I accept this as her demonstration of that care and concern. You wouldn't let me have the relationship with her—with any of you—that I deserved to have. So I'm keeping what she gave me and not giving away any of it to them. I'm just not doing it."

"I'm sorry, dear." Mercy is in tears. "I've done this all wrong."

Those doe-like eyes look up at me and whisk away my rage. I sit with her.

"You haven't done it all wrong. You took care of your siblings as your heart told you to do and as the adults in your life instructed. You just forgot about me. And you forgot about me because of Billy, my father. You had to keep me at a distance. I get it. I don't like it and it has messed with me, but I get it."

I feel her distress and appreciate her honesty.

"And now, back to it." I turn my back to her and keep sorting Eleanora's things into a giveaway pile.

I had removed Nellie Jane's casket quilts early on. I don't want to explain them. When the time comes for each to be offered to the deceased, I will do so with a note, offering condolences and explaining who crafted the quilt.

It's hard to shake free from the way of life she taught. I found her way of thinking to be a comfort. I have no other coping methods. Her guidance strengthens my resolve to work harder and smarter to heal and to overcome.

I want to believe that she saw me as I am, an abandoned and broken child. But still, it strains my thinking to imagine how she—and Mercy, for that matter—could have kept me at arm's length while knowing full well I needed to be welcomed into loving arms. Fair and cruel she was to me. Fair and cruel. But I get it now. I hate it, but I get it.

Mercy and I spend a week together, emptying out Eleanora's house. Some of the contents go to Jack. I let him pick what he wants. He's thorough and thoughtful in his selection, obvious in his silent gratitude as he receives Eleanora's things.

I love Jack, my Uncle Jack. I do want to see him with Nellie Jane's things. He too was left in the dark on the night of the murders, when he ran away into the woods with his brother.

Jack is my opposite. He's tender. He's uncomplicated. His scars are visible. He's the person I'd like to see reflected back to me from my own mirror, but I know that will never happen. How is it, I wonder, that we can be so different?

I picture Billy raping me and at the same time, I hear Nellie Jane's drum. I have my answer. They were raised in a way of seeing whole things. I was not.

Most of the furniture and household items are sent back to the reservation. That place with those people brought Nellie Jane back to life for us, not for themselves. She taught me the importance of giving back. This is a way to honor her.

I keep a rug in addition to her chair and the quilts, which are already home. Mercy salvages a few items.

The windows are opened, the floors and walls are washed, and the porch is swept. I sit on the top step, burn some sage, and thank everybody.

"*Mitákuye oyás'iŋ. Pilamaya*. It's all yours." I stand, turn back, and close and lock the door. "Goodbye for now," I whisper as I walk to my car.

And it's done. *Wašté*.

Mid-April to late May is seed-starting, birthing, and cleanup time. Ned reinforces the animal pens and cleans the sheds. I rake and shovel and till the gardens once the ground thaws. Cold frames protect young sprouts and boast success in the form of collards, kale, curly spinach, and pea tendrils. We open the greenhouse for the onions and celery started in March. I can see the buds fattening on the apple trees and the raspberry canes.

Before heading back to the house, I walk to the shed to put away my rake and garden gloves. The smell in the air is rich with earth. Bird songs are energizing. I love this time of year up north, almost more than any other. It's easy to see how what is old can be reused in some way to help what's coming along into new life.

The force of life in a seed that rests in a cupboard for six to seven months can pop right through its dried shell into a lively green sprout. I know we can nourish families of all types of creatures for three seasons, even longer if we harvest and store some of its fruits as seed.

All the fresh green that emerges from the last of the snow in the pasture is luscious forage for the goats. It is made for nutrient-rich milk and cheese.

I love my perennial flowers too. They need little from me yet provide beauty and, from some, even sustenance. The tiny violas, the lungwort, the brunnera, and the crocus all signal the passing of winter but can easily survive a sneak return of a mild frost.

This spring, I feel I can breathe again. My lungs let loose from all I've been holding back—the grief, fear, all of it. It exhales out of me into the spring winds.

Ned gets lucky, often. He's been generous with his support of me and my array of struggles. I've come to welcome him for me—not just to me. He is steady and reliable in his quiet, deliberate way. He loves me and, finally, I love him back the way he deserves.

The season brings renewal to my mind too. I realize now that Billy not only tried to kill Eleanora but also tried to kill my spirit. Even as I age, I have to work to keep alive love and desire, even want.

Some days, I tire of the labor. It's those days I'm most grateful for the farm, for Ned, and even for Jack. In the past, this was an evil place, but I feel it has, with our care and Jack's guidance, come alive again, to create something wonderful for now and into the future.

"Coyotes!" I hear a shout from outside.

I run outside to see Jack herding the goats back into their shed. I jump and yell all at once. Ned, from the den, grabs his rifle and runs out into the dusky twilight. I'm right behind him. These are no shape-shifting trickster Indian spirits. These are two warm-blooded, four-legged coyotes on the hunt.

Ned fires a warning shot into the air that sends them scurrying for the time being. We know they'll be back, but probably not tonight. It's springtime in the woods. Wild babies of every ilk are quick to catch and be killed for a meal. Jack secures the goats in the barn and makes a quick inspection of the fencing outside the chicken coop.

Ned jumps in the truck to give Jack a ride.

"Thanks, Jack," I say before he climbs in next to Ned. "I thought you'd gone home."

"Nope. Waiting for Ned." He speaks in the same deliberate monotone as though nothing exciting has happened.

My adrenaline is kicked into full gear, making my heart race. On my way back to the house, I feel something new, fresh rise inside. I feel grateful and happy and safe.

CHAPTER 33

I learned from Nellie Jane that to feed others is to feed them your prayers. "Be careful in the preparation of your mind and heart before preparing food to eat," she would often remind me.

Preparation of food is Ned's area. I eat as I think—on the move. And I'm constantly on the move. Since I care so little for most other people, to be prayerful or thoughtful of them is outside my reach.

But when Ned prepares a meal, it's a blessing wrapped up in the bliss of biscuits and savory sausage gravy or any concoction that flows sweetly from aroma to palate. It looks simple when he does it. It tastes like home and love and sometimes adventure. I can cook a chicken in all kinds of ways, but it's never great, just okay, certainly never memorable. When Ned does it, it's all kinds of wonderful.

I've been out in the garden all morning, tilling and soil-prepping, hauling straw bales to mulch rows. At my age and rate of speed these days, what gets done before I'm done in is less and less. Mike stops by with his brother, who is visiting from Colorado. I wave them off to the barn, where Ned and Jack are clearing brush.

I don't know how Jack accomplishes all that he does so quickly. I don't think he ever smoked. That may be the thing that makes all the difference. I used to smoke and drink and carry on as though I meant each day to be my last. I don't feel that way anymore.

Wait. I do feel each day may be my last—especially when I'm tipping a wheelbarrow full of manure—but I don't want it to be my last. I want my "now" to sustain and to continue on.

Each day, I wake up more open to Ned and to my life with him. I know life is temporary. I've got twenty or thirty years left maybe, but I want more from it now. It's about time I feel real love, the abiding love offered up by the poets.

I'm healing. This place, with all its ugly surprises, has brought healing. I am no longer orphaned to evil. I am home. I ache for CiCi and Nellie Jane and LuLu. But I'm okay—better than okay.

Back at the house, I walk through the cooking smells in the kitchen to get to the bathroom for a deep cleansing shower. There is little contrast to the hot of the kitchen and the hot of my body from the outside work, even though the spring temperatures are still in the low 40s. The shower feels great.

In my bedroom, I bundle up in my oversized, bunny-headed fleece robe, put my hair up in a clip to air-dry, and head to the den to pour myself a stiff Sunday pre-siesta drink. Halfway down the hall, I let out a scream like a rabbit caught in the jaws of a fox. Fucking Lydia, the Uninvited, ambushes me in the hallway, waving a cardboard cylinder.

"Hi, El." She pushes past me. "I'm just going in there for a moment." She points to the bathroom door.

I'm sure she's never spoken the word "bathroom"—probably always calls it "the ladies" in the most demure, coquettish way.

The apology for scaring me half to death does not come. Big surprise. I head to the kitchen. Ned is nowhere in sight. He must still be outside with the other men. I check on the meal. Nothing needs immediate attention.

I veer back toward the den to continue my pursuit of Sunday afternoon libation. But no, hard liquor is not calling. I turn to plod back to the kitchen to check in the fridge for an open bottle of wine. And again, I run, literally, into Lydia.

"Lydia!" I can't help my exasperation.

"Excuse me, Ellen."

She speaks with her trademark sweet lilt. She leads me into my own kitchen and seats herself at my table. The definition of *gall* is . . .

I find the wine in the fridge, but now I shake my head. I shut the refrigerator door and move myself back to the den to snare a bottle of the hard stuff after all. I pour a glass of bourbon, neat. I slog back to the kitchen. My mood is blown from a healthy, vibrant, prideful, little-bit-happy state to gloom and dread.

"Why are you in my house?" My exasperation is clear, loud. But the shot goes wide. Lydia ignores the question.

"I saw Ned out by the shop and he waved me into the house. I want to talk to you about Eleanora's place. Is this a good time?"

Still fresh from the shower, dressed in my bunny-headed robe, and with my clipped-up hair dripping onto my shoulders and back, I realize she is incapable of recognizing a good time.

So I say, "Sure." I sit down to take a swig of my drink. "What about the house?"

"I want to let you know we'll be expanding the structure. I wonder if you'd like to see the plans." She holds up the cardboard cylinder.

I don't know what to say. She's such a twit. I stare at her, glass in hand, and try to think of some way—short of a shotgun shell—to get her ass out of my life.

She and hers will be here to stay for generations beyond me, I imagine. They'll likely own this farm some day and Jack's place and

Mercy's. Like a glacier, they'll creep over any claim I may have and turn my story into a footnote, if that, to their own grand saga.

Ned and Jack come in, smelling of brush smoke. Their cheeks flush with heat from the fire. They're laughing. I don't often hear Jack laugh. It's not a belly buster, but the softest roll of sounds of pleasure. But Lydia's presence hijacks my moment of enjoyment.

The men hang up their coats, remove their boots, and one after the other head for the bathroom to wash up for dinner. Ned returns first to check on his meal.

"The other guys had to get home. We ran later than I thought we would. We got to talking, and the time just went along and away." He's smiling as he lifts a pot lid and comments to himself, "We'll freeze the extra for the next poker night. You staying for dinner?" This request is directed at Lydia.

"Oh, I hadn't thought to—"

"Lydia, go home," I cut her off.

She looks to Ned for support. To my surprise, she gets none.

Instead, Ned gives her instructions. "Thanks for coming by with the plans. We'll look them over later."

"Oh . . . I . . . yes. We'll talk then."

As she rises from the table to leave, I head back into the den for another shot of booze. When I hear the door shut at my back, I release my anger into a guttural sigh of relief.

Ned serves up the stew with the roasted carrots glazed in maple syrup, twice-baked potatoes, and a colorful salad of red and green romaine, tomato slices, feta cheese, figs, and vinaigrette I put together. He gives me an approving nod. Peach cobbler with fresh cream ends the feast. I revel in every bite.

After dinner, I clear the table and clean the kitchen, leaving Jack and Ned to study Lydia's blueprints. I notice a beautiful glow on Jack's face brought on by hope, I suppose—hope of a familial future. And he, out of all of us, should be the cynic. At this moment, I'm grateful he is not ruined as I am ruined. I'm grateful to witness the blush of innocence on his rugged, white-whiskered old face.

Before bed, Ned and I sit together in the den, reviewing Lydia's plans to transform the old house. Nellie Jane's former home will have a grand front porch and patio. Three new sleeping rooms are to be added. The kitchen will be expanded and modernized. It will be the largest home in the town. There will be little land left, as the gardens will be razed for bathrooms, a family room, and storage space.

This is not to be a summer cottage at all. This is a planned retirement compound for the Carl McInnis-turned-Farnsday clan.

And why on earth, I wonder. There is nothing here in Capitol but wilderness and aging family members. Why here? The fishing isn't that great. The summer is short. It's a long drive to anywhere for groceries and gas. What are they thinking?

Ned can read my confusion. "Honestly, Ellen, I don't know what to think." He pauses. "She told me she'd also like to buy this farm when we're ready to leave."

Apparently, Lydia spoke to Ned at some length before he "waved" her into the house.

"For now, she'd like to lease the land we're not using and begin to prep it for future farming."

"I don't want her here. When we're gone, I don't care what she does. But I don't want her in my space all the time—and she would be. I don't trust her."

Ned listens, knowing I don't trust much or many, anyway.

"You can't take Nellie Jane's place back. And you wouldn't want to. Mercy and Jack are happy to have their family here. Lydia could be on the hunt for a foundation, like you were. That's what brought us here. I'm sure Carl made it clear to her that this is a place that few know exists and where less would want to live. But a living can be made here, if you know what you're doing."

It is true. Families have been here since the town was founded. People still know acres by the family name of the original owners. We found warmth here and welcome by the locals. I feel more accepting of life as it is each day because of being here.

But these Farnsdays, man—they're not casual people. Lydia is determined in a way that unnerves me.

"And don't forget," Ned continues, "Carl and Jack's story is the stuff epics and sagas are made of. They're the heroes, the winners, in this tragic tale of good triumphing over evil. Maybe in Lydia's mind, Capitol, the old farmstead, is hers to reclaim."

Is it possible that my hero's story plays a bit role next to theirs? How do I wrap my mind around that? No wonder Lydia rankles me.

"You may be onto something with the hero's tale idea," I tell him.

"What do you mean?"

"Well, what you said gives me a new perspective. She might well believe she and hers are superior to me, that I am a minor character to be brushed aside as good takes all."

"I know, I know—you're family too, and that hits a nerve. You don't think they see you as part of that."

Anger rekindles into a roaring blaze. "Part. They only see me as an extra because their story is the only story. But it isn't. Billy's effect is every bit as powerful on my life as on theirs."

Ned winces at the rage in my voice, but I continue, now on my feet.

"And to keep them comfortable, I must concede that truth, every time I'm with any of them. They are in it together, and I'm on the periphery, letting them have their story, their way. I'm generous, and they don't know."

Adrenaline pumps my heart hard as the truth, the core of it, spits out of my mouth.

"I feel crazy. I feel Billy all over me while they willfully ignore his attacks."

"First, Ellen, I get what you're saying." His look is sincere. "Second, you need to sit down. I can get you a pill, if you want. I don't need you to have a stroke. You should see the veins in your neck and your head. You're on the edge of something I don't want to see happen."

His arms around me now, he walks me into the den as he would a child. He settles me into my favorite chair by the window. I feel the residual adrenaline nesting in my muscles and mood. My eyes stare, focused on nothing, as the truth settles in.

"Wow. That's the whole of it, right there, isn't it? We came here together for me. I wanted family love, support, inclusion. I fell in love with the farm. You fell in love with the farm. You have friends here. But I have nothing now. Nothing."

Ned is frustrated. "That's not true. You have me and a lifestyle that's new, and you like it. Yes, your family disappointed you again. Where is the surprise?"

I'm so tired of trying to find ways to explain myself to him and everybody else. "Think of it this way. I'm like that sapsucker, Ned—the one I tried to save in the winter by feeding it syrup. It died anyway. It died because it was fucking winter! No amount of nature's sweet nectar was going to save the hide of that poor bird. I'm like that bird.

I'm trying to stay alive under the harshest conditions. I can feel the sticky crap of trying all over my mouth, and it tastes like Lydia and the rest of them and their agenda. Do I just keep sucking up the syrup until I freeze to death?"

"I'm not sure I follow—"

"Every interaction I have with these people—Lydia, Carl, Mercy, even Jack in some ways—feels like they're taking something from me. Billy. They're all like Billy. To make nice, I shut up about it. I have to allow myself to be used by people who cannot love me and who can't even be interested in me unless they want something from me. I do this because I don't want to leave what we've built. I don't want frustration and, yes, disappointment to run me off. But that doesn't stop the invasion. I'm dying inside, little by little, because I'm so hurt to still be the outsider, out in the cold."

I'm starting to feel guilty. After all, Mercy and I had a come-to-Jesus moment about this, yet I'm still stuck on it.

"Aren't you overthinking this? Can't it be an imperfect new day?"

"I'd like nothing better, asshole!" It's not normal for me to call him that.

I shrug. Ned winces. "It's not just over-thinking, it's over-*feeling!* It's too much, with the lies and the denials. And you know what I struggle with the most? They don't seem to suffer any consequence while I'm in agony."

"No consequences? You think they've suffered no consequences?"

"That's not what I mean. I know in the past, yes, it was awful. But they have something now that is whole and happy, and I don't get to be included."

Ned has reached his limit. "Maybe you exclude yourself."

"Oh, Jesus. This again? Sure, I can be the suck-it-up Pollyanna. 'Everything is fine. No matter how we got here, it's good now, so that's good enough.' Well, it isn't good enough for me."

"Honestly, Ellen, if we're to stay here—and we don't have to, you know that. But if we do stay, you'll have to figure this out in a way that doesn't hurt you. And here's the thing for me" His look puts a knot in my belly. "I don't want to be in agony with you all the time, wondering when the next meltdown is coming."

I can tell we've reached the edge of this argument. It's making a turn, going the wrong way. I feel punched in the face.

"Fuck you."

"I'm telling you my truth now. I want to enjoy the rest of my life, with you if possible. But I do not want to be jumping on and off this carousel of drama all the time."

"Well, Ned, I'm going to let you in on a big, fat truth. The fallout from child rape and neglect has no expiration date. Fuck you!"

I storm off. Ned objects, and I tell him to fuck off again.

Screaming and muttering, I disappear out of the house and into the shack. I curl up in a recliner, shocked again by too much emotion.

Let's see—is this the eighteen-hundredth time I've been in shock since Billy's death?

I don't know what to do, but I'm determined to not give in to devastation this time. In some way, Ned's challenge clears the fog in my head. Maybe I need to see that I can take him to his limit.

Or maybe, just maybe, I need to see clearly that everyone, absolutely everyone—except CiCi—thinks I'm broken and need fixing. They think there can only be a good outcome if I just do what I'm supposed to do and make everything easy for them.

It doesn't work that way!

I stand up with conviction and return to the house to face Ned. He's in the living room, sitting, staring out the picture window. He turns his head toward me, his face without expression.

"Thanks, Ned. You've helped me enter a new level of hell. Nice for you that nobody ever hurt you or tore up your soul and body. In this level of hell, we all can tell the truth—that this shit doesn't get cured. It is who we are. We are here together with our abusers. We cannot escape."

I can't keep doing this. But I have to. I feel like I'm buried alive, crying for help. I have to keep screaming until someone hears me, finds me.

"Here's the good news. Here's what you want to hear, I can heal from this, too. But here's the news you don't want to hear. You are not allowed—nor is anyone else—to ever again suggest that I should do anything for *your* fucking comfort."

I take a step back from him and rein in my rage.

Ned stands, fills the space I've opened between us, and takes my hand.

"The next time you call me an asshole will be the last crack you get at me. We can either sort this out together or apart. This has been a tough couple of years, and you're wearing me out. It's not my job to fix you, nor is it to unconditionally support your every moody eruption. You have a therapist. Go see her."

I am thunderstruck. A tear puddles in my eye and slips away like a thief with a precious jewel. It is smug as it trickles down my face.

"That's so ugly." I crumple to the floor. "I meant to see her." I say in a small child's voice, barely loud as a whisper.

"I don't care. Figure it out."

I flash on Nellie Jane in her kitchen, an empty chair waiting for an unexpected guest and enough food prepared with hope and love to fill the belly of anyone who might arrive. She would have taken Lydia in, just as she took me in. She would have taught me to see a larger world beyond my own pain.

Eleanora as Nellie Jane wasn't healed, she was covered up. But she was given into a family who gave the gift of love. Now I see why she gave me her house. She couldn't give me the truth, that there is no cure for my illness. But she could give me love and shelter. The least I can do for her is to pass that shelter on to Lydia. As for Ned, I need to leave him alone for a while. I pack for the cabin and write him a note.

Message received. In Ely.

CHAPTER 34

I see her—Grandma Flora. I see her on a walk through the woods. She is smiling—no, laughing. Her fingers are weaving through a young boy's hair. Billy. This is Billy and his mother. She is beautiful. He is loved.

I wake with a start. *Billy was loved by his mother.*

Billy's loving, gentle mother died as her beloved son raged against her youngest daughter, Eleanora, in the way his father raged against her, forcing her soul into heaven. And from the long-suffering Flora, I imagine, not a whimper.

Up and dressed, I sit with a mug of fresh, steaming coffee out on the porch to let myself think about this dream. This is the fourth day at the cabin and time to go home. Mental notes stack up about work and my therapist. I already feel better. Ned gave me the kick in the pants I needed. I'm ready to start over without tantrums and wallowing.

At home, I see Ned walking from the barn to the storage shed. Mike Patterson's pickup is here. The men are doing whatever men do when women are not watching.

He is happy here, I think. He likes the engineering opportunities of a small farm. He's installed three high tunnels—one will grow an orchard of dwarf apple trees. He attended a farm tour five hours west of here earlier this summer and was amazed to learn how high tunnel technology could speed up the growth and maturity of these trees, allowing them to produce a viable crop in only one year.

I'm on board with anything that produces a fruit pie or cobbler. I know we can't leave this place.

The guys are working on a hydroponic system too. Fresh greens year around is their goal. They've submitted numerous grant applications to help them set up a rural distribution center for their produce. They want to store and deliver locally grown foodstuffs to the isolated families here in the northern forests, a more sustainable plan than Mercy's pot roast deliveries.

We won't be moving anywhere, which means I have to get my head on straight here at the McInnis family farm.

Billy was loved. Why does that come up now? *You were loved.* No. Neither parent . . . *Eleanora loved you.* She loved me from the beginning of me, but I didn't know.

I run into the house, tear into the stash of Nellie Jane's quilts, grab one plus the car keys, and race toward Mercy. I see it now. I see.

Please don't let Lydia be there. Please.

No one is at Mercy's house, not even Mercy. Up at Nellie Jane's old house, signs of preliminary construction are everywhere. But there in the small, untouched garden of perennials is Mercy, snipping a bouquet and probably harvesting herbs.

"Hello, dear," she says. "I hoped you would stop by today."

She's hoped that every day for weeks, I bet. I snatch her up and hug her. "Let's have some coffee and a chat."

She accepts a sound and grounded kiss on the cheek, and back to her house we stroll, arm in arm.

It feels good to serve Mercy coffee in her kitchen, to sit talking as we did so often before Lydia.

"I went to Ely for a few days," I tell her. "You know how that settles me. Ned and I had an awful fight. The argument forced me to take a hard look at my behavior and reasons for my behavior."

"Are you all right now? And Ned?"

"Actually, I haven't seen him to speak to yet. I wanted to see you first. I had a dream about Grandma Flora and Billy. She showed me how she loved her boy."

At that, Mercy's face relaxes, with decades of relief falling away. Her eyes are moist with tears. I never allowed Mercy her horrors or the raw pain of her battle to keep quiet the baby of the lie that wanted to scream to the world, "My sister! My sister! My ma!"

Her tears flow as I hold her against me as any mother would a suffering child. It is my turn. This, I believe, is the legacy left for the women McInnis, to find the mother who will birth the love lost to each one. I grieve silently for myself, that I didn't know to open my arms to Eleanora, who would have collapsed utterly into my offering of mother love.

"I don't know what went wrong with Billy," I tell her as I hold her, "but I could almost hear Grandma Flora's voice pleading with me to end the pain. And I knew at that moment that I had turned all love to fear and hate and pain and competition. I couldn't get here fast enough to tell you that I will stop now—or die trying. I can figure this out. I can stop hating Lydia and Carl. I can figure it out."

Mercy's soft and kind old face shines with love and thankfulness. I want to look over my shoulder to see if her Jesus stands behind me. I suppose this is what it means to be on the cross for others—you give it all up, ghost and all. But you come back, resurrected into new life, a life that can see forgiveness without judgment. Life can only cloud the view. It takes death to clean the slate.

Wašté.

At the house, we settle into the kitchen chairs. The kitchen is full of light. I share with Aunt Mercy a dream I once had. In the dream, it was Christmas, and I was young. I crept into the living room, dark but for the colored lights of the season. They dressed up the night with a welcome to magic, a wonder to my child's eyes. I could hear laughter and quiet chatter coming from the kitchen. I peeked into the room to see her and Uncle Terry wrapping gifts, their faces happy in smiles.

Mercy nodded to Uncle Terry, who looked up from his wrapping to see my small face sneaking a peek through the doorway.

"Come here, child," he beckoned to me. "Come and sit with us and have some warm milk."

I crawled up into one of the wooden chairs at the table and waited in silence for the milk to come.

"Why are you out of bed?" Terry asked me.

"I woke up."

He smiled at me. Mercy set a mug of warm milk in front of me on the cluttered tabletop.

"Did you have a dream?" he asked.

"I did." I nodded and sipped at my milk. "I did have a dream." I started to cry. "I had a bad dream."

"Well, you're awake, and you're safe now. You'll always be safe with us, safe from any harm." He patted my small hand. "You know we love you, don't you?"

I nodded, knowing it was true—that they loved me and I was safe. I was happy.

"This dream of Billy and your mother, it was like that too," I tell Mercy. "It was warm and full of peace and promise." I start to cry. "I'm so very sorry for all the trouble I've caused."

Mercy reaches for my hand, but I'm already up and out of my chair, and turning toward the door.

"I'll be right back."

And I leave her there alone to live with my words as I rush out of the house, to the car, to get the quilt I brought along. It is the one Nellie Jane made for her sister. I want to tell Mercy about the quilts and to let her put hers aside for the day she will join Eleanora.

Back in the house, Mercy is slumped over the table. At first, I think she's thinking, maybe, about what I said before I went outside. But she doesn't move. She doesn't lift her head to see me carrying her quilt, her death robe.

I've killed her by crossing the threshold of life and death with this floral prognostication draped across my shoulder. A screech billows up like rancid smoke from my chest. I can taste her death on my tongue. The room spins. The pressure builds. I cannot stop screaming in my head. I punch in Ned's number and leave a message to come to Mercy's, now. I know I have to get to the co-op. I have to get help. I have to tell someone, anyone, that Mercy is dead.

Across the street, in the store, I yell at the few people inside. "Hurry—come quickly. It's Mercy."

I race out of the building and jump off the porch with Abel Gunderson, one of the store's proprietor brothers, hobbling along behind me. He is well over eighty years old, wiry, small, and plenty spry. I hear the town bell and know that everyone will come now. The sound can be heard for four or five miles, depending on the wind and thick of the forest. Most living at the edge of telephone range have a phone tree and will call their neighbors, who will race to neighboring homes. For a good sixty miles away, people will know something is happening in Capitol. Details will follow, or you can come see for yourself.

That same bell system brought the townspeople to the McInnis farm on that horrible night of devastation so many years ago. It rang not that long ago for Nellie Jane. Now the bell sounds for Mercy. Her death will break the hearts of many. I'm sure it will harden mine. I left her alone. I left her.

I don't want to tell Jack. Oh God, Jack. But there he is, on his way, to find out what the fuss is all about. I duck back into the house before he can get to Mercy. I take the quilt delivered with exquisite timing and cover her. I do not want him to see the fact of her dead body at the table.

I turn to see him coming through the kitchen door. He looks at the quilt-covered body, then looks at me, then sits down. He pays no attention to the other people filling the room. I push them all out to leave him alone with his sister. I send Abel off to find the midwife—our local medical professional—who is probably fishing at Scrub Lake.

I feel horrible for Jack. I feel horrible for me.

Ned arrives. *Thank God for Ned.* I touch him on the arm as I leave the kitchen. He brushes a kiss through my hair.

In Mercy's bedroom, her bed receives me as she would have, with warmth and comfort. Her pillow takes my head, her blankets surround my body. The raging cold of shock overwhelms me. My eyes close. My system shuts down.

I remember Ned's friend Davis Porter describing the day he was electrocuted. He'd been working on overhead wiring in a school gymnasium. He thought the power was turned off. His grip on a live wire completed an electrical loop in his body. He wanted to let go to break the circuit, but he couldn't. Like him, I just want to release, to drop, to land, to let go.

It's quiet back at the farm that night. A clear black sky sparkles with the glitter of eternal gods. A vast frigid universe encompasses the above and below. I feel the gentle kisses from Nellie Jane on Mercy's sweet aged face. I sense distress from Missy as she boards a plane in Paris. I can see the slight wisp of form made by my grandmother with her arms extended into all time to receive one more baby girl.

And I can hear now, breaking the silence, a coyote. He is not far away.

CHAPTER 35

Mercy's funeral is the funeral to beat. I've never seen so many old men in plaid shirts with clean hands and bare heads and caps stuffed in pockets in one place at one time. Not a lot of wives or daughters remain in the region—dead and buried or move away. The handful of local women who remain, are preparing the first reception luncheon in the basement kitchen of St. Michael's Evangelical Lutheran Church.

A smattering of Catholic families present themselves in the chapel to honor Mercy along with the Protestants. They keep to the back, except for Lily Huttunen, barely five, who is too hopped up on cinnamon buns to settle down. She is making friends with everyone in each and every pew. Even those deep in prayer for the dearly beloved Mercy Marie Miles lift their eyes from God and the angels when Lily offers a handshake and an endearing, "How aw you dis mowneen?"

At any other funeral, Mercy would have that child in her lap, loving and fussing over her, until Lily, itching to get down, would have likely kicked her. Then Mercy would have, with reluctance and a wince, given up her hold.

And after the service and the church ladies' basement buffet, we would have all made our way to Mercy's for weeping, "What will we do without So-and-So?" There would have been storytelling, coffee, sweet cider, and more food well into sundown. The men would migrate to the co-op back room for beer and setups.

It will be that way today as well, though without Mercy to preside. Missy's flight is delayed, so until she arrives, it is my turn to step up, since Mercy has stepped out with the Lord. It is my turn. I rise in the ranks today to the fill-in-the-blank space left by Mercy.

It is natural that the community, as one, will make this assumption. They know I am the most able female of Mercy's family, knowing the community and its ways as I do. It is my turn because I am married to Ned, whom everyone loves and respects. It is my turn because I am Jack's niece—equally well-loved and respected. It is my turn because it is assumed that I can make a decent pot roast dinner.

I hear nothing of the service and remember less. I keep my place in the receiving line and eat with the old codgers at the buffet. Then I make my way, unnoticed, out of the room, up the stairs, and over to Mercy's for a few moments of quiet before setting up for visitors. Ned stays at the church. He will be gone most of the day into the night now, hanging out with the old guys.

But when I arrive at Mercy's, I am horrified to find Lydia and her crew hard at work preparing food, brewing coffee, and welcoming me as if I am one more village mourner in need of comforting by the bereaved family. They've taken over. They are in Mercy's cupboards, touching her things. Carl sits in the overstuffed easy chair with a bottle of booze on the side table and a glass half full of liquor, neat.

The community enters Mercy's home after their short hike from the church. Like ants to a spill of honey, the mourners find themselves at another bountiful table. It is irrelevant to them who prepares or hosts the feast. They are mourners and eulogizers, not chief cooks and bottle washers, as Jack once said. Mercy has died, and it is left to the community to grieve and continue. In this harsh environment, it is understood that memories are beautiful, like quilts and other needlework, but they are not the stuff of survival, unless one is speaking of the soul.

I retreat to Mercy's bedroom, only to find Judy and her girlfriend sprawled on Mercy's bed, playing games on an iPad. I make it to the bathroom in time to throw up. Then I sink to the floor and sob from loss of Mercy and rage at Lydia.

Without warning, given no time to plan for this, I'm knocked over by this latest assault from Lydia. Her mindless usurping, her intrusion into all things not Lydia's, disorients me. I'm blind with anger, stumbling about in my grief. Someone has stolen my cane and guide dog. I am locked in a room of suffering without an exit strategy.

I hear Jack's voice and Lydia's following in a singsong of conversation. I look down at my body, stiff and rigid, sitting on the cold tile floor. I want to crawl out the bathroom window and go home. I slither snakelike up the wall until my feet are sound under my full body weight. There is no one to be seen outside the window. I make my escape.

At home, the sound of the backdoor opening startles me. Ned should not be back so soon. But then Beulah Dickson, Madeline Flost, and Geraldine and Winnie Small Dog enter my home like apparitions, carrying their own feast and mourner's chatter. Each one passes by me with a condolence and a kiss or a pat to my head. As if in a trance or waking dream, I feel them walk through me and around me as they might in a ghost dance, putting the fire back to my ash, creating wood from burn, and then they grow a tree from the downfall. They build me up in a moment, creating space for love and renewal and recognition.

Their feast is unwrapped and placed on counters and the table. The smell of coffee and pot roast and some kind of pie swell to stifle all but a sense of luscious yearning. My gratitude diminishes me. I see the Little People moving about, in and under things and us in the room, a room made Holy by wholeness. I put my head down and soak it in. There is nothing in all the world like a room filled to bursting with a bunch of old women who mean to take care of someone in need. I can imagine their Jesus sitting back to take a lesson.

As we prepare to share a meal, we reminisce about Mercy and Nellie Jane. The women tell me they knew all along Nellie Jane was Eleanora.

"We were children ourselves when everything happened, but we knew our friend when she moved back here," explains Beulah. "We never told Mercy that we knew, but we often talked about that—should we, shouldn't we? We didn't know. We knew Mercy and Nellie Jane both believed your father might hurt them again. So we kept their secret. We made friends all over again and made sure we were all friends forever, regardless of life events."

She tops off my coffee. "When you moved to the farm, I'll admit we were worried—you being William's daughter and all. Of course, we didn't know your intentions at the time. We didn't understand why you came here. We kept an eye on you and Ned to be sure you wouldn't harm them. But then we got to know you."

Winnie speaks up from behind me as she carves the roast. "We didn't know William. He missed a lot of school. And then when it all happened, he and Terry were taken away. The little boys went missing, and for all we knew, they died out in the woods. Mercy was the only one left, or so we thought."

She places the meat platter and gravy boat on the table.

"Of course, my family on the rez knew everything. It was just a matter of time before we kids learned the truth too. We were sworn to secrecy, but we were used to keeping secrets about everybody!" She flashes me a smile. "Your people, whites, made liars of us all!"

The women laugh as they arrange themselves around the table. I still can't believe they're here.

"Why aren't you at Mercy's house with everyone else?" I ask.

Madeline chirps in. "I arrived at Mercy's to witness your escape from the back of the house. I called the others and suggested we meet up here at the farm."

"I can't thank you enough. You may know I am not a fan of Carl's Lydia. I just couldn't believe she was at already Mercy's, running the whole reception. She didn't talk to me about her plans. Of course, I suppose I didn't tell her my plans either. I just assumed . . . it doesn't matter. I fled."

I hesitate to ask them about Carl, but I plunge in anyway.

"Tell me—what do you all think of Carl?'

Beulah nods her head as if already agreeing with me. "He's not a cuddly one, not warm like Jack. But he's done right by his brother. We talked the other day. He told me he's worked with death all his life and feels he's earned the right to come home and drink a good whiskey."

"Spoken like a true Scotsman, eh?" Madeline snorts a laugh.

I hesitate again, then decide to open up a bit more. "You didn't know my father, but here's the thing, Carl looks exactly like him, only bigger, taller. And you also don't know—and I'm not going to elaborate—that my father's violence did not end with the attempted murder of his sister. So, Carl—the look of him and the smirk on his smug face full of booze—scares the bejesus out of me."

Beulah stands from the table, armed with his defense. "Well, that may be, but as I said, he's done right by Jack. And Mercy was thrilled to have him home. She glowed with peace and a settled soul after all these years. I believe you and don't doubt a word you say, but I don't think you need to worry about him. We'll keep an eye out, just in case."

While the ladies clean up, I sit quietly by myself in Eleanora's rocker. It's reassuring to know now that they've kept a watchful and protective eye on my aunts—even viewing me with suspicion, for no reason other than I am Billy's daughter. How is it that one person can cause so much fear in so many? But that is my father's truth and legacy.

I nod off and fall asleep, only to wake up inside the nightmare of my life. It's a recurring fright fest. Billy stands threatening in my bedroom doorway. I can feel the attack in every part of my body, but I cannot scream or cry or move at all. I can smell him on me.

But the dream morphs this time, into something even more terrible. I am no longer the victim, and the assailant is not my father. The menacing figure I come to see inside the dream is my grandfather, and his victim is my own father as a small boy. The attack is relentless.

I awake drenched in sweat and race to the bathroom to vomit. A cold washcloth applied to my face does nothing to help me recover. The dream is alive in me. I can't rid myself of its horrors.

I crawl in bed and grab the sheet and blanket tight to my chin. Somehow, I fall asleep.

In the morning, Ned's head is on the pillow next to me. I'm careful to creep away from him, then quietly shower, dress, and make coffee. I'm sure Ned will sleep for another hour or two. He'll have plenty of stories to tell me when he's up and about. Until then, I need be alone, to try to clear the nightmare's residual feelings out of my heart and mind.

Jesus Christ—the animals!

I jump to my feet, grab my boots, pull them on, and race from the house to feed and water everybody. Of course, when I reach the barns, I see that Jack was well ahead of me this morning. I look out from the goat shed to see him heading home.

"Jack! Come for breakfast!" I shout.

He turns to saunter back toward the house.

I place a mug of coffee on the table for him and assemble the ingredients for applesauce muffins. I can hear Ned moving around at the back of the house. *Everything is already back in rhythm. How is this possible?*

CHAPTER 36

I will wait before confronting Lydia. I need to calm down. Armed by faith from an army of four old women at my back, I feel brave and righteous to strike, to win the battle for first rights to Capitol. I was here first. That should count for something.

Lydia disrupts my forward thinking. She pisses me off. She makes me act like a child. Yeah, yeah—nobody can "make" anybody do anything. Not true. Not true.

I will tell her to back off and stand down. I wait. I obsess. I struggle. I make plans to strike her hard.

The community of Capitol has had little time to recover from the loss of Mercy Miles before shifting into fall, facing winter. I can feel the subtle change of seasons from August to September, even though the day is sunny and still. The leaves make a different sound in the most gentle breeze. It happens the moment they reach their peak of growth and begin to wither, having given their all to fruit or seed. A new language of autumn speaks of harvest and preserving the gifts brought from the earth and the barns.

Wood smoke wafts across the yard, exciting my senses. Ned and Mike are out with some of the local men burning five acres of brush land. The light smoke smell is invigorating, and the bit of ash that falls in the other areas of wood and garden will help to enrich the soil. The management of this land is critical to maintaining habitat for small game birds such as grouse and woodcock. The burn should have been done in the spring, but sometimes should-haves turn to when-we-cans. It's been cooler than normal this August, with little wind, making today's burn easy to manage.

I hear laughter and friendly shouts back and forth. I've promised Ned to keep watch on his beef ribs and buffalo stew. He's planned a hungry man's feast for later. Already we have some butternut squash and the last stash of early red potatoes ready to roast and add to the table. Onions, tomatoes, and cucumbers tossed in mayonnaise with a touch of dill will provide a vegetable side.

There's a hearty harvest of raspberries, strawberries, and blueberries this year. The raspberries will continue to produce into October, if winter will hold off. That's happened only twice in the last decade, I'm told. The berries have made their way into two cobblers to finish off Ned's meal.

I am content with this day. The goats are a little skittish because of the smoke in the air. I've left the shed door open for them to come and go as they please. I don't know if this will provide comfort, but there is nothing else to be done. I sit down on the west porch with the latest novel by Gerald Lincoln Mosier, *A Dying Species*, and a glass of iced tea.

Shoes off, hand-knit socks in a clash of colors, I curl up on the porch bench and am deep into a story of murder, mayhem, and madness when I hear a car pull into the driveway. Assuming it is someone else to help with the burn, I ignore the sound and keep reading.

But then I hear steps. I look up.

"Lydia."

"Ellen." She nods to me. "I feel we need to talk."

She stands tall above me. I am always both awed and angered by her beauty.

"About what, Lydia?"

"About your disappearance at the gathering for Aunt Mercy, among other things."

I sit erect, allowing the book to slip onto the porch floor with a light thud. I bend over to fumble for it, outraged. Aunt Mercy, my ass.

"I've tried, my family has tried everything we can think of to be warm and welcoming to you," she begins. "Ned embraced us. Aunt Mercy, Uncle Jack, and even cousin Missy from overseas have both welcomed us with such love and care. The locals all are open, friendly, inviting us into the community as the long-lost residents we are. But you—you are cold, nasty, and smug about us for reasons I can't grasp. What is your story, Ellen? What is this about?"

"Well, aren't you just the perfect family." I would like to punch her in the face. I really would. I keep my hands where I can see them. "You rolled in here on the coattails of your drunkard father's name, which he changed to protect *himself*. You rolled up on Mercy and ran her down with your intrusive, heavy-handed plans for her sister's home, her community—everybody's community. We, the people of Capitol, are not garments hanging in your backroom for tailoring, waiting for redesign and adjustments by you and your big plans. I—my Ned and I—are not available for your consumption and regurgitation into your notion of model citizens of this town." I can barely breathe. "You and your—"

Lydia sits down on the porch step, lowering herself to me, displaying her elegant profile with a slight bow to her indescribable head of Scots-bred red mane. Her virginal, penitent posture of submission lacks only a halo and choir of heavenly truthbearers to sing of her innocence.

And this is my undoing. I leap to my feet, jump past her to the ground, nearly breaking my neck in slippery sock-shod feet. It is not a graceful move. I look up at her, blocking her gaze to anything but me.

"Do you have any idea what it means to give you an inch?"

I glare and stop talking. This is not going according to plan. How did she know to come today, to preempt my strike?

"Ellen, no good can come from us shouting at one another."

Oh, how I want to take a swing at that glistening porcelain skin, a delicate setting for her lightly freckled nose. She hasn't begun to hear shouting. This is civil discourse.

We'll get to shouting. Hang on.

"You came here today snooting about my bad behavior and your acts of great generosity toward me and mine. What the fuck did you expect from me? You want passive agreement? I'm not heading that way. That way is not on my map."

"Ellen—"

"Lydia, shut up. You wanted to get a rise out of me, and now you've got it. We are not in the negotiation stage of this event between us. We are in the rip-the-duct-tape-off-the-third-degree-burn stage. I don't play passive, and I don't play cute. Shut up and get from me what you came for."

Lydia begins to cry. Her face collapses into her lap, not to show weakness, but to accentuate the actor's state of pain. Grabbing my book, shoes, and iced tea, I walk back into my house with a "Fuck you!" trailing behind.

I immediately smell the burning ribs. One more "fuck" and a few other expletives wrap around the name "Lydia" as I flip open the oven door, yank out the tray of ribs, and set about fixing what is almost ruined. By God, I will not let that woman wreck anything for Ned!

In the bathroom, I cool my face and attempt to calm my pounding heart. I bend over to touch my toes fifteen times for the purpose of distraction.

Thinking I might live to fight another day, I leave the bathroom, only to physically bump into Lydia, again in my house, uninvited and in my way. *Jeeeeesuuuuus Christ!*

"Get out of my house, Lydia!"

"I have to use the washroom." She speaks in a whisper, averting her eyes from mine.

I don't buy the act for one minute, but I let her through and return to the kitchen. It will be hours before the men come in to clean up and eat—plenty of time for me to calm down. And then she's back, talking, still talking.

"This bullying of yours has got to stop."

She speaks with tremendous control. Her posture has transformed from submissive—which didn't work—to her true colors as the aggressive, manipulative bitch I know her to be.

"We are the heart of gossip. I'm trying to make a legacy home for my family. And you're making it impossible for any of us to feel comfortable—especially my dad. What is it that you want from me, from us, Ellen?"

"I want you to go away. That's what I want. I don't understand why you're here. I thought Capitol was a summer place for your group. Now it's your forever home? I don't like it. I don't like your father. I don't like what he did, leaving Jack on his own. I don't like his drinking, and I don't like his rude, entitled attitude. I don't like you and the way you barge in everywhere you please, whenever, always uninvited."

Lydia is an exhausting human being. I hate the sound of the woman's voice. I stare at her as she begins again to plead her case of family innocence. For the first time, I see lines on her face and strands of untouched gray at the crown of her hair. Ha! She dyes it that color! I feel smug and fueled to finish her off.

But she keeps talking. "You know nothing about us. You haven't asked a single question about me, about him, about my life, my mother, or my siblings. Yet you don't like us. You know you don't like us. Don't you need *some* information to form such a critical opinion?"

"I have information, Lydia. I have you in my house uninvited far too often. Your pushy behavior tells me all I need to know to dislike you. When your father makes an appearance, it's with booze in hand, looking for more. And then there's Mercy's reception. When did you ask *me* about the preparation of *that*?"

"Ask you? Why do I need your permission to go to *my* aunt's house to prepare to receive her grieving friends? All you had to do was walk into the kitchen and help. But no. You stormed off in a fit of rage. Because why? Because we were there first? Is that what this is? Do you think you're the alpha member in this pack, and the rest of us are expected to fall in line behind you?"

I sigh, then pour myself a glass of wine. Why will she not leave, not shut up?

But I know why. I understand. It is the defense of the childhood tantrum, turned on since the first episode of neglect and abandonment. I don't have to know Carl or his wife to recognize his orphan daughter. I want to feel sympathy. I cannot. The image of Lydia, the sound of her, represents every ounce of struggle I've lived, fighting myself all the way, to heal the broken spirit of an unloved child.

"You say my dad's a drunk. He's not."

I fool with the wine in my glass, shifting the liquid from side to side, stuck in a moment of near defeat.

"Yes, Lydia, he's a drunk. He has every right to be a drunk. He lived the nightmare, did the best he could. I see his effect on Jack. It's a beautiful thing, really. But you—you have got to stop pretending that he deserves a defense. Grow, for God's sake!"

Lydia ignores my words. "He still feels ashamed for running away from his dying mother and everything that happened that night. Jack's scars? His eye? Did you know he was shot too? Dad didn't know until Jack fell when they were running away. Dad got him back to Jake and Millie's, where they hid until the sheriff left. Jake got the doctor, and Jack was patched up. They got him to safety as quickly as they could."

I want to scream at her to stop talking.

"He's also ashamed for leaving Jack, but he knew he had to. Dad had to make something of himself so he could take care of Jack. Jack wanted to stay close to his family home. So Dad built him a house. At any time, you could have asked. You could have . . . I don't know."

"That's all bullshit! Jack didn't even know who your father was when he built him that house. Your father is a fucking coward, and that's why he's a drunk!"

I am fully exasperated and sick of Lydia. I don't care about her spin on the story. I want some peace. I want her to go. I want to look forward to the fun that is to walk in the door when the men return from a long day of fighting real fires—fires with smoke and singed leaves and charred wood and grasses. A fire you can smell, taste in your mouth, cough up from your lungs. All my resolve to forgive is in ashes.

I'm still outraged at Lydia's intrusion the day of Mercy's funeral. She shows no respect to anyone but herself and her immediate clan. The relationship I built with Mercy changed my life, saved my life. Mercy is the warming ember in my cold house. Yes, I love Ned, but it is a love I believe can come undone at any time, like a leash on a dog. I loved Mercy and Nellie Jane with unintended abandon—something I know Lydia will never feel.

I concede my life to the effects of Billy and Virginia. At least I know what makes me the way I am. Lydia has no capacity for self-reflection. She is an emotional vampire. Vampires have no self to reflect upon.

I can't keep talking to her, reacting against her. She is an apparition, another family ghost.

"Lydia, get out of my house."

I don't look up as she rises in slow motion with all the drama she can emote. She leaves, uncharacteristically, without the last word.

I stare into the empty room and appreciate the calm that settles in around me. There it is—the peace I crave. I sip my wine and wait for Ned. I'm anxious to talk to him, to tell him about my exchange with Lydia.

When I saw Billy as a child loved by his mother, I caught a glimpse of what was on the other side of my window to the world, the one constructed for me by my parents. I didn't know then that there was a window or a side or any world but my own. My parents shaped me to see one thing only: fear. Yes, I built a screen to filter out complete madness in order to function, to pretend to have my own life. But I was never ever anyone but a child looking through a window, touching only glass.

The men return from the burn, and the feast begins. Afterward, Mike offers to take Jack home. Ned takes a shower before he joins me in the living room. I'm looking forward to quiet time with him. He calls to me from the hallway, asking if I'd like some wine while he grabs a beer for himself.

"No, I'm good with the three bottles I have here in front of me." I laugh.

He sits next to me on the couch and tells me every detail of his day with the guys. He talks of fighting fires they started and whatever other manly things he can recall to fill in his report. I feel how happy he is. Through all the turmoil of the last two years, he maintains a welcoming sunny side that I envy. I kiss him, and settle back in his arms.

"You know, Ned, I think sometimes I'm going to lose my mind. Really. After all this time, holding it together, I feel it's inevitable. Nellie Jane used to talk about 'saving the ghost.' I feel like I'm about to give up the ghost. The fight is out of me. I'm so tired."

Ned pulls my head to rest against his chest.

"I realized something today: Lydia's father's tragedy, however that played out on her, is her universe, sun, and moon. It's no different than my lifelong obsession with Billy and Virginia—who they were, are, what they did. Everything is their fault. I can't like in Lydia what I can't stand in myself."

Ned's kiss in that moment means everything to me.

"I may be on the verge of understanding something new about myself," I add. "Seeing Lydia in action is like watching a movie about me, only I'm better than her in so many ways. I'm smarter . . . Okay, maybe just smarter."

Ned chuckles. "And more beautiful."

"Oh, that's right. You know, I could dye my hair. Oh, and get extensions. Then we'd be twins."

"Please don't." Ned pushes my head from his chest and looks me in the eyes. "Please, please, don't!"

"But honestly, I do feel like I'm finally getting somewhere in my own life. Of course, I thought I *was* fine until Billy's death. I had no idea how screwed up I was. No idea."

"To be fair, Ellen, you built a good life for yourself. You let CiCi and her family step in and keep you anchored. I don't want to imagine what might have happened to you without their support and guidance."

"Weird to think that I've been lucky, but it's true. CiCi, her family, and of course you—made all the difference. But my real life was locked away beneath a façade of normalcy. Even though I spent time in therapy, all that did was put a polish on my unfinished edges. I felt better, but I wasn't better at all, only better managed." I run my fingers along the hairs on his wrist.

"You're tickling me!" He laughs and rubs his hand across his itchy wrist.

Ned's arms around me feel warm and strong. I feel we might be in full synch for the first time. I tell him about the little girl looking out a window.

"They didn't leave me much of a view. Everything was scary. And yes, I did cover it well. I did not know before today how separated I have been from everyone and everything. I could not connect. But Lydia—Lydia brought it all into focus for me today. Can you believe it? Lydia!" I look up at him and smile. "I'm done. I'm okay. And I have worlds upon worlds of living to explore. I'm free. It's exhilarating."

Tears sting my eyes as I fight to hold them back. There's nothing left to cry about.

"I love you, you know that, right? But more…I can love you more."

"I do know that you love me." He strokes my hair.

"I want to jump up from under the evangelist's palm and shout and dance, 'I'm healed! I'm healed!' I'm not cured, but I am healed. Nellie Jane used to talk about that. She'd say to never pray for a cure. A cure could be a death. Healing is what we want." And then I start to laugh.

"What?"

"I'm sorry. Marvin Gaye jumped in there.'"

Ned picks me up off the couch to carry me in to the bedroom, singing the lyrics of "Sexual Healing." His hands linger on my chest before kissing the flesh above my heart.

"Let the healing begin."

CHAPTER 37

In the morning, thoroughly loved and appreciated, I gently remove the bedcovers from my side and tuck them back down to keep heat from escaping. Ned doesn't move, and I leave him to sleep.

It's early, maybe 5:00 a.m. Too early to be at the barns, although there's a puff of dust rising above the tamaracks. Mike must be on his way with Jack.

Dear Jack. How he plods through his life—deliberate, intentional. He never expects anything, he's lost a lot, yet he welcomes what's offered—for the most part. Mike drops him off and I watch Jack shuffle off to feed the goats and chickens, head down, inspecting the earth on his way. Mike waves to him out of habit, knowing Jack won't look back, and pulls out of the driveway.

I'm trying to get hold of whatever genius thinking I had going on before Ned swept me off my feet last night. That I'm healing. Healing.

I'm swirling now in images of rape and torture and CiCi's singing and life before and after all the death and devastation. It's the stuff epic films are built from, that dams are built for. But everything is opening in me like it's spring and I'm a tulip. Petals fall back to let the bees have at the pollen. That is the life force, right there. Yellow dust makes the world go 'round. I've never felt this alive.

The crash will come. I know it will. Euphoria has its place. It's temporary. But for now, I know the difference between open and closed.

I think of Uncle Terry. I see him as a rock at the side of an abandoned road. I want more for him. As old as he is, there is still a chance. Maybe.

Later, at breakfast, Ned agrees to try, one last time, to visit Terry, still hanging on to the life that has tortured him for over eighty years. I want to tell him it's okay now, that the secrets are out in the open. Not only was his sister alive but his little brothers were found soon after they ran off, and they are safe and back in Capitol. I want him to know. I want to help him out of his pain. I imagine he will smile—maybe for the first time since he was a boy. I want to give him that. He deserves that.

We arrive at the assisted-living home on Wednesday. I look at the clock above the registration desk before Ned comes in from parking the car. It's 3:35 p.m. The receptionist advises me that residents will begin going to dinner at 4:30. We want to make sure to catch Terry in his room. I called ahead, but of course Terry did not answer the phone. I left word with his nurse that we were coming for one last visit.

We walk down the hall, hand in hand, sad and happy all at once. I'm glad to be done with the secrets. I'm ready to relax into my future with Ned, to cease from struggle.

I knock at the door. There is no response. I knock again, then try the knob. I slowly open the door, calling out to not catch him by surprise.

"I told you not to come here!" I hear Terry growl in protest.

There's a loud noise. The doorframe shatters. My fingers, gripping the doorknob, won't let go. I feel the air at my face change in a way I can't identify. There is something on my cheek.

In slow motion, my hand releases the doorknob to touch my face. Blood and bits of wood lay like puzzle pieces in my palm.

Ned has fallen. He's not standing by my side anymore. I see blood on my shirt and blood at my feet. I don't know what's happening. What is happening?

"Ned?"

I look at him. His eyes are open, and his right arm is moving, like he's swimming. But he's not swimming.

"Ned!" My screams fill the nursing home hallway.

I see bodies running toward me. I hear an alarm. And I hear that noise again. Like an explosion in my head. I think I'm screaming. Someone is screaming.

The staff pull me back from the doorway and away from Ned. I'm frantic. There's a stretcher and first responders and noise, so much noise.

I pass out.

Ned spends three weeks in critical care. His brain is bruised, and he suffered a stroke. Only time will tell how he might recover.

My past troubles speed away into a vast tunnel of time long gone and irrelevant. Ned is everything to me, everything good. He's in danger, and there is nothing I can do to help him.

I remember little about this time while Ned is in the hospital. I remember a nurse telling me that Terry shot at us when I opened the door. One of the old timers saw it happen. Somehow Terry got hold of a pistol. It was loaded and ready for me. But the bullet went wild, shot through the door, shattered the frame, and grazed Ned across his temple.

The nurse can barely catch her breath. "Then your uncle shot one more time—killing himself."

I don't know how Terry got his hands on a gun or concealed it from staff. He knew we were coming, and he was prepared to kill me. Why?

A couple of weeks after the shooting, I receive a call from Terry's doctor, a psychiatrist retained by the county to oversee treatments provided on the county dime.

"The psychiatrist wants to meet with me," I tell Ned as I sit next to his bed, holding his hand.

Ned blinks and reaches for his water. I help him take a drink before continuing. I wish he could advise me. I wish he could stand and walk out of this awful room.

"I turned him down. I know all I need to know. He's insistent, though. He says he has information to share that might help us understand what happened. How fucking much more do I need to know?" I try to keep the anger from my voice and let my words do their work.

Ned smiles and squeezes my hand.

"Okay. Okay." I nod in agreement with his desire to comfort me.

I make the appointment.

The doctor's office is in a nearby clinic, walkable from the hospital. I arrive, on time, with an attitude, and check in with the front desk. Soon after, a nurse approaches to lead me back to the office.

"I'm Dr. Stein." He rises from his desk to greet me. He extends his hand and, without permission, takes mine in his.

"I'm so sorry for what's happened. I've heard that your husband is recovering well." His voice and manner seem sincere. "Please, sit down."

I position myself on the edge of a soft brown leather chair, placed across from his desk. He sits down in the chair next to mine. Too close. I stiffen.

"I want you to know how truly sorry I am."

He hands me a cardboard banker's box, lid off, containing a number of student-style notebooks.

"Each quarter, when your uncle met with me for his med check, he left me with another notebook. After the first year or so, the notes he made were less and less coherent. In later years, the pages were mostly blank. He fell into the habit of leaving the notebooks with me in what I believe became a sort of confessional ritual for him. I stopped reading them after the first two years of blank pages, although my nurse always scanned them on the off chance he might write again."

I hear him speaking as I dutifully cradle the box in my lap. I want out of here, but I can't move.

"And he did. Earlier this year, he made a new entry in a new book. I realize now I should have seen a problem. But still, with HIPPA laws and no stated threat, there was nothing to be done." He touches the notebooks in the box. "You'll see that the notebooks are numbered. There is one older notebook, number five, that I recommend you read and that last one, number 19."

He pulls those two out of the box and places them on top of the others. He expresses his condolences again, then urges me toward the door.

I now stand with a box full of Terry and his troubles at the edge of a waiting room in a psychiatrist's office in a clinic not five blocks from where Ned lies with a near fatal wound. I want to toss the lot of the notebooks across the lobby and watch them flip out of the box and scatter.

But I don’t do that. Instead, I drop them all, but the two singled out, in a trash bin near the exit.

CHAPTER 38

This is the best day of forever. Ned has been home for a week, getting around with assistance from a walking stick whittled from diamond willow, made by a local old geezer. The men are assembled over poker and whiskey in the shack. All my friends, Mercy's cronies, are with me on the back porch and filling up the kitchen.

While I was nursing Ned back to health and life at the hospital, a quit-claim deed arrived in the mail. Lydia signed Nellie Jane's property back to me without explanation. I handed it over to my attorney and forgot about it. Apparently, Lydia decided to make her family compound elsewhere. Good riddance. Don't care the reason, although Beulah thinks I should.

"Terry's violence against you was too much for Carl," she says. "He told me himself. He said he didn't know how he could manage to see you. He said you didn't matter a bit to him until the shooting, and then his childhood came back to him. He said, 'I saw her in it,' as though you might have been there that night, in some way. He said he couldn't face you and was too old to try to figure it all out. And then they up and left."

He always was the runner, right? That explains it.

Ned's homecoming gathering is wearing on the elder ladies. One by one, they pack up their platters and utensils, give me kisses, and disappear into the oncoming twilight. I know the men will be here most of the night, if not through the entire of it. I'll leave Ned in their hands, clinging to the hope that they'll know to send him to bed when he's ready.

Before dark settles, I want to walk to the old Who-rock and give thanks, for what it's worth. On my way out, I check in on Ned in the shack. He's fine. He's beautiful, and he's fine. He gives me a wink, and I duck out the door.

The goats rustle in the straw as I pass their shed, but the chickens, roosting, are quiet. All is quiet except for old men sounds of happiness and the tread of my shoes through the grasses. I reach the spot where the rock rests. Only a tip is visible above leaf and pine needle litter. It's been too long since I've been here. I clear its face to accept the moonlight when it shines.

I feel an urgency to hurry. It's the predator's time of day. But there is another, even more primal urge, and that is to make a prayer.

I stretch my arms to the four directions, then to the heavens, home to countless worlds, and then to the earth, my home. I offer tobacco I've saved from Nellie Jane's stash. I offer my soul, my right to be here, as I call the relatives.

"*Mitákuye Oyás'iŋ*."

I see CiCi gliding between saplings. I imagine LuLu running with wolves. I hear Nellie Jane's rattle, soft as a rain of sand through the Creator's fingers. I feel the rise of freedom. I do not have tears. There is no more loss. It is done. I brush one palm across the other.

"*Wašté*."

A few days after the party, Patsy arrives for a month-long stay. We haven't seen each other since the move, yet she did not hesitate to drop everything to come and help us. God love her. With Ned at home now,

I need the help. There's a lot of planning to do for winter, and I can't do it all. Mike is all in too, he says, to help with farm chores.

Jack is all but retired now. This last round with Terry took some life from him too. He doesn't say anything, but he looks broken. All his siblings are dead, except for the one who once again left him in the lurch. As glad as I am that Lydia and Carl moved away from here, I am sad beyond words for Jack. Still, Jack comes every day when Mike comes. He mostly sits in the barn, petting the goats.

Patsy is sprawled across the worn plaid couch. We're in the shack, drinking.

"So where is Ned today?" But then she interrupts before I can answer. "God, I love this place!"

"He's in Twin Bays until tomorrow. He's got physical therapy and other tests. Routine follow-up stuff."

"But he's okay, right?"

"Exceeding all expectations."

We review the last year's events. Patsy's new girl is now steady, and there's a plan to marry next fall.

"We have two cats. Can you believe it?"

I can't. I love to see her so happy.

There's not much wine left in my glass, and Patsy is downing the last of hers.

"Another bottle?" I offer.

Patsy winks. "Keep 'em coming. By the way, you look good, you know."

"Why, thank you."

"No, I mean it." Patsy sits up straight, twirling her glass. "The last time I saw you, girl, you scared me. I thought you'd lost it for sure."

"Patsy, my friend, what I lost can stay lost." I sit next to her to fill our glasses for a toast to myself. "Here's to survivors!"

Our glasses clink, then Patsy pushes her feet against my hip and shoves me off the couch so she can resume her lounge position.

"So that's it? Survival? That's it?"

"Yes and no. Turns out, survival had been my lifestyle all along, but I didn't understand that. When you held me through my hysteria, what you witnessed was my defenses peeling away. It felt like my skin had ripped off muscle. And it got far worse before it got better."

Patsy closes her eyes while holding her glass in one outstretched hand. I wonder if she will try to bring it in for a sip, slowly, like landing a plane in the dark without runway lights.

"When Terry shot Ned—by accident to be sure, because he was aiming for me—everything came into focus. I was done whining. I was shocked out of shock. I was knocked to my feet instead of knocked over."

Patsy's arm moves ever so slightly toward her face. One eyelid lifts at half-mast to navigate her glass. She gives up, though, just in time to avoid a spill. She fully opens her eyes and repositions herself.

"What made him do it, Terry? Do you know?"

"I do, and I don't. His doctor gave me journals that Terry kept most of his medicated life. I threw all of them away, except for two the doc culled from the others. He said I might want to read them. They might help me understand my uncle better."

"And did they help?"

"I never read them."

"What? Why?"

"I don't have the nerve, and I don't want to understand so I'll have to forgive him."

"Do you still have them?"

"I do." I eye her carefully. "You want to read them, don't you?"

I ignore my own hesitation. Maybe it won't be so bad. Or maybe it will be worse than I can imagine. At least with Patsy here, I won't have to find out on my own.

"Yes, I really do."

"They're at the house."

We agree to go back to the house, find the journals, and read them together. I stroke the cover before opening the first book, feeling afraid now. I look up at Patsy, who is eagerly awaiting the reveal. I feel like I'm in a horror movie scene with a creepy hatchet guy behind me.

I open the notebook and stare at the first page, the first entry. Other than some scribbled notes in the margins, it's written neatly. Terry's handwriting is quite good. I wonder where he learned to read and write. And then I remember I'm touching the pages of a dead man who nearly killed my husband. I close the book and look again at Patsy, who smiles and waves me onward. I begin to read aloud from Notebook No. 5.

There was blood everywhere. There was crying and screaming and death and dying. I didn't know what to do. I'd lost my mind, gone too far this time. I knew it, but Billy kept on. He wanted damage. Anyone could see his fury. He couldn't stop when he was like this. I could, but he couldn't. Now he'd turned on Mercy. I could join him or be flattened by him. I knew he'd kill me too, given time and opportunity. I also knew our father would finish him off first before he ever got to me.

I explain to Patsy that this entry is about the night when my grandfather murdered my grandmother and when Billy, with Terry's help, nearly murdered Eleanora.

"Intense." she says. "He's a decent writer. Strange. I can feel his fear."

I don't want to do this anymore. I feel sick. The wine and nerves are churning my stomach.

"This isn't a novel," I snap at her and close the notebook.

Patsy is quick to apologize. "I'm sorry. That wasn't what I meant. I meant that his writing lets me feel him. I know this is real and horrible. But isn't this like reading the family obituary? Doesn't it help?"

"I don't know."

I open the book again, aimlessly paging through it until I'm stopped by the words, *It has all been too much for me.*

It has all been too much for me. Living every day with the pictures in my head and the feelings I have and the things only I know—it is worse than being dead. This is the fire and brimstone of hell that the preacher warned us children about. The invisible fire never stops burning me up. There's no break from it. There's no end to the screaming for help in my head.

I close the book and set it on the floor. My mind is quiet. I savor the silence and breathe deeply. I look at Patsy and smile.

"I'm done. I'm done. It is over. Over enough. Ned and I are good. We're happy here. We look after Jack. We have a good life. I can't tell you what it was like when Ned came home from the hospital and the whole town came out for him."

We're both tired. We pick up the bottles and glasses, take them to the kitchen, and say goodnight.

As I walk back to the bedroom, I remember that I have a gift for Ned, a coming-home present. I pull a round paper box from an upper shelf of our closet. I set it on the bed and brush the top in a gentle sweep, as if brushing away a cobweb or a light layer of dust.

The word *Stetson* is stenciled in black on its side.

67707655R00176

Made in the USA
Columbia, SC
31 July 2019